Catesby: Eyewitness to the Civil War

By Bob O'Connor

ISBN 0-7414-4642-1

Cover artwork
"From the original painting by Mort Künstler
Distant Thunder
© 1998 Mort Künstler, Inc.
www.mkunstler.com"

Published by:

PUBLISHING.COM

1094 New DeHaven Street, Suite 100
West Conshohocken, PA 19428-2713
Info@buybooksontheweb.com
www.buybooksontheweb.com
Toll-free (877) BUY BOOK
Local Phone (610) 941-9999
Fax (610) 941-9959

Printed in the United States of America

Printed on Recycled Paper

Published May 2008

Dedication

To my daughter Kelli Ordakowski;
great daughter, wonderful mother, and faithful friend.
Thank you for the blessings you have brought
to my life. I love you.

Also by Bob O'Connor

The Perfect Steel Trap Harpers Ferry 1859

The Virginian Who Might Have Saved Lincoln

www.boboconnorbooks.com

Harpers Ferry, West Virginia
Saturday, October 27, 2007

Pst. You over there. Don't be afraid. I won't hurt you. I'm over here, hiding behind the old pickle barrel in the corner.

Everyone around here calls me "old man Newberry." Pleased to meet you. You're new around here, aren't you? I've never seen the likes of you or your family before. I would remember. As for me, I've been hanging around here for years and years.

You'll have to excuse me. I'm kind of on edge. I'm trying to keep my eyes and ears open. If you hear a clicking noise, let me know, so I can duck back behind this barrel.

There's a man who has been chasing me. He says he has a score to settle with me. His laugh frightens me.

Let me know if you see or hear him. He's a big colored man — about yea tall — and has a metal crutch that makes a clicking noise. I can usually hear him coming about a mile away if I'm quiet. He hasn't caught me yet, but I ain't taking no chances.

He worked for me years ago. Can't imagine what he wants with me now. Oh, all right. If you want to know the truth. I do know why he is after me. Didn't he ever learn you should just forgive and forget?

You and your family probably were expecting to find someone like me here tonight as you took the walking tour of Harpers Ferry with Miss Shirley. Well, here I am — big as life. And perfectly harmless.

I guess you are curious, like the rest. You are not afraid of me, are you? I admit I am a frightful sight for your eyes. No need to be afraid though. I'm way too old to be of any concern to you.

We get a lot of tourists. Many have cameras like your father's so they can snap a photograph to show the folks back home.

Ask your father if he would like a group shot. You stand here. If your sister is afraid, she can stand on the other side of you so she doesn't have to get too close. Might get germs, you know. That's a joke, son. Tell your mother to stand in front, but not to block me. Now we are ready. Smile.

Let's take a look, sir. Sometimes on these new fangled digital cameras I don't show up much — just a blur. I must have moved. I have this natural twitch. Here, try again. Smile kids.

Oops, that one didn't take either. You can see me. I'm right here. It's not like I'm just a figment of your imagination. It must be your camera, sir. A malfunction, perhaps? You might want to get that checked.

Hear that clicking noise? That's him. I've got to go. You won't tell him where I am hiding, will you?

Nice talking to you. Maybe we can try taking that photograph again the next night you are in town.

Chapter 1
Seeking the Treasures

December 10, 2006
Charles Town, West Virginia

I have known Doug Perks for some time. He and I worked together on several projects at the Harpers Ferry National Historical Park. Now in his retirement as a high school history teacher, he is an administrator at the Jefferson County Museum. At the museum he introduced me to his friend, Jim Glymph.

Between the two of them, both having lived a long time in Jefferson County, West Virginia, I can get the scuttlebutt on just about anybody or anything that ever happened in the area. I am full of questions. They have many of the answers.

We have quite different personalities, but are interested in history and the history of this area in particular. There is a great deal of local history to be learned.

They have taken an interest in me and my historical research. I have learned from them. I think they have learned from me too.

Having grown up in Illinois, in the "Land of Lincoln" and in the hometown of Ronald Reagan, I am a staunch Republican, a Yankee, and a conservative. I am the new kid on the block, having only lived in Charles Town about seven years.

Doug is a liberal, and a die-hard Washington Redskin fan. Because he taught history and knows history, I can count on him to help me find whatever I need.

Jim is a rabid Confederate and a "Yankee Dog" hater, one who would be willing to resume the fight in the Civil War at the drop of a hat. Jim knows the history beyond the history in the books. You have to watch him though, because his yarns are as true-sounding as the honest to God's truth. That doesn't make him a bad person or an unreliable source.

He is just a mite eccentric. In fact, I may be the only "Yankee dog" he actually converses with on a regular basis.

We all seemed to hit it off from the get-go, though Jim could not accept that I referred to the famous battle in the War Between the States in nearby Sharpsburg, Maryland as the Battle of Antietam. That's all I had ever heard it called.

To Jim there is no such thing. The event is either called the Battle of Antietam Creek or the Battle of Sharpsburg. And it was definitely not the War Between the States. He calls it the War of Northern Aggression, a term I had never heard in Illinois. So now I stood corrected, trying valiantly to remember the proper nomenclature in his presence.

Jim is an avid relic hunter too. He has amassed thousands of Minnie balls and artifacts, while still looking for a particular item that will make him rich and famous. He has donated several fine collections to the museum.

Doug and I laugh about Jim's attitude on days he isn't at the museum. I suspect on days I am not there, they laugh about my attitude.

Here's a good example of how Jim sees things. One day a man asked Jim about Michael Shaara's book on Gettysburg, "Killer Angels." Jim laughed and said, "That's a novel and Longstreet's view of the battle anyway. We can't have a serious conversation about that."

Today we were going to go with Jim to the Beall Air mansion near Charles Town and along the Washington Heritage Trail, a National Scenic Byway. Colonel Lewis Washington, great grand nephew of George Washington, had once owned the plantation.

Jim knew liberals didn't relic hunt, but coaxed Doug to come along anyway. Jim had learned the farm was in the throes of development and told us several old buildings on the property were to be demolished the next day. He invited us to join him as he had been granted permission to search and take anything he found.

On this fine Sunday morning we met at the Sheetz store and jumped into Jim's truck. We had a couple of hours before Doug had to get back to watch the Redskin's game. We headed east from Charles Town on Rt. 340, turned north on Country Club Road for about a mile, and then east onto a road along the old Winchester and Potomac Railroad tracks.

We bumped along the dirt lane back toward the historic house. The road split the Sleepy Hollow Golf Club. A few golfers were out enjoying the splendid winter day. Normally that would have caught my attention, as I like to golf myself. But today we were on a more important quest.

We cut across the railroad tracks and followed the road past the mansion. I was appalled how bulldozers had already raped the pristine pastureland to make way for the building of huge new houses within a stone's throw of the delicate old mansion.

Developers and their bulldozers at this location had pushed dirt right up to the front steps of the old mansion house. I guess they thought it was alright as long as they gave people like us one last chance to rummage through the ruins and take anything of value before leveling the old buildings. Perhaps in this particular instance, we should be grateful they allowed us to be here at all.

The mansion house itself had been restored. Now at least it had a decent coat of paint. I hadn't seen what they had done to the inside. The massive acreage around it had been sold off and the original plantation was now down to just a few acres.

We passed Colonel Washington's house and parked behind it. We went on foot from there, back into the fields and away from the development being started on both sides of the house. Jim said the ruins were at the back corner of the lot where he told us we would find a large barn and several out buildings.

We speculated as to what we might find and tried to determine even before the treasures were accumulated, what we would do with the loot. If we found money, it was to be a four-way split, with each of us getting our share and the

Jefferson County Museum getting one-fourth. We also knew our chances of finding money were probably about as remote as winning the Powerball lottery.

If we found something identifiable to the Confederacy or some kind of firearm, Jim would get them. Papers of any sort would go onto Doug's pile as he loved researching old documents to see what information they might reveal. I was willing to give any of those items to them without any fuss at all.

And as for me, I am an author. If anything we found was determined to have value for my next book, I would get first crack at it.

It sounded like a losing proposition for me, but I was just happy to be here. This was my first-ever relic hunting venture. I was determined to have a good time.

Jim pointed to where he knew the buildings were. We marched off in that direction. I followed them through deep grass, appreciating that Jim told me to wear hiking boots. We trudged back a quarter mile or so.

Over the last hill we found parts of three structures. The area around the buildings was marked with "No Trespassing" signs. We passed the signs by as if they weren't there. After all, Jim said we had permission to be here today. Who were we to question him?

We started in the largest building -- part of a barn. The roof of the old structure was gone. The walls were falling in. It was not the safest place I had even been. Our job was to pick up anything of interest and make a pile of our loot in the center of the barn so we could sift through it and sort it out later.

I watched as Jim's metal detector swept back and forth in his hands. Every once in a while he stopped and dug, seeking whatever had set his instrument to pinging.

I turned on my flashlight, put on my gloves and began my own exploration. Being chicken-hearted, I stayed close to the center of the dilapidated old barn, away from the walls. It looked like a good wind could topple the building, causing serious injury or even ending my life.

Before long I had found a horseshoe and some square nails, a broken pitchfork and a part of what I thought was a wagon. I piled them in the center of the room and went back for more. On my second round, I scored what looked like a leg bone, several other bones and an old decayed saddle. I brought them to the treasure pile and headed back out again.

Meanwhile, I kind of lost track of the other two. It didn't seem like I had turned up much of anything of value, but perhaps the others had.

When I was finished with the area on the ground, I glanced up and noticed a partial loft over my head. The ladder to the loft loomed in front of me. I yelled for the others. Doug came by to see what I needed.

"I'm going up," I said, pointing to the loft, not wanting to be stranded up there without someone knowing that's where I was going.

"Go for it," Doug insisted. And so I did.

I climbed the ladder very carefully because the rungs were all rotten. I knew the same would be true with the floorboards once I got to the landing. I was thinking all the way up that I must be nuts at the age of sixty-one to be doing this. But I carefully moved onward and upward.

There was nothing much in the loft except for something in the back corner that my flashlight shined on. I skirted the edge hanging on to anything that looked substantial until I got close enough to determine what I had seen was a small box. I picked it up and tiptoed back to the ladder.

I yelled down to Doug again for him to hang out at the bottom of the ladder as I climbed back down, lest I fall. Now with the box in hand, the journey down the ladder seemed even more perilous than my trip in the other direction.

I couldn't see where my feet were landing on any of the descending rungs. I carefully climbed back down, breaking the last rung and practically falling into my friend's arms.

"Look what I found," I stated proudly, holding up my little box. "Could this be my next book?"

"Not if it's got money, Confederate items or papers in it," Doug reminded me.

"Yea, I hear you," I announced, still clinging to my little treasure chest.

Jim came around the corner. "I think we're finished here. Let's look through the other two buildings."

We followed as he explored the smaller buildings. One building was more like a storage shed, only big enough for one of us at a time to enter. It was in much less stable condition than the barn. Jim scoped it out quickly but found nothing of interest.

The other building Jim said was the blacksmith shop. I could see that it had a stone fireplace at one end. There wasn't much left today. Jim picked up a broken piece of wood from the floor and brought it along. There was nothing else there.

We walked slowly back into the barn and over to the pile in the middle of the room.

Doug and I sat on the floor and watched Jim pour over the booty. He held each item up and decided who would get it. He had found several Minnie balls and a Confederate belt buckle. I would not have known the difference, so I was assuming since Doug didn't protest, they were indeed what he said. They went in Jim's pile.

He showed off some papers, announcing that they were receipts for items purchased for Beall Air. He put them in Doug's pile.

Jim sent crumbs my way, probably to keep me from protesting. I got to keep the dilapidated saddle, the nails and the horseshoe. So far my future book was looking mighty thin.

After about thirty minutes, the other items were all divvied up. My pile was by far the smallest. A couple of items went unclaimed including part of what I thought might have been a sign on a broken board with the letters "Cat" on the top and "Blac" on the bottom.

It wasn't until Jim got to the end of the loot that they finally noticed I was still holding the box. It was like I didn't want it piled in the middle.

"OK, O'Connor," Jim announced. "Let's see what you've got."

I reluctantly handed him the box. Jim held it up. We all visually examined my treasure chest. It was about 10 inches long, 5 inches high and 8 inches across. The box had brass hinges and was in quite good shape. It was locked. We argued for several minutes about opening it.

I expressed concerns that the box was much more valuable than whatever was in it. I was not in favor of injuring the box to open it. Jim argued that it might contain money or some fabulously important Confederate artifact lost for all these years. He insisted that we look inside. Doug was for opening it too, but agreed with me that we shouldn't injure the box just to see what was inside.

The vote was in. We would open it carefully, so we did not damage the box. Jim asked Doug if he minded that I be given the box, sans the contents, and Doug agreed. I was grateful, but had already decided it would go into the Jefferson County Museum if it ended up in my pile.

Doug suggested we guess what might be inside before opening it. Jim guessed a stash of rare Confederate bank notes. Doug speculated that the box contained documents signed by Robert E. Lee. If either one of those guesses were right, we truly would have had an outstanding day.

I was next. I thought for a moment, remembering my friend's remarks about capturing positive energy and making things happen like I wanted them to. I guessed someone's diary.

Jim pulled out his Swiss Army knife and opened the lock. The hinges creaked as he carefully forced the lid open. Doug and I crept closer for a better look.

Jim lifted out an old battered book. My hopes soured. Was this my dairy? "One well-used old dictionary," Jim announced. He put it aside and reached in to pull out an old photograph, the early kind from the Civil War. "Colonel Washington," he said, showing us the photograph. We shook our heads in agreement as we recognized the owner of Beall Air.

Jim and Doug both knew of my interest in those kinds of photographs. Jim looked at Doug and with his approval, Jim put the photograph in my pile. I thought I had won the jackpot.

"That is it for the box," Jim said, holding it up and offering it to me. I was excited. I carefully put my photo inside, and then stopped. Something just wasn't right. The inside bottom was higher than the outside bottom.

"I think there's a false bottom inside the box," I shouted. "I'd like to investigate."

"Be my guest," Jim told me. "It's your box."

"What if that's where the Robert E. Lee letter is hiding?" I asked.

"It's all yours now," Jim admitted, kind of angry that he had missed this important discovery.

"I agree," Doug added dejectedly, acting peeved that Jim might have given up the box prematurely.

I borrowed Jim's knife. I carefully pried open the false bottom. Within a few seconds, the bottom popped open.

My heart was thumping loudly in my chest. My treasure awaited me. Even if it was the rare bank note or a Robert E. Lee letter, either could be worth a fortune.

I reached inside and found what looked like a journal.

I carefully pulled out the book. My positive energy had paid off. I read the markings on the cover out loud, "The Life of Catesby."

I couldn't wait to read it. Jim wondered aloud, "So, who's Catesby?"

I walked over and picked up the broken sign with "Cat" and "Blac" on it and the very worn dictionary no one had claimed. I put them in my pile. "I think these go with his story," I announced.

And now we are all about to find out the answer to Jim's question.

Colonel Lewis Washington

Beall Air mansion today
Colonel Lewis Washington's home
(Clubhouse for private development)

Chapter 2
In the Beginning

October 1, 1859

Ever since my mother, Willa, taught me how to read and write, she encouraged me to practice my writing. She gave me this journal for that purpose. She wanted me to write about my life so that someday others would find out who I was. This is my story.

My earliest memories were of running around and playing at Beall Air, a plantation belonging to Colonel Lewis Washington. The plantation was located along the Winchester and Potomac Railroad about halfway between Harpers Ferry and Charlestown, Virginia.

As a youngan, life was easy at Beall Air. There were a bunch of boys all about the same age. We played in Flowing Springs Creek that flowed through the plantation. And we tried to outrun the trains passing directly in front of the big house.

Together we caught frogs and fished, swam and chased dogs, and threw lots of rocks. And we made up stories especially about what we were going to do when we were older. We were kind of dreaming about that last part.

I was better than the others at running. There was nobody who would catch me when I got started. I was also bigger and stronger than my friends. I loved playing from the first light of morning until way after dark. Any game you could come up with, I was ready and eager to play. Being a young child on the plantation was always exciting.

Besides being the fastest, the biggest and the strongest, I was also the smartest of the bunch.

When we got older, the play turned into work. Us boys did not get much chance to be together during the day. Each of us had our own jobs to do. But in the evenings, we still acted like four brothers. We developed a bond that you could not put your finger on, but you could not break with a hammer either. Perhaps we were blood brothers.

My friends are Jim, Sam, and Mason. My name is Catesby, pronounced like "cats" and "bee." I did not know who my daddy was. I had no last name. Neither did the others. We were just plain old Jim, Sam, Mason and Catesby.

Beall Air was home to me. I was born here and have lived here for many years. I do not know for how long -- about twenty years I would guess. It might seem funny to you that I do not know for sure when my birthday is. If you know I am a colored slave, you would not find it so odd.

It was common for slaves to be born with no birthday and no age. I think that was to our owner's advantage. When it came time to sell us, he could say we were younger. That way he could get more money for us.

The law said it did not matter if our father was free or slave. Us coloreds were sorted out by the status of our mother. Since my mother was a slave, that made me a slave. Jim, Sam and Mason were slaves too. If our mothers would have been born free, we would have been free too.

I was born into slavery. I did not particularly like it any, but there was nothing I could do about it for now.

October 2, 1859

Jim, Sam, Mason and I shared dreams most nights of what it might be like when we would be able to purchase our freedom and become free blacks. We talked about going to school, owning property, and being able to make our own decisions. We laughed that someday we might marry and have children of our own. We knew it would be smart of us to marry a free woman so our children would be free.

Mason was the youngest. He was always talking, even when he didn't have anything to say. His mouth often got him in trouble. Seemed like he was talking first, and thinking about what he had to say later. Many times we laughed at him just because of what came flowing out of his mouth.

Mason disagreed with anything you said. If you said the sky was blue, he'd say it wasn't, just so he could get into an argument. Before long he would have you convinced that you had been wrong about the sky color.

He had a younger sister, Sissy, on the plantation. His mother had been sold away. He had no idea where his mother was or whether he would ever see her.

That was one of the hard parts of being a slave. Your owner could sell you or your kin to separate plantations. You may never see them again. My mother told me the threat of splitting up families was a way the plantation owners had to keep slaves on their best behavior.

She made me promise if we were ever sold to different owners, I would never stop looking for her.

Mason and his sister worked in the field and were called field slaves. They worked at plowing, picking and caring for all the crops grown here. They tended the corn, barley, oats, and wheat and the large orchards. Mason had to cut firewood all year long.

Sam was the runt of the litter. He was small but mighty. There wasn't anything he couldn't do. He was not afraid of anything or anyone.

When we picked sides for any game, Sam was always picked first because he was good at most anything. Sam's team almost always won the games.

He was light skinned and was said to be a mulatto. Mother said mulattos were the result of white masters loving the slave women. Mother told us, "That was the way slave owners made more slaves without having to buy them. They grew more by loving slave women." Mother hated that part of slavery. She said it was disgusting. She promised that if any white man ever tried to love her, he would be sorry.

Because Sam was small, people tended to pick on him. But after the first time, they didn't come back again. Sam could beat up even the biggest of the other lads.

Sam's mother, two younger brothers and an older sister were here at Beall Air. They were all field slaves too.

Jim was the oldest and my closest friend. We had this understanding where we could almost know what the other was thinking. He could just look at me or nod. I would know what was up without saying anything at all. He was also the best looking. All the women on the plantation, even the white ladies, found Jim to their liking.

Jim had no kin at Beall Air. All his family had been sold to other plantations and split apart. His mother was a beautiful fair-skinned woman who all us boys really liked. She had been sold about three years ago and had not been heard from since. Jim was a field slave too.

October 3, 1859

My job at the plantation was learning to be a blacksmith. It took some powerful lifting and carrying. I enjoyed the work though it was mighty hot and dirty. If you asked me, I was real good at it too, though no one ever asked me.

I could keep that fire going forever. I loved being able to heat up the iron to a red hot color and then bend it like it were butter. My job was tougher than anything Jim, Sam and Mason had to do. I thought I had the best job of all.

The blacksmith, Billy, who was my teacher, had been at Beall Air for about forty years. Billy had been born into slavery but had recently purchased his freedom. Billy was the biggest and strongest man I had ever seen. He was over six feet tall, with arms like tree trunks. His hands were huge and hardened. His arms and hands were covered by ugly burns. He was a very good blacksmith and an even better teacher.

At first I started just working the big bellows. And then I was able to help more and more in the shop. There were lots of projects to complete. I tried to learn fast so I could move on to the other jobs in the shop. As I learned more, I was able to make repairs on the wagons and harnesses, fix all the plows and sharpen the scythes and corn knives used by the field hands. And I kept the horses shod.

Billy told me I might be good enough someday to be a real blacksmith. He would help me buy my freedom. With Billy's help I could learn everything I needed.

Billy taught me how to know when the iron was ready to be worked. He showed me the hottest spots in the fire. If the fire was too hot the metal would burn up. If it was too cold, the metal was not as easy to bend. And if I took the metal out of the fire too soon, or too late, the job would become harder to finish.

My other teacher was my mother. She taught me to mind my manners and be respectful. That was what I tried to do. I have a couple of lash marks on my back from years ago, but haven't been in any trouble for a long while. I guess you could say I learned my lesson.

Jim, Sam and Mason were a bit more trouble than me. They took their beatings every once in a while. Got so I could tell from their screams which one of them was taking a licking at that moment. It hurt me to hear them being beaten. From the talk in the evenings, sometimes those boys had been up to mischief and probably deserved every lash they got. Colonel Lewis never hit any of us but his overseers, Morgan and Bishop, were cruel to the slaves.

Bishop was a toothless savage. He had no sense at all. He had worked at the plantation for years and years. He got his kicks by knocking slaves around.

Bishop had way more muscles than brains. He liked to drink. The more he drank, the more he beat on the slaves. The only good thing about Bishop was he would get so drunk, when he was supposed to count out thirty lashes, he often forgot partway through and ended up giving less.

Colonel Washington's other overseer was Morgan. He wasn't near as mean as Bishop. Morgan had a couple more teeth and a couple more brains than Bishop. Morgan's problem was he liked to chase girls and capture them for his pleasure. Quickly the young girls on the plantation learned to steer a wide path when Morgan was around.

Both Morgan and Bishop thought beating us slaves proved they were better than us. They were the overseers of the field slaves and their word was law. Seems like they punished Sam, Jim and Mason more than any of the others. Maybe it was because my brothers were quick with the comments, speaking up first without really thinking about the trouble they were getting themselves into.

It was an unspoken rule that slaves did not fight back when being punished. We slaves knew that. If the day ever came that we needed to fight back, Bishop and Morgan would have been no trouble for any of us boys to lick. If that ever happened, we would need to skedaddle out of here as fast as we could.

All of us wished we were not slaves. Someday we were going to purchase our freedom. It was not something I thought about every day because I was not being mistreated like some of the others in nearby plantations we heard stories about. If I were being whipped and beaten everyday like some, I would be jumping on the train that went right by the house never to be seen again. Or I might just start to run and run until I was far away.

But for now I was not going anywhere. I still had learning to do because I was not ready to be a real blacksmith.

October 4, 1859

Colonel Washington was a respectable gentleman on most days. For a white man, I kinda liked him. He was a "I am better than you are and we both know it" kind of man and full of himself, but he had a funny kind of charm about him.

He was short and pudgy. His large mustache was his trademark. The colonel had a large open forehead where many men had hair. His look was that of a successful plantation owner. He was about fifty years old.

Colonel Washington's wife had died, leaving him to raise three children. His son, James Barroll Washington, was away at school at West Point most of the time.

His daughters, Eliza Ridgely Beall and Mary Ann, were both younger than me. They were hardly ever around. They lived with their grandmother in Baltimore, Maryland.

Colonel Washington was not a real colonel. I was told his title colonel, was honorary, meaning he was not in a war or anything like that. Someone just gave him that fancy title.

President George Washington had other kin in this area too. The nearby town of Charlestown, Virginia was named for his youngest brother, Charles. Other relatives lived close by at Harewood, Claymont, and Blakely Plantations.

The colonel had some fancy guns in his collection given by General Lafayette and a sword from the King of Prussia, all passed down from George Washington. Anyone who visited got to see the colonel's collection of George Washington items.

There were other slaves on the plantation, including my mother, who was a house servant. Some of the other girls and the older men worked in the house too. It took my mother a long time to get into the mansion house and into Colonel Washington's trust.

There were days my mother acted like she was a member of Colonel Washington's family. She was treated very well. Mother told me she thought there were times she was treated like a white woman.

There were several youngans running around too, playing everyday as they were not old enough to start doing any of the work.

Some days I wished I was still running around with them.

October 6, 1859

My mother was trying hard to encourage all the slaves to read even though it was against the law in Virginia. She said it was another white man's law to keep the blacks depending on them forever. She promised whether it was against the law or not, the children at Beall Air were going to learn.

I could read and write. Learning seemed to come natural for me. I was doing my ABCs before some of the others were still learning how to walk.

I was not allowed to go to school, but there were books in the mansion house. Mother borrowed them often and read to me when I was young. She read as long as there was oil in the lamps to burn in our shanty.

She read me books like Aesop's Fables, Robinson Crusoe, and Uncle Tom's Cabin. My mother kidded me that my birth was so difficult for her because I passed from her holding a book in my hand. That must have been something to see. As I got older, I started reading books to her.

Mother taught me how to write using a book that she traded from the peddler's wagon when it came to the mansion house with supplies. The book showed me how to form each one of the large and small letters of the whole alphabet, from *A* to *Z*.

I would spend one whole night forming big *A*'s and small *a*'s, and then show them to my mother. If I did most of them the right way, I could go on the next night to the big *B*'s and small *b*'s. If not, I would have to start over with the *A*'s and *a*'s until I got them right.

When I got all the letters right from *A* to *Z*, she taught me how to spell words, starting with Catesby. I liked to write Catesby over and over again.

And then she started teaching me all the little words that started with *a* like as, an, and ant. She taught me longer and longer words, like apple, alert, aunt, after and along, and then even longer words that started with *a* until I could spell and write out words like agreement and August.

When I learned all the *a* words, I got to do the short *b* words, like be, but, and bee. She taught me the longer ones like before, beyond and bath. Finally I learned the real long *b* words like beginnings, and of course, my favorite, blacksmith.

Later the peddler's wagon brought a wonderful book called a dictionary. Mother traded for it. She gave it to me as a present. On every single page there were lists and lists of words starting with all the letters of the alphabet. It was one of my favorite books. I almost wore out the pages of that book trying to learn each and every word in it.

Learning to read and write took me about five years of hard work. I did lessons every single night. When I was ready and could do it, I made myself a small wooden sign with the word "Catesby" on top and the word "Blacksmith" underneath. Billy let me nail it up in the shop.

Mother thought learning was the way for me to be a free man. By teaching me, she had given me a valuable gift. I thought with my skills as a blacksmith together with reading and writing, I might succeed.

October 8, 1859

The days at Beall Air were long and hard, starting at sunrise and going through until after dark. We worked everyday except Sunday, which was a day set aside for the Lord. Mother was teaching me from the Bible on those days off.

Each week was pretty much like the week before. I looked forward to Sundays and days when sometimes Colonel Washington would let me drive him into town in the wagon.

October 10, 1859

Everyday was a busy day at the blacksmith shop. We always had a long list of jobs to do. Seemed like whenever we would get all of Colonel Washington's wagons fixed, he would have us work on one of the neighbor's wagons. Billy and I worked long and hard to put everything in working order. There were times we got so busy Billy brought in a striker to help us.

I had not known there were so many things to learn as a blacksmith. Not all the tools were alike. We had about fifty hammers including large, medium sized and small ones, and ones with round peens, straight peens and crossed peens. Billy said I had to learn which tool best fit which job.

He showed me how to use chisels and panches. I learned how to forge, upset and weld the iron and steel. Billy encouraged me to watch the first few times he worked on something new. And then he would stand back and let me try it by myself. If I made a mistake, he would shake his head and show me again. He didn't expect me to make that mistake again.

With Jim, Sam, Mason and the others in the field, there was always one of Colonel Washington's men overseeing their work. That was not the case in our shop. Most days it was just me and Billy. I think because Billy had been here so long, he was trusted. He had Colonel Washington's respect and the respect of the neighbors. He was left alone. Billy said colored blacksmiths were more respected than most coloreds because of the skill it took to learn the trade. I was hoping I could earn that respect someday too.

Billy's hands were the biggest I had ever seen. Even the big hammers looked like toys when he held them. He was strong as anyone. I never saw him fight because he was gentle by nature, but he could probably break most any man in half without trying too hard. I am sure he could have beaten up Bishop and Morgan at the same time with one hand tied behind his back. I know Bishop and Morgan were scared of Billy.

Blacksmithing was a grand job for me. At the end of the day I could line up jobs I had worked on and feel like I had done something good. Billy always praised my work. He said there was nothing he taught me that I couldn't do well after just a few tries.

Besides blacksmithing, Billy taught me about life. He said I had a good mind and needed to think and talk about things. According to Billy, it was important to have my opinions heard. He told me about his life as a slave and how wrong slavery was. "God made us people too," Billy insisted. "We ain't property. Most white folks ain't no worse than we are…but they sure ain't no better than we are, either. It's just they are the ones who make the laws."

And you know. I think Billy was right about that.

Recently Billy had talked to me about being a free black man. "Catesby, you need to be sure you do two things. Be a real good blacksmith and be a free man."

Seemed like there were a bunch of free blacks in Jefferson County, Virginia where we lived. Billy knew James Roper, a free black, who was the wealthiest landowner in Jefferson County. These freemen were allowed to have jobs, own their land and earn money because they were free, just like Billy. They could live wherever they wanted to and did not have to be owned by anyone.

I decided I wanted to someday be free. When I asked mother about it, she said being free should be one of my main goals. She would be very happy when I was able to buy my freedom, even if that meant leaving her at Beall Air and moving somewhere else. She said the laws of Virginia only allowed free blacks to stay for one year after they became free. And then they had to move somewhere else.

Billy thought a war was coming to this country. It was time for the coloreds to fight back for our rights God had given us.

Billy told me of his dreams of finding him a good woman and even having children someday. He didn't think he was too old to still do that. He wanted his children to go to school, just like the white children. He wanted them to grow up better off than he was. He knew colored children weren't allowed to go to school, but that was wrong too. Blacks needed to fight for the right to go to school.

Because the others were not as learned as I was, Billy said I needed to lead them and help them improve their place in life.

Chapter 3
Taken by Force to Harpers Ferry

October 16, 1859

We had celebrated the harvest on Sunday, our only day off for the week. It was a festive day. We ate ham, turkey, potatoes, yams, cabbage and squash pies. We were dancing, singing and drinking. Drinking was allowed only on certain special occasions. After all the activities, I was mighty tired.

I went to bed early, to get ready for the start of the week. Billy had prepared a long list of items that I needed to get done. I wanted to be well rested for the tasks ahead.

October 18, 1859

The last few days have been a blur. I want to write about them while I remember them.

After midnight on Sunday, October 16, I was awakened by armed men and dragged outside. Jim started to fuss, but I grabbed his arm and told him to hold back, we were outnumbered. Our other slaves including Sam, Mason and Billy had been captured too.

The men also brought Colonel Washington out of his house in his nightshirt. I asked about my mother and he told me the women had fled. He thought for now they were safe.

We were ordered onto one of the colonel's wagons and driven to John Allstadt's house nearby. There Mr. Allstadt and his son and all his slaves, Henri, Ben, Levi, Phil, Jerry, George and Bill were rounded up and put on another wagon. Mr. Allstadt yelled and screamed, but when one of the armed men put a gun to his son's head and told him to be still, he got real quiet.

We rode the wagons into the lowest part of Harpers Ferry along the two rivers. There we were pushed into a building at the armory. Colonel Washington, Mr. Allstadt and his son were put in one corner. All us colored were given long poles with a point on top and were told to guard the others.

Talk among the men who captured us was that they were with a gang who had been sent here to free the slaves. An old man with a beard, who the others called captain, was giving orders. He looked to be in charge.

As the sun rose in the morning of Monday, October 17, more prisoners were brought in for us to guard. The captain left and came back with a cart full of food. I heard him say he had swapped a prisoner for breakfast for everyone.

Colonel Washington shook his head from side to side. He didn't want us to eat. We didn't, even though we were all mighty hungry. Later I was told the colonel feared the food might be poisoned.

As the day went on, men outside the building started firing their muskets at us. I ducked down to keep from getting shot. Men inside were shooting back.

Jim and one of Mr. Allstadt's slaves, Ben, motioned for me to come with them as they talked to the captain. I watched but didn't join them. I thought my job was to protect the colonel. That's what I was trying to do.

Jim and Ben left to go outside with several of the captain's men. The captain had sent them to ask for a truce. One man returned. He had been shot. He lay on the floor, bleeding terribly. No one made a move to help him.

More prisoners were brought in for us to guard. They were wet from the rain that was falling outside. The captain had himself a sword that I think might have belonged to Colonel Washington's collection, and was swinging it around, giving orders. More shots banged into the building where we were being held.

I hung on to my pole, wondering just what I might do with it.

The captain brought some of the white prisoners together. He gave them paper and pencils and told them to write a letter. He said they would be released if an able bodied slave would be traded in their place.

Late in the day, when there was a fuss outside, the prisoners broke the back window. Several of them escaped. The colonel motioned for us to stay put.

Another of the captain's men was wounded and fell beside the first one. He too was hurt badly. The first man hit lay silently. I feared he might be dead.

It was quiet after dark. I dropped to the floor. I was too tired to stand any more. The captain's men asked where all the men were who were coming to help them. The captain said he was disappointed, as not many showed up to help.

On the morning of Tuesday, October 18, a man knocked on the door and told the captain he needed to surrender. The captain refused, and slammed the door. He shouted instructions, readying his men for an attack. It sounded like someone was trying to break down the door. I huddled behind a cart with a fire hose on it. I readied my pointed pole.

The door was smashed in. Soldiers ran into the building. The colonel pointed out the captain and his men, including a colored man who had taken up a pole pretending to be one of us. Within a few minutes the gang was either dead or captured. We were released along with Colonel Washington.

Outside the building there were hundreds of soldiers. They wanted to hang the captain's gang right there.

Colonel Washington got us some food and told us to wait as he talked to some of the officials there. He asked about Jim and Ben. Ben had been captured. Jim had been killed.

We hung around the rest of the morning. Colonel Washington pointed out Colonel Robert E. Lee, who he said led the troops in capturing the captain and his gang. I was surprised to see Colonel Lee was not wearing a uniform.

As we returned to Beall Air, the colonel thanked us for protecting him. He said we should always remember being captured and held prisoner by the famous John Brown.

I was sad that my friend, Jim, had died and that Ben had been captured. He was now in jail with the rest of them. I was puzzled as to why Jim and Ben had joined John Brown. I wondered how it would have turned out for me if I had gone with them.

Engine House at Harpers Ferry
Drawing by David Hunter Strother
<u>Harpers Weekly</u>   November 5, 1859
West Virginia and Regional History Collection
West Virginia University Libraries

Chapter 4
Results of the John Brown Raid

October 29, 1859

For several days in a row, I have driven Colonel Washington to nearby Charlestown for the trial of John Brown. The colonel has been called as a witness.

Each day I took the colonel to the courthouse building in the center of town and tied up the horse in back of the building to wait for him. Several armed soldiers asked me why I was there. I showed them the official pass the colonel had left with me.

The colonel told me that he thought the men who had held us hostage were all likely to be found guilty. He said there was talk that they would be hanged.

He also had found out that Mr. Allstadt's slave, Ben, had died in jail.

November 2, 1859

Today Colonel Washington told Billy that he heard John Brown had been found guilty and had been sentenced to be hanged on December 2. The trials of the other men were starting up. He would have to go back in town to testify at those trials.

November 10, 1859

The colonel had been right. He told us today the other four men had also been found guilty and were sentenced to hang. Two of those were colored men, including the one who had hidden among us at the armory building.

November 25, 1859

Tonight I took Colonel Washington into Charlestown. When I went in past the courthouse, there were more soldiers than when Colonel Washington had gone there before. Several times soldiers blocked the streets. We were stopped and the colonel showed them his official pass. The soldiers let us pass.

Two streets past the courthouse Colonel Washington told me to turn right and pull up in front of a church building on the next corner. I helped the colonel climb down. I tied up the horse and waited.

There was a big crowd there that evening. I could hear someone talking and loud clapping as the side windows of the building were open.

It was late when the program was over. I watched for the colonel. When I saw him walking down the front steps, I pulled the wagon to the front. He climbed onto the wagon. The colonel said he had been listening to some readings of Shakespeare from a soldier from Richmond at the reading room.

On the way home, we were stopped again for questioning by the soldiers.

December 2, 1859

Today Colonel Washington ordered me to hitch up the wagon and drive him and my brothers into Charlestown to watch John Brown be hanged. Colonel Washington told us, "I want you to watch this because you men remained loyal to me when we all were taken hostage."

Once again the streets were blocked by hundreds of soldiers. Colonel Washington had to show his pass several different times before we were allowed to go through.

Colonel Washington told me where to turn and then where to stop the wagon. I tied the horse to a post. We walked to an open field not too far from the jail and the courthouse. Soldiers would not let us get any closer.

There was a large crowd of soldiers in long rows surrounding a tall platform. We watched from behind the soldiers. All were armed and stood ready. There were not too many other people behind the soldiers.

We watched a wagon come down the street with lines of soldiers on each side. Captain John Brown sat on a casket in the wagon, his arms tied behind his back. He was dressed in red slippers, a black coat, pants and a black hat.

Men on the platform made short order of old John Brown. They put a rope around his neck, slipped a bag over his face, and chopped the rope to let him fall through the trap door and into the hole in the floor. He jerked a few times and then was very still. He hanged there for a long time. I guess they wanted to be sure he was good and dead. I was sure he was dead right after the rope snapped his neck as easy as me squashing a bug. He didn't move at all after that except for twisting in the breeze.

People said old John Brown wanted to die like that, to prove a point. I cannot wish that on anyone. It was difficult to watch. Maybe the others liked watching hangings, but old Catesby did not enjoy the moment.

Colonel Washington had seen enough. We all walked back to our wagon and climbed on board. The colonel spoke to a young soldier. When he climbed back on the wagon, he told me that was the soldier who had performed for them at the reading room, J. B. Wilkes. I took notice of the man before nudging the horse forward.

I drove us all back to Beall Air. Billy, Mason, Sam and I talked about the hanging when we got back. "Coloreds seem to be hanged a lot more often than white men," Billy said. And he was right. I thought back to what Billy had said about the whites making all the laws. I wondered what things would be different if they let the coloreds make the laws the next time around.

December 16, 1859

I drove Colonel Washington's wagon back to Charlestown this morning. He wanted us to watch the hangings of four other men who had been at Harpers Ferry with John Brown.

Two colored men were among the four men who were to be hanged today. Colonel Washington said the two blacks, John Copeland and Shields Green, had both come to help John Brown free the slaves. Today they would give their lives for that cause. He told us "the colored men were found innocent of treason in their trials because men had to be citizens to commit treason. It had been argued in court that the two colored men were not citizens; they were property."

It didn't much matter that they were found innocent of that, because they were to be hanged anyway. I wasn't too sure about Ben. I was happy that I didn't have to watch his hanging, but sad that he and Jim had died.

While I didn't agree with what happened at Harpers Ferry, I admired the two colored men and their attempt to be free. Someday I would do something to be free too – though I wasn't sure what that might be.

After seeing one hanging already, I really did not want to watch the others. This time they were hanged two at once. When the rope was cut, the trap door opened and two men fell through the hole in the floor. The colored men died in the morning.

We waited for the white men to be hanged in the early afternoon. They included the local man who had visited Beall Air before taking us prisoner. His name was John Cook.

Many more people watched these hangings than the one on December 2. Hundreds of soldiers still were guarding the town.

January 2, 1860

I got the buggy ready to take Colonel Washington to Washington City. We were to be gone about a week. I was happy Colonel Washington asked me to drive for him on such a long trip.

We were going so that Colonel Washington could be a witness in the Senate hearings about what happened at Harpers Ferry. I had never been to Washington City before.

It had been snowing, so the roads were muddy and full of ruts. The journey took three days. Colonel Washington didn't have to speak until the fourth day, so we didn't have to hurry.

He stayed each night at an inn along the way. I slept with the horse at a nearby stable. As usual, the colonel sent food out to me before he bedded down for the evening.

Washington City was the biggest place I had ever visited. Colonel Washington pointed out the White House to me, telling me that was where President Buchanan lived.

He told me to stop at the Willard Hotel just a few blocks from the White House. It was a grand hotel for important folk to stay overnight, like Colonel Washington.

I found a bed in a straw pile at the nearby livery and slept with the horse and buggy.

January 6, 1860

Today I delivered Colonel Washington to the Senate hearings and waited outside. In late afternoon, when the colonel came out, we started back to Beall Air. The colonel was tired and did not say very much on the return trip other than the Senate committee had been trying to find out if anyone else from outside the area was involved in helping John Brown and his men at Harpers Ferry.

March 16, 1860

The colonel told us two more of John Brown's men were to be hanged today in Charlestown. That made seven all together. He was not interested in watching. I was happy to stay home. I had seen enough hangings to last me a lifetime.

With these hangings the Harpers Ferry incident was over in Charlestown. The soldiers left. The newspaper I read at the general store, however, continued to carry news about Captain John Brown. I heard the youngans in Charlestown singing a song about John Brown's body lying in the grave, but his truth kept marching on.

The more I read about John Brown, the more confused I got. He came to Harpers Ferry to free the slaves, the newspapers said. Then why did he take Colonel Washington's and Mr. Allstadt's slaves as prisoners?

And why would a white man be in charge of freeing this country's slaves? I would have thought someone like Frederick Douglass, who seemed to be a national colored leader, would have been assigned that job. I think Mr. Douglass could have led us to freedom better than some old white man. I did not understand.

I asked Billy to explain that too. He was just as confused about it as I was.

The field slaves mentioned tonight that Bishop and Morgan finally were starting to leave them alone following our capture at Harpers Ferry. Perhaps Colonel Washington had said something to them since we protected the colonel from harm. The beatings stopped at least for now.

April 12, 1860

As I worked in the shop, Billy and I talked about the puzzling events at Harpers Ferry.

Each time I was sent into town to pick up supplies in Charlestown, I heard people talking about it. A man at the post office said John Brown believed he had been chosen by God to lead the slave revolt. If that was the case, I wondered why God chose him for that job.

Another man said John Brown had murdered five white men in the new state of Kansas. Another said five of the Captain John Brown's men had actually escaped Harpers Ferry and had not been recaptured.

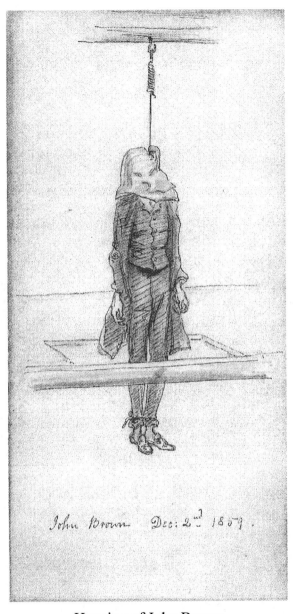

John Brown   Dec: 2ᵈ 1859.

Hanging of John Brown
Drawing by David Hunter Strother for <u>Harpers Weekly</u>
West Virginia and Regional History Collection
West Virginia University

Chapter 5
Mother Takes Sick

June 20, 1860

One of the house servants came into the shop this morning to tell me my mother had taken sick. I went to the mansion house. She was lying in the upstairs bedroom. Because she was a slave, I knew she would not get any medical care.

She had the fever and chills real bad. Her face and her dress were wet from the fever. Her eyes were closed. She was breathing very slowly. I took a wet rag and wiped her face. She was too ill to talk, but I spent some time with her. I held her hand tightly. I told her how important she was to me.

I told her in a few days she would be back on her feet and working again. She smiled when I said the mansion house could not get along without her, so she had to get better. I kissed her good night when I left.

June 21, 1860

Colonel Washington returned to the shop this morning early. "Catesby, your mother died in the night. I am real sorry that she passed. She was a fine woman." He reached out and touched my shoulder.

I was in shock. I didn't think she was that sick. There were so many things I would have wanted to say if I'd have known she was going to die. I never got a chance. I felt cheated.

My mother was the most important person in my life. She was the only kin I had. I felt empty, wanting to scream at God for taking her from me.

June 24, 1860

We held a funeral service for mother today. I was allowed to bury her in the Washington family graveyard behind the house.

Mason and Billy, some of the other slaves and Colonel Washington's family talked about my mother's life. Colonel Washington said "Your mother was a very good woman. We will all miss her."

We said some prayers and sang spiritual songs. I was thankful for all that.

I spoke too, telling the others how important my mother had been to me. "My mother taught me everything I know except for what Billy has taught me. She prepared me for life. She taught me how to read and write. She said I should be generous to others. She held my hand when I was little, picking me up and brushing me off when I fell. Mother sang me songs. She told me stories about people and places I would never have known. Her stories of her own mother, my grandmother, took me back to an earlier time when slaves had a much different life."

"The lessons she taught me," I told them, "have stayed with me. Love thy neighbor. Thou shalt not steal. Be truthful in everything you do. Give thanks to the Father for even the smallest blessing. Do unto others as you would have them do unto you. Don't look at people's color — get to know what is in their heart. Be not afraid."

That evening I cried. I was already missing my wonderful mother.

June 28, 1860

Billy helped me make a metal marker in the shop for mother's grave. Today we planted it where she was buried. It said "Willa, loving mother. June 21, 1860 R.I.P."

July 2, 1860

For days and days I couldn't keep my mind on the work. My mind kept wandering back to my mother. I missed her more than I thought I would.

I regretted not having spent more time with her thinking that she would live forever. I thought some day we could sit and talk some more. I did not tell her I loved her enough.

Her death was so unfair. She was still young -- I think around forty. Certainly for a healthy woman, it was surprising that she was gone. Those at the mansion house told me my mother had never been sick.

I missed her every single day. The hurt and emptiness did not go away.

July 10, 1860

Billy told me today I was about ready to be on my own as a blacksmith. I had learned about all I needed to run my own shop. He said that meant Colonel Washington would probably sell me to someone else, as there were always others who were looking for good blacksmiths.

I went to the mansion house in the morning and asked Colonel Washington about it. He explained, "Catesby. You are a good man and a fine blacksmith. I can get a grand return by selling your services to someone else. Now that your mother has died, you have no reason to have to stay here with me. Yes. I am searching for someone to purchase you."

Everyone I knew and loved was at Beall Air. Now that mother was gone, perhaps this was my time to move on. I had known someday that this would happen.

Chapter 6

Colonel Washington Brings Home a New Wife

August 14, 1860

Today Billy and I were called to the mansion house to make repairs on several latches and hinges. Inside the house, servants were painting, cleaning and repairing things in every single room. When Billy asked why all the fuss was being made, he was told the colonel was courting a fine lady from Virginia.

Sissy, Mason's little sister, who had just been moved into the kitchen of the mansion, stopped us. She thanked us for being so good to Mason and her. She said she liked her new job.

Sissy said last week Morgan had grabbed her and dragged her into the cellar. On the way down the stairs, she grabbed a loose rock and smashed his hand as he started to undress her. She didn't think he would try that again, at least until his hand started working properly.

I smiled, thinking how surprised Morgan must have been to have gotten hit by a colored girl.

September 1, 1860

Billy started teaching me about the business parts of the shop. He taught me how to determine the price of the work. I learned how to figure out how long a job would take. He showed me how to keep track of the cost of all the parts I used so I could find out my profit.

He taught me how to keep records. If I fixed a wheel before, and I could find the information when the next broken wheel came in, I could save lots of time just checking back to the record of that first job.

Billy helped me copy some of his records to take that would help me get started. He showed me how to keep track of time I spent doing each job. He said I needed to copy each bill, so the customer had one and I had the other.

Up to this time I thought I knew everything there was to know. There was still much I had to learn. "It isn't enough to be just a blacksmith," Billy said. "You need to be a record keeper too."

He said if I could do all that, I could be a real blacksmith soon.

October 12, 1860

I continued to read the newspaper about the unrest in the South and the election coming up in November. A new president was due to be elected. As a colored man I had no right to vote. But I was interested in who might be elected.

I traveled to Harpers Ferry today to pick up supplies at the Baltimore and Ohio depot next to the Wager House Hotel.

It was good to be trusted to take the wagon myself. I thought about driving off to freedom, but I needed to plan more on that idea. I was determined to wait to see if I would be sold before I made any big decisions.

I hadn't been back in Harpers Ferry since the John Brown raid a year ago. It was certainly much quieter today.

As I waited for the clerk to have time to show me to the colonel's order, I walked around.

The armory building where we had been held captive seemed smaller than I remembered. The door the soldiers smashed had not been repaired. There were Minnie ball holes in the wood.

Christine Fouke, a lady who worked at the hotel, told me Heywood Shepherd, a free black man who worked for the railroad, had been killed by John Brown's men. It seemed strange that this free black man had been killed by the men who were supposed to be freeing the slaves.

The colonel's order was finally ready. I loaded the wagon and left Harpers Ferry with the horse pulling the heavy load up the steep hill on High Street. I drove back to Beall Air.

November 1, 1860

Colonel Washington came into the shop today. He asked me and Billy to fix up his best buggy for November 4. He wanted me to drive him to Clover Lea in Hanover County, Virginia. The colonel was getting married. He said I would take him there, stay overnight, and then bring him and his new bride back.

He told us that Miss Ella, who he was marrying, was a direct kin to Betty, President George Washington's only sister. He said he knew everyone at Beall Air would like Miss Ella.

Billy and I put all our projects aside and readied the colonel's buggy. We polished all the metal on the harnesses and bridles, repaired the torn seat cover and painted the wheels. When we were finished, the buggy was ready for the wedding.

November 4, 1860

This morning I brushed down Miss Abigail, Colonel Washington's finest mare and hitched up the buggy by mid-morning. I waited patiently for the colonel to send for me.

Morgan came over a short time later. He told me to take the buggy to the mansion house and load the large empty trunk on the back. Morgan's right hand was bandaged. I was smiling inside thinking that hurt hand was from Sissy's hitting him with a rock.

When I got the trunk loaded, Colonel Washington boarded and we headed south. He said the trip would take most of two days. He knew of an inn where he could board for the night. After giving me the directions, he fell asleep. We arrived at the inn after dark.

The inn where he boarded was not fancy. But I am sure it was better than the ground I slept on out back. The colonel brought me some chicken to eat before he retired for the evening.

November 5, 1860

We continued our travels in the morning, arriving at Clover Lea in the late afternoon. I dropped Colonel Washington at mansion house. Several coloreds helped take the empty trunk into the house and directed me to the barn.

I walked Miss Abigail into the stall and brought her water, feed and straw. Richard, the man in charge of the barn, welcomed me. He told me I would be boarding with him. Supper would be brought by shortly.

I enjoyed the evening with Richard, eating roast beef and peas provided by the kitchen and talking about the colonel, Miss Ella and the wedding.

We listened to music late into the night as the people celebrated the upcoming wedding.

November 6, 1860

I watched this morning as buggy after buggy of well wishers came to the house. The mansion yard, Richard said, had been set up for the reception. He pointed to the church where the wedding would take place -- St. Paul's Episcopal Parish Church across from the mansion house. Richard said we were just to watch and be ready when they wanted to leave.

The area was beautiful. The mansion house was built between two rivers. The family here appeared wealthy as the plantation was very large. Richard said he was one of over one hundred slaves at Clover Lea. That was by far the most slaves I had ever known on any plantation.

Richard told me Miss Ella Bassett was about twenty years younger than her new husband. I think that made her about thirty years old.

He said Miss Ella was a fine lady, and was very pleasant, but she was real head-strong too. He laughed, saying if the colonel didn't watch out, Miss Ella would be running Beall Air before he knew it.

That evening when the guest buggies started leaving, Richard said it was time. He helped me hitch up the colonel's finest horse, Miss Abigail. We rode to the mansion house in the buggy together. The trunk was waiting on the stoop near the doorway. We loaded it on the back of the buggy. It was quite a bit heavier this time, loaded with all of Miss Ella's treasures.

It wasn't too long before the colonel and his new bride appeared on the porch, saying goodbye to the remaining guests. I helped them into the buggy, climbed up onto my seat, and drove down the lane toward Charlestown. The colonel told me to take the same roads back. Within minutes, I heard Colonel Washington snoring. The excitement of the day must have worn him out.

I introduced myself to Mrs. Washington. I told her everyone at Beall Air was preparing for her arrival.

She laughed, saying, "I hope everyone there likes me. Not everyone here does."

Mrs. Washington was handsomely dressed. She had rosy cheeks and a broad smile. I took to liking her right off.

I drove the newly married couple toward Charlestown. Colonel Washington woke and directed me toward another inn.

I slept on the ground. Tonight I went hungry. I guess in all the excitement of his wedding day, the colonel forgot to bring me some supper.

November 8, 1860

In the morning, the couple boarded the buggy and we traveled back to Charlestown.

The word spread quickly as we approached the mansion house in the late evening. By the time the new Colonel and

Mrs. Washington arrived, all the slaves and family surrounded the buggy, shouting their welcomes to Miss Ella.

November 20, 1860

Richard had been right. Mrs. Washington took over the operations of the plantation almost immediately upon arriving at Beall Air. She also fired Bishop and Morgan. We were all quite happy about that. A new man, Gregory, was hired. He was down right decent to us coloreds so far. That took us by surprise.

November 25, 1860

I was sent to Charlestown today to mail a package for Mrs. Washington. While there, I saw a newspaper that announced a Republican Abraham Lincoln had been elected president. The men at the post office had nothing good to say about the new president. They said "the rail splitter from Illinois is going to be nothing but trouble for the South. The southern states were deciding soon on whether to leave the Union. We hope Virginia will follow the others."

I was confused. If Virginia left the Union, where would Virginia go? I lived in Virginia and feared what might happen.

December 25, 1860

We celebrated Christmas on the plantation today. Mrs. Washington's gave us more food and more drink than any holiday before.

We sang and danced and hooted and hollered all day long until I was right tuckered out.

My day was saddened because it was my first Christmas without my mother. I sat by her grave at night, crying because I was missing her.

Chapter 7
Talk of Virginia Leaving the Country

January 25, 1861

I took Colonel Washington to the courthouse in Charlestown today. I overheard men there talking about how South Carolina and other states had voted to leave the Union. These men hoped Virginia would leave the Union too.

I asked Billy what we would do if Virginia left the Union. He didn't know the answer to that.

March 20, 1861

I read in a newspaper left by one of my customers, President Lincoln had been sworn in. In his talk, the president told the southern states he would not interfere with slavery where it already existed. I was disappointed in that. I thought someone needed to step forward and to interfere like John Brown had.

April 15, 1861

Colonel Washington brought back news from town today. He said men were saying the country was now at war.

He said no one expected the war to last very long, but it might be a problem for the businessmen in Charlestown. It could give him trouble because much of his trading was with nearby Maryland. And he wasn't sure that Maryland would join the southern states or stay in the North.

April 25, 1861

I heard the colonel say that Virginia had left the Union. Harpers Ferry had been attacked, with men taking guns and supplies for the southern cause. It didn't seem much different than when John Brown tried the same thing a few years ago, though the cause was different. No one made any fuss at all this time.

At the general store men said there were no prisoners or killings this time around, but many of the armory buildings were burned down and the train bridge had been blown up.

May 29, 1861

Billy, Mason and Sam weren't real interested in any of the war news. It was distant. "You talk about war, but what's that got to do with us?" Billy asked. This time I did not have an answer to his question.

But war news was important to me. I tried to learn about the war because whenever I went to Charlestown, men were talking about it. Every newspaper I read had articles of the war.

The men in town were on the side of the South. The town's people were very opposed to the Union and President Lincoln.

For me it was confusing because President Lincoln was said to be opposed to slavery and maybe even a friend to the coloreds. And if you asked me, the slaves needed a president who was opposed to slavery. Maybe that was why the white men didn't like President Lincoln much.

June 1, 1861

Colonel Washington talked in town today about the war. I listened while pretending not to be interested. He told the men at the post office he was having financial problems and wasn't sure just how long he would be able to continue to operate Beall Air. He said he was going to ask members of the southern government if they had a job he could do for them.

June 5, 1861

Today Colonel Washington asked me to drive him back to Charlestown.

Along the way, he told me, "Catesby, you are someone I can talk to because you are smarter and better informed than most of my friends. I hate this war. Our plantations here might not survive the conflict. I fear Union troops who have recaptured Harpers Ferry may ride out and burn Beall Air because I am known to support the South."

Many Charlestown lads enlisted proudly in the rebel army. The colonel was happy so many of them answered the call. He said he was too old to enlist.

I offered to fight. He laughed. "Slaves are more important staying and working on the plantations. But I appreciate that you are willing to fight for the cause."

Chapter 8
Beginning a New Life in Maryland

June 9, 1861

Colonel Washington told me today, "Catesby, I have sold you to Mr. Newberry from Keedysville, Maryland. Mr. Newberry has a wagon company and needs a good blacksmith. Please pack your things. Mr. Newberry will pick you up on Friday."

I told the others at supper. Their reactions were like mine. They were sad to see me go but happy for the chance I had to be a real blacksmith.

I didn't have much to pack. All I owned was my journal, a few pencils, my dictionary, and some receipts I copied from Billy. I put them in my duffel so I would be ready to go.

I knew leaving Beall Air was an important step to being a real blacksmith and being a free black man. Billy and my mother had got me ready for this. In situations like this my mother would have said, "Be not afraid."

I stopped by my mother's grave tonight and told her I was leaving Beall Air. "I promise, mother, that I will never forget you. I will visit your grave whenever I am able."

June 14, 1861

Today I said goodbye to Colonel Washington and Mrs. Washington. They thanked me for my services. The colonel presented me with a small photograph of himself. "So you don't forget me," he offered.

I said good bye to everyone, saving my friends, Billy, Sam and Mason, until last.

It was difficult to leave them. They were my brothers. Billy gave me a bag of coins to help me buy my freedom as he had promised to do. He told me to hide it and save it until I needed it. Sam and Mason wished me well.

"You'll do great, Catesby," Mason insisted. "Come back and visit us when you are free." I promised I would return.

Colonel Washington led me to meet Mr. Newberry. Mr. Newberry gave the colonel some money. They signed papers making the deal official. And then the colonel shook my hand. He said, "Goodbye and God speed." I thanked him and loaded my bag on the wagon.

I climbed up next to Mr. Newberry on the seat. He pointed to the back and told me to ride back in the bed of the wagon. That was not a good sign.

Mr. Newberry was an older man, short and squatty. He smoked a big old cigar. His clothes were quite fancy. Even though he didn't say anything to me at all, I did not like Mr. Newberry from the first moment. Sometimes I can tell by just looking. I don't think he liked me none either.

We rode for quite a while, crossing the river at Shepherdstown and passing through Sharpsburg. We stopped at his farm in Keedysville. It was quite a large spread. He had a few slaves. I was assigned to stay in a shanty with Robert and Thom.

They welcomed me like a new brother. Both were happy I was there. Their last blacksmith had been a white man who had not been friendly to them.

They told me in the first few minutes, "Mr. Newberry is a mean man. We hate him. There are regular beatings, sometimes for no reason at all other than it is our turn. He breaks the whip on us regularly." They joked that it was my job as the blacksmith to keep the whip in good repair. They did not want old Mr. Newberry missing out on any of the beatings.

June 16, 1861

Robert was older than me. He was born in the Tidewater, Virginia area. He had been sold to Mr. Newberry when he was about 5 or 6 years old. He didn't remember much about his family. They had been split up and sold to other plantations.

I liked Robert. He acted mature and had a take-charge attitude. He was field smart, but admitted he could neither read nor write. He said the slaves looked up to and respected him.

Thom was younger than me. He was a frail little fellow who I could have picked up and tossed clean across the room with hardly any effort at all. He said he was born here, but was alone as his mother had died. Thom talked constantly. Before long he told me everything he knew about the farm.

He said old Mr. Newberry was a "lying, cheating, son of a bitch" who beat his slaves regularly. Thom said his mother told him Mr. Newberry even beat his own wife and children. According to Thom, Mr. Newberry had nothing good to say about any man, white or colored and was hated even by the white men who knew him.

Thom announced that their little gang had been plotting to run away. They wanted me to help. This was just my first week here. I told them I would work with them as their brother but it was much too early for me to be planning to run away.

June 18, 1861

Blacksmithing at Mr. Newberry's was difficult. His many wagons all needed to be repaired. They were lined up along the fence for me to fix. I guess he had been without a blacksmith for a while. There were fancy buggies and work wagons. Some were broken and others were just banged up a bit. I took on the ones that needed the most attention first, just like Billy had taught me.

The shop here had a bigger work area and a larger variety of tools than at Colonel Washington's shop.

June 20, 1861

I took Mr. Newberry into town today. There was a large group of people right at the beginning of Sharpsburg, where the turnpike goes off to the north. He ordered me to stop the wagon. He climbed down and told me to wait for him.

A large crowd of white men surrounded about thirty slaves – men, women, and children – all in chains and linked together.

I watched in silence as a colored man in chains was marched up some stone steps. A white man yelled out, "What will you offer for this fine, 20 year old, muscular, healthy black man?"

"400 dollars," someone shouted.

"I'll give 450," another one yelled.

"500," a man in the back shouted.

My mother had told me about slave auctions. I had never seen one. It didn't take me more than a few minutes to figure out what was going on.

A colored man cried out begging that his wife be purchased by his new master. The new owner showed no interest. The slave knew if they were split up, chances were he would never see his wife again. She was sold to someone else. I watched them being led off in opposite directions. That was just another bad side of slavery.

I felt sick to my stomach. The event was more difficult to watch than I could have imagined.

June 25, 1861

Mr. Newberry ordered me to pick up supplies for him today. It was the first time he sent me out on the wagon by myself. I knew this was an opportunity to run away. But I needed more time to plan. I was going to stay put for now.

I followed Mr. Newberry's directions onto the Chesapeake and Ohio Canal to the Grove Feed and Grain Warehouse.

The canal, I had been told, always was a place to get the news from both up and down river. Today I heard there had been small battles at Philippi and Fairfax Courthouse, in Virginia.

Two men who were also waiting there were arguing over whether President Lincoln was going to help the country end the war. I felt sure they were soon going to start settling things with their fists.

July 15, 1861

My new brothers and I had long talks nearly every night. They asked about Beall Air and my life there. They were surprised to hear I had been captured by John Brown and had witnessed his hanging.

Robert said John Brown's men had been holed up in the Kennedy farm just south of Sharpsburg. The man who ran Mr. Newberry's blacksmith shop had repaired a wagon for an old man named Isaac Smith one day. Mr. Smith turned out to be old John Brown.

They wanted to know how many beatings Colonel Washington had given me. They asked "Was a blacksmith treated differently than just a field slave in Virginia? How much did Mr. Newberry pay for me? How long did it take me to become a real blacksmith?"

They were surprised I had not been beaten in many years. I told them a blacksmith often got more respect from the white men because of the skill needed to do the job.

I had no idea how much Mr. Newberry paid for my services but I had heard him bid $800 at the Sharpsburg auction for a man who was not a blacksmith. And I told them I worked about three full years with Billy before I was able to become a real blacksmith.

July 18, 1861

When I got all of Mr. Newberry's wagons fixed, he invited neighbors to bring their wagons that needed repairs.

As I worked, I listened to them talk about the war.

There was an argument about which side Maryland would join, the North or the South. They said Mr. Newberry would probably follow the money. I thought it might be smarter for him to pick the same side the state of Maryland joined, since he lived in Maryland

Robert told me the Potomac River nearby at Shepherdstown divided the states between North and South. Shepherdstown, Charlestown and Harpers Ferry and all my old friends were now in the South.

With each passing week, the war was all that everyone talked about. The men in town said President Lincoln had called up troops from each northern state to fight to preserve the Union. I didn't hear as much talk in Sharpsburg against President Lincoln as I had heard back in Charlestown.

Some of my customers read newspapers while I worked on their wagons. They often left the newspapers in the shop when they were finished. I read every word I could about the war to Robert and Thom. At first they weren't much interested, but after a while, the more the war went on, the more they wanted to know.

July 30, 1861

The newspaper reported today the two armies had their first major battle at Bull Run. I read that folks dressed up in their Sunday clothes, took their best buggies and packed picnic lunches to watch the action in Manassas, Virginia. Many fled when the battle started, frightened by the fighting they saw. The losses on both sides were about 3,500 men. The South won this battle. Men here in town didn't think the war would last much longer.

September 15, 1861

My first beating came today. I think my new master gave me time to settle in, and now he wanted to give me a welcome.

Mr. Newberry came into the shop carrying a whip. He accused me of being lazy. He said he had given me three things to do the day before and I hadn't completed them.

It didn't matter that I had completed them all. In fact I had even finished several wagons he didn't even know needed repairing. Whether I had done a good job was not considered. It did not count that I could have broken Mr. Newberry in half with one hand if I had wanted to. It did not matter that he couldn't have caught me if I had run away. All that mattered was that he was the master and I was his slave.

He ordered me to turn around and take off my shirt. I got thirty lashes on my bare back. I counted. I wanted to know how much I was going to owe him some day when I was ready.

He really didn't hurt me. He was too old and weak to hit me hard, though I'm sure he was trying his best. I was more angry than actually hurt even though I was bleeding by the time he was done.

I was angry that he was allowed to own me. From that moment on I decided I would work even harder to be free.

October 5, 1861

I couldn't get that beating out of my mind. I had not ever liked being a slave before. I liked it even less being Mr. Newberry's property. I was sure that the only way to save myself was to become free like Billy.

Chapter 9
Being a Real Blacksmith

November 1, 1861

The blacksmith business was good at Mr. Newberry's shop. Billy had been right. I was a good blacksmith. Everyone said so. I was beginning to like it here at the shop. As long as Mr. Newberry wasn't bothering me, I thought I would work hard, keep learning, and wait.

I was going to be free someday. I knew each day I was getting closer to the day that would happen. I didn't know when it would be. Right now I was not in any hurry. When that day came, I would be more ready than I am now.

Meanwhile, I was working to get all the jobs done that I was supposed to do.

November 29, 1861

I was tired each night after working in the shop, while at the same time pleased at all the work I was getting done. I was doing things I had not learned from Billy. I am learning by doing. Billy had told me that was sometimes the best way to learn. I know Billy would be proud of what I was doing here. I wished there was some way to tell him. I was determined to return to Beall Air someday to let him know how I was using all the things I had learned from him.

December 25, 1861

Christmas at the Newberry farm was nothing special like it had been at Beall Air. Mrs. Newberry sent us extra food and gave us all the day off. I doubt if Mr. Newberry knew about that or approved it.

The slaves all sat around, eating and drinking. They listened as I told them about my adventures in traveling to Washington City with Colonel Washington. None had been there. They thought I was a great traveler.

January 10, 1862

I loved being a blacksmith. For Billy's sake, I wanted to be the best blacksmith that ever lived. That made me try to be better every single day.

The heat and soot didn't bother me at all. The hotter it was, the better I liked it. The extreme heat on my hands and arms excited me. I breathed in the smoke of the fire as if it were the smell of a flower.

The feel of the iron in my hands was power to me. The cold metal soon became bright red from the flames. The heat flowed up the shaft of the metal and into my rough hands. I enjoyed working the metal as it melted with the heat.

I could tell by the glow of the charcoal in the fire whether I had the right amount of heat to bend the metal. That came from the teachings of Billy and from experience. The heat needed to make candle holders was different than the heat needed to make a horse shoe. There was no way to measure, but I knew by looking whether the charcoal was ready. I liked the clanging of my hammer on the metal. The sound was like music to my ears.

If no one came into my shop at all in a day, that was fine by me. I worked well alone, not wanting to be bothered.

February 10, 1862

It was snowing and blowing quite regularly this winter. Robert and Thom sought refuge from the cold in the shop. Several times they did help me move a wagon into or out which was easier than me doing it by myself. But on most days they were more mischief than help.

March 19, 1862

On many days sparks landed on my arms, burning my hair and skin. I remembered the burns on Billy's arms. I knew those were just the marks of my job. Billy said when the day came that my arms were burned like his, I would know I was a real blacksmith. That day had finally arrived for me.

I had to keep close watch because a spark falling on the straw on the floor could cause a fire. The shop was mine, in my mind. I wasn't going to let a spark burn it down. Of course, I knew too, that the shop and the tools really weren't mine. But it was important for me to at least claim ownership and take care of the shop as if I owned it.

Mother had told me that more than anything, slavery was about the chains on a person's mind, much more than the chains on a person's leg. I was beginning to better understand that lesson now.

June 1, 1862

On Sunday, our only day off, we slept late. And then we walked down to the stream. We played and splashed in the water.

I brought my books and old newspapers along to read to the others. I helped them with their letters and words from a book I had purchased in Sharpsburg called *The New York Primer and Spelling Book*. I knew how important education was. I felt I needed to help the others learn too. I had eager students.

I would say a word and then spell it on a small blackboard. Each one would say it and spell it back. I thought they would learn best by saying words out loud. We repeated the lessons many times. It had worked that way for me. They liked the learning. We all agreed Sundays were our favorite part of the week. Thom especially was a quick learner. He always thanked me for my help.

Chapter 10
No Laughing Matter

June 20, 1862

It was my turn to be beaten again. Maybe Mr. Newberry thought I had it coming. I certainly didn't do anything else that deserved a whipping.

He came in the shop with his whip in hand. He accused me of setting the others to plot against him.

I was silent. I wanted to tell him how crazy that idea was. I realized I had no legal right to defend myself. He said he was going to punish me with fifty lashes. Perhaps that would teach me a lesson.

Each lash was slow and deliberate, but because I was so much bigger than he was, he didn't have the strength to hurt me. When Mr. Newberry was done with my beating (he was now owed for eighty lashes), and my back was bleeding all over everything, I looked him in the eye and laughed at him. I couldn't help myself. He tried so hard to hurt me. But he hadn't hurt me at all. I wanted to make sure he knew that.

I found out real quick that laughing at Mr. Newberry was a big mistake.

He reached over and grabbed an iron bar I had left in the fire and stabbed it into my leg. The red hot poker drove into my right thigh like a flaming arrow. I went down hard, in horrible pain. And then it was his turn to laugh.

It felt like my leg was suddenly on fire, inside and out. I wanted to run to the pond and jump in to put the fire out. But I couldn't run to the pond. In fact, I couldn't even move.

I didn't want him to know that my leg hurt, but I couldn't help it. The pain was worse than any pain I had ever had in all my life. I screamed out. The more I screamed, the more he laughed. I hated Mr. Newberry as much for laughing as for injuring my leg.

My brothers came running. They tried to calm me down. Mr. Newberry left quietly while they were tending to me.

The others pulled the metal bar out. They poured cool water on my leg. The water boiled in the open wound.

I could not stop screaming. I thought dying would be less painful. I begged God to take my life to ease my pain.

The burned flesh left a stench in the air. The pain finally was too much. I don't remember what happened next.

June 23, 1862

I was told that I didn't wake up for three days. By that time my wound had been dressed by one of the colored women. When she took off the bandages, I saw an ugly festering sore and a hole in my leg. It had burn marks all around the edges. The hair on my leg was burned. The sore bled through the bandages.

June 26, 1862

My leg was in bad shape. The hole wasn't healing. I was stiff and sore. I tried to walk, but I didn't have the energy to stand without holding on to something. I fell several times before I finally decided I needed to just rest.

July 1, 1862

Day after day I tried to get up to walk. I got stronger every day, but I knew that I was not ever going to be able to walk like I had before. I would always limp. Suddenly my plan of running away seemed impossible.

Mr. Newberry came to visit today. He could not look me in the eye. He talked to the ground as if I were not there. He said, "Work in the shop is piling up. If you are not back in the shop by tomorrow noon, you will be taken out back and hanged. Your usefulness as a working slave will be over." With that he left.

I didn't care how much my leg hurt. That was not going to happen. If Mr. Newberry thought he could defeat me, he didn't know Catesby very well. I was going to be free. He wasn't going to stand in my way.

I was not going to let Mr. Newberry hang me on the morrow, or on any day. I promised myself that he would die a painful death before my time on earth was finished.

Tomorrow, I would start back to work in the shop.

July 2, 1862

I was in the shop before the sun came up this morning. Mr. Newberry came by, looked in to see if I was working, and quickly left. I am sure he was disappointed that I was there.

I promised myself, from this day forth, I would not dare miss work. I hobbled to the shop, limping around in pain. I swore that Mr. Newberry would pay for this. I would be free and get my revenge. But not today.

July 16, 1862

I continued to work each day. The pain did not go away. Some days it hurt so bad, tears ran down my face. Fortunately the heat of the fire dried them. Even so, I was determined and stubborn. I was not going to give up. I learned to work around my leg. I was never going to let it be an excuse.

I built a crutch from a metal pole and padded the top where it fit in the pit of my arm. It helped take the weight of my body off my bad leg. My brothers laughed because the crutch made a clicking sound so they could hear me coming.

July 30, 1862

Mr. Newberry was avoiding me. I know it was because he was scared what I might do to him. He hadn't come into the shop for the whole month except for that first day. That was fine with me. I hated him more than anyone on earth even though my mother told me hating was a sin.

With every single step, I was in pain. It made me think of Mr. Newberry's ugly face.

I plotted ways to get even. Killing Mr. Newberry was out of the question. That would have let him off without any suffering. I wanted the man to suffer every day left of his miserable life.

I thought of stabbing Mr. Newberry with a hot poker in the exact spot as mine so we could have matching injuries. I dreamed of taking a red hot iron bar and stabbing him in his eye. I thought of pounding his hand with my largest hammer, shattering his knee or pouring hot coals on his lap.

But instead I waited. I hoped he slept with one eye open at night, and worried that I might come after him while he was asleep. I hoped he was uneasy thinking what I might do and when I might do it.

I removed the bandages and let them dry out during the night, trying to be careful not to get them close to any dirt. In the morning I put clean rags over the sore so it wouldn't bleed through to my clothes. One of the house slaves stole old rags from the house to help me out.

August 5, 1862

Every day I thought of worse injuries to repay Mr. Newberry. It raised my spirit to think of his pain. I could have used any of a dozen tools in the shop to injure him. But I also had to be very careful so as not to push him off the edge, because he could kill me under the law and have no punishment. I finally decided I wanted to be free more than I wanted to hurt Mr. Newberry.

No punishment or revenge on Mr. Newberry was worth giving up my life. For now, the only satisfaction I got was in my mind. My hopes were to someday pay Mr. Newberry back.

I would wait instead. I tried to focus on my work. The pain in my leg distracted me. I hobbled everywhere I went.

Chapter 11
Getting Some Help

August 6, 1862

Today Mrs. Newberry made her first visit ever to my blacksmith shop. She asked me to take her into Sharpsburg. She wanted me to be ready by mid-morning. I found her asking rather odd, as Mrs. Newberry had not spoken to me since my arrival here.

I pulled the buggy up to the house and helped her get on board. I drove into town. When we arrived, I tied the buggy to the post in front of the general store, and then helped her down.

"I want you to follow me, Catesby," she whispered. I followed her about a half block down the street. She entered a doorway to the left and motioned for me to follow. I limped along as quickly as I could, trying to keep up. She hurried up the steps to the second floor. At the top of the steps, she entered a doorway. I followed her into a room that smelled bad. A man in a long, soiled, white coat stood in the room.

She announced, "This is Doctor Harnish. He is going to look at your leg. Mr. Newberry does not know we are here, Doctor Harnish," she added, turning toward the older man, "and I trust that he will never find out." With that she walked out the door leaving us alone.

The doctor told me to remove my pants and lay on my back on the cot so he could see my leg. I did what he told me to do. He removed my bloodied bandage. Then he slowly and gently prodded and poked where the stab wound was very sore and fresh. I jumped several times when he hit the most painful spots.

"This leg is quite bad," he told me. "But I think I can help the wound heal," he added, leaving the room when he stopped speaking.

The old doctor returned with several white cloths, dripping with some liquid on them. He laid them across the wound. The liquid was quite cold. I jumped again when the liquid touched my sore leg. The bad smell I had noticed earlier was coming from the cloth. "Relax," he said. "I'm going to leave these on for about an hour." I closed my eyes and fell asleep.

The doctor came back in and woke me up. He took all the cloths. They were red with blood. He put a new fresh bandage over my wound. And then he told me to get up and dress. Mrs. Newberry arrived shortly after we were finished.

"That's all I can do for now. I think that will keep the infection down and help the healing," he added. "You will not have much use for the leg, I'm afraid, but it should heal quicker."

And then he asked, "How did you injure your leg?"

Mrs. Newberry took charge before I could answer. "Well, Catesby, it's time to go. Thank you, Dr. Harnish. Good day." She grabbed my hand and dragged me out into the stairwell right past the startled doctor.

"Thank you," I said to the doctor, following close behind Mrs. Newberry. She hurried down the stairs and was waiting for me at the bottom.

She looked me square in the eye and said, "Catesby. If you want no more trouble, forget you ever met Dr. Harnish."

"Yes, ma'am," I responded. "I don't remember meeting any doctor today."

"I'm beginning to like you, Catesby. But don't tell anyone that either," she said with a little laugh.

"No, ma'am. That'll just be between me and you. Thank you, ma'am, for taking me to see that doctor who I didn't really see up there."

"You are welcome, Catesby," Mrs. Newberry added. "You didn't deserve what my cruel husband did to your leg.

I am doing my best to try to help you. Now let's get some supplies at the store before we go back home."

With that she opened the door. We stepped back onto the street as if nothing had ever happened.

August 14, 1862

The word must have been getting out that Mr. Newberry's blacksmith shop was doing good quality work, because each day I got more and more business.

Folks from Boonsboro, Hagerstown, Funkstown, Sharpsburg, Keedysville and Smithsburg brought in projects for me to work on.

The few times Mr. Newberry looked in on me he saw I was working hard getting the projects done. He didn't say anything. He didn't stay long. I was sure he was quite afraid of me. He knew I owed him. I hope he was worried that I might try to get even.

August 15, 1862

Every so often Mrs. Newberry would come by and show me notes someone had delivered to Mr. Newberry thanking him for my good work. She thought it would be good if I got to see them too. Here's what they said.

"Best job anyone ever did in repairing my saddle. Thank you." Jackie

"That Catesby is the best blacksmith in the area. I have told others about his work." Diane Grimes

"Catesby did a real good job fixing my gate." Jean

"Your blacksmith did a fine job repairing the buckle on my harness." Pat Grossmann

"Please thank your blacksmith for a job well done. The door latch is working quite well now." Susan

"The fine iron kettle holder your blacksmith made was a perfect gift for us. Please let Catesby know his work is admired and appreciated." Edith and Chris Sweigert

"I am very pleased with the work done on my carriage." Mary Rutherford

I thanked Mrs. Newberry for sharing the notes. She started to leave and then she added, "Catesby. Thank you for what you do. You are a good man. You make Mr. Newberry look good with everything you do here in the shop. I am sure he doesn't appreciate you."

I was pleased to hear what she said. It was good to hear my customers were happy with my work.

I was a good blacksmith. There wasn't anything I couldn't fix. If I didn't have the right materials or the right tool for the job, I made do with what I had and finished the job anyway. I never got even one complaint except from Mr. Newberry the two times he beat me. But he had no complaint either of those times. He just needed an excuse to show me who was boss.

August 17, 1862

I noticed about this time that I started to think about things differently. I thought about how much money my work was bringing to the shop. Mr. Newberry, a man I had no respect for and who I hated for injuring me, was making a nice profit. I thought often how easy it would be for me to start taking just a small amount of money for myself from each of the jobs. He would have never missed it. And it certainly would have been fair. I was doing all the work. Mr. Newberry wasn't helping any. What would have been the harm in it?

He got hundreds of dollars for my work, and I got none. I wondered how much harder I would work if this were my shop and if I were free and allowed to keep the money. That was easy. I would work no harder. I was working as hard as I could now.

But my mother taught me better than that. The words "Thou shalt not steal" she said were from the Bible. There was not one bone in my body that could steal from Mr. Newberry.

Was that fair? No. So what was I going to do about it? Become a free man.

August 18, 1862

My bad leg interfered with all my work. Everything took longer now. I had to plan better, making sure to keep my tools close by so I didn't have to keep moving to the other side of the shop to find what I needed.

Each morning I worked to try to move my hurt leg so it wouldn't stiffen. The pain lessened over time, but the leg was still pretty useless. There were times I thought it might be easier if I just cut my leg off, but I couldn't quite bring myself to do that.

At night I massaged my leg and soaked it. But it never really got any better. I just had to drag it along behind. It was as annoying as if I had a ball and chain attached. The crutch I had made helped me get around. It became one of my most useful tools.

August 19, 1862

Often I was asked to drive the wagon into town for supplies. Much of the talk in town I overheard at the post office and general store was about the war. With each passing week, the thoughts of a short war seemed less likely.

Virginia and Beall Air were now part of the South. But just across the river here in Maryland, folks weren't real sure. I could tell they were having trouble deciding just which side they wanted to be on. They argued often.

No one I heard talking in town had been to the war or had seen it. They were just passing along what they read in newspapers including the *Harpers Weekly* newspaper or *Frank Leslie's Illustrated* newspaper. Occasionally I got to read those newspaper accounts too.

The war might as well have been in another land because it had no affect at Mr. Newberry's farm. My job was the same.

Suttlers who brought our supplies often stopped at the shop for minor repairs. One had actually seen the battle at Bull Run. He described it as brutal and bloody.

Neighbors told me of troops being called up. They complained that the war was stringing out longer and longer. With all the battles in the South, they said food was scarcer there.

To me the war seemed distant. The newspapers made the battles sound exciting and interesting. Some battles were declared Union victories, and the others Confederate victories. It didn't sound to me like either side was winning. I read that thousands of men were dying on both sides.

The men in town said as long as the war was in the South, we didn't have to worry about it in this little town in Maryland.

Local men had enlisted and had gone off to join the war. Many lads who had been hanging around in town for as long as I had been here were suddenly gone. Their mothers and sisters and sweethearts waited at the post office each day for a letter from them with news of the battles.

Thom, Robert and I talked about the war too. Thom thought it would be lots more exciting to be a soldier than a slave. We agreed, knowing full well that the only soldiers that were allowed to enlist were the white lads.

I thought silently to myself that if I were in a war, several of the slaves at Beall Air and at Mr. Allstadt's house would have made grand soldiers. I would put up their bravery and courage against any enemy. I had offered my services to Colonel Washington to fight as a soldier for the cause. I would never have made that offer for Mr. Newberry's cause. Besides I was not sure what his cause was.

August 20, 1862

Robert and Thom were pushing me hard daily to get even with Mr. Newberry.

"Catesby," they begged. "We have to stop Mr. Newberry before he kills or injures someone else. Any normal man would have died with the injury you got."

"You were just too stubborn to lie down and die," they argued. "You are content here and are not working on a plan to get rid of Mr. Newberry. You do not have to fear him because he already crippled you — but what about us? Which one of us will be next?"

They were right. Something must be done. And I could have easily died from my injury. One of them was probably next in line. They were afraid. And rightly so. Waiting was not something any of us was particularly good at.

I did not blame them for being afraid. But I didn't want them to take the law into their own hands. I did not have a plan other than keeping them from taking any quick action.

I told them I would start right now. I asked their suggestions.

Robert insisted, "We will murder Mr. Newberry in his sleep, steal a horse and a wagon, and hightail it north to freedom."

Thom's plan was more realistic. "I think we should poison Mr. Newberry slowly to make it look like an accident so that we will not be suspected. Life around here wouldn't be so bad without him. After his death, we could take our time planning our escape. I want Mr. Newberry's death to be very slow and very painful. Robert's plan makes his death come too quickly."

I thought they both had some good ideas, but we needed to think this through. I asked Robert, "How will we kill Mr. Newberry? How far do think three colored men driving a stolen wagon would be able to go before we got arrested and hanged?" He admitted he hadn't thought it out that far.

I asked Thom, "Where will we get poison? How will we make sure Mr. Newberry eats it and it doesn't poison Mrs. Newberry or their children?" He too had not planned out any of the details.

None of us had any of those answers. We all agreed we were moving toward some kind of plan. I promised them I would think on it.

For now they listened. I did not know how much longer I could hold them off.

August 24, 1862

Whatever Dr. Harnish had done for my injured leg, it actually helped. The wound dried out and crusted over. It no longer leaked or bled. I was able to remove the bandages. The injury was certainly healing as the doctor said it would.

The visit was never mentioned again. I was thankful though I knew I could not tell Mrs. Newberry. I thanked both Mrs. Newberry and the good doctor in my prayers.

August 25, 1862

Today I was sent to the high bluff above the Chesapeake and Ohio Canal to a home called Ferry Hill to repair a farm wagon and fix several bridles. The home was owned by the attorney Henry Kyd Douglas.

While hobbling to look at the wagon, Mr. Douglas stopped and asked if I had been a slave for Colonel Washington. He said he thought he had seen me driving the colonel's buggy at the trial of John Brown and the others.

I told him that was me. And that I had been sold to Mr. Newberry.

He said he had gone to the trials as an observer. And that he had run across John Brown too. "I helped an old man by pulling his wagon out of the mud along the canal just below the house," he explained. "His wagon was piled high with heavy boxes. The old man said they were miner's tools. I think now they were probably pikes and rifles. When I got to the courthouse, I recognized the old man I helped was John Brown."

August 31, 1862

The next time I saw Mrs. Newberry, she asked me to take her into town. I picked her up at the house. When I helped her up onto the wagon, she was crying.

Her eye appeared to be swollen shut. When I asked if she were all right, she said, "Yes, Catesby. But thanks for asking."

At that moment I remembered Thom telling me that Mr. Newberry not only beat up his slaves. He beat up his wife and children too. I wondered to myself what this nice lady might have done to deserve this. Since I did nothing to deserve my beatings, I was pretty sure Mrs. Newberry did nothing to cause her beating either.

I thought about that injured eye as I drove the wagon. To hit the slaves you owned was one thing. I didn't think anyone had a right to hit his wife. It only made me work harder to plan my escape from mean old Mr. Newberry.

September 2, 1862

I took Mrs. Newberry to Shepherdstown today. She tried to hide her eye from me, but I noticed it was still black and puffy. I pointed out for her the house where Henry Kyd Douglas, my shop customer lived.

We were stopped by soldiers at the river. Mrs. Newberry had a pass to allow us to go into Shepherdstown.

As we crossed the Potomac River, I asked Mrs. Newberry if this was the same Potomac River that was in Harpers Ferry. She laughed, explaining if I got in a boat at Shepherdstown and floated down the river, soon I would be in Harpers Ferry.

In Shepherdstown, we stopped at the farmer's market and the Mecklenburg Tobacco Warehouse. The warehouse was where I had to go to pick up the special cigars Mr. Newberry smoked.

Shepherdstown was an active town right on the heights overlooking the river. Mrs. Newberry said President George Washington had favored the town once for the national capital, before settling on Washington City instead.

Mr. Newberry had given me directions to Jay Hurley's blacksmith shop to pick up a tool Mr. Hurley had borrowed last spring.

Mr. Hurley had the reputation of being the area's best blacksmith. We spoke for only a couple of minutes as he fetched the tool. He seemed like a real nice fellow.

I remembered that crossing the river, according to Robert, was the dividing line between the North and the South. I was now in Virginia, the South. There didn't seem to be any dividing line I saw anywhere along the way splitting the country into two pieces. Robert must have been mistaken.

Chapter 12
The War Comes to Maryland

September 6, 1862

While in Sharpsburg today picking up supplies, I heard that the southern troops marched into Maryland just a few days ago. Their army crossed the river near Leesburg, and were marching toward Frederick, Maryland.

Men in town were confused as to what to do. Some wanted to take food and drink to welcome the soldiers to Maryland. An equal number wanted to get their rifles and muskets and kill them or at least chase them back into the South.

Several big arguments occurred in Sharpsburg. I wouldn't have been surprised to see a little war start right there.

With the rebels in Frederick, men argued that they would go next to Washington City to try to take the national capital. Good thing the capital wasn't in Shepherdstown, I thought, because they would be marching right through Sharpsburg to get there.

Men were placing bets on where the troops would go next. The pot had reached twenty gold pieces with the postmaster holding the money. There were bets placed on Hagerstown, Harpers Ferry, Washington City, Baltimore, Westminster, and other places I didn't even know. Someone was going to win a lot of money soon.

September 14, 1862

Today a man on horseback rode through the area announcing that troops were heading along the National Road and would cross South Mountain near Boonsboro soon. I don't remember anyone betting on that place.

Before long I heard cannons and guns being fired along the top of the mountain. The fighting had begun.

September 15, 1862

Today I heard a man tell Mr. Newberry, "There are hundreds and hundreds of dead and wounded of soldiers, blue and gray, lying on the mountain top. The rebels dug in, but were overrun by the Union boys. I think they are all marching your way now, sir."

Mr. Newberry, who had pretty much left me alone since crippling my leg, told me the armies may need his horses and wagons. He ordered me to spend all my time to keep the wagons ready and available. I knew Mr. Newberry wasn't sure if he was for the North or the South. He was going to play it by ear, and come out on the side of whoever was winning.

September 16, 1862

Soldiers dressed in gray uniforms passed the farm by the thousands today, heading from the direction of Frederick and marching toward Sharpsburg.

It seemed like everyone that lived here in Sharpsburg was heading out of town as the soldiers marched in. The line of soldiers passed by for hours and hours. Most marched on foot; many without shoes. Some had horses and others were on board wagons.

I remembered all the shooting at Harpers Ferry when I had been taken prisoner. I feared for my safety and my life that day. Having this war come here, to where I lived, after reading about the awful battles at other places, was frightening. Would any of us survive?

The soldiers in gray took many of Mr. Newberry's wagons and horses. I reckon he got paid for them. It was less wagons I had to worry about. Many of the officers brought their horses to the shop to get shoes. I was busy throughout the day and night working to repair the rebel wagons and shoeing their horses.

Mr. Newberry was trying to be friendly to all the rebel officers. He brought by an officer he told me was General Robert E. Lee.

I was ordered to shoe General Lee's horse separate from all the others. Mr. Newberry talked to the general like he was an old friend, on the other side of the shop, while I took care of his horse.

I heard Mr. Newberry say the general was riding in an ambulance, with his horse walking behind. The general had fallen off his horse and injured his hands. General Lee was not able to ride.

The general's horse was good natured. Unlike some, she was not bothered by my work. I stroked her mane as I hobbled around between the shoes. I kept apples in the shop to eat whenever I got hungry during the day. I gave one to the general's horse. The horse chomped away as if thankful for the food.

Mr. Newberry insisted I hurry up because the famous general, the head of the Army of Northern Virginia, and he were dining together. There was no time to waste. I wanted to tell him I was working as fast as my injured leg would let me, but decided that would not help matters any.

I looked up and saw the general, wondering if he was the same Robert E. Lee who had been at Harpers Ferry when I was a prisoner of John Brown. I couldn't be sure. The man in Harpers Ferry had a mustache but no beard and wasn't wearing a uniform. This man here today had a full gray beard and a fancy gray officer's uniform with full boots.

I kept still. It was not my place to ask.

September 17, 1862

Loud explosions woke me from a deep sleep. I looked out but couldn't see anything because it was still dark. The booming of the cannons never stopped for even a minute. Neighbors said there was fierce fighting nearer to town. The Pry farm, near Mr. Newberry's farm, had been set up as the Union's headquarters.

I had never heard such loud noise. It sounded today like God was angry, and with each passing minute, he was getting angrier and angrier.

Smoke filled the air so I could not see the sun or the sky. The noise grew louder as if the battle was on the next farm. I wondered if we should run for our lives if they came this way.

I kept on working through the day, but never could totally think about my job because the ground was shaking under me.

By late afternoon dozens of wagons full of wounded men in blue uniforms passed out of town toward Frederick. The sounds of wailing and screaming drowned out the sounds of the cannons over the hill.

The fighting had been down by Antietam Creek. No one could quite figure out who won the battle. I guess that muddied the waters for Mr. Newberry taking sides in the war.

Chapter 13
The Fields of Battle at Antietam Creek

September 18, 1862

Mr. Newberry ordered me to drive the wagon for him today. He didn't say where we were going.

The only good wagon left was battered, but it was still working. I hitched the old plow horse to the wagon after realizing the rebel army had taken away all the best horses and wagons.

Mr. Newberry climbed aboard. He motioned for me to drive toward town. As we rolled slowly down the hill into Sharpsburg, I saw a few soldiers from the gray army marching out the other direction toward Shepherdstown. They were battered and torn — bleeding and crying — wandering around, stumbling and falling.

Mr. Newberry pointed for me to turn right onto the turnpike.

I was not prepared for what I saw just over the hill. At the fence line I saw hundreds of bodies of dead and dying soldiers. Many were probably the same gray soldiers that I had seen marching into town. They were now lying in heaps, left behind by the rebel army.

We passed a small white church still smoldering and battered from the battle. Men were being carried there to what was now a hospital. The building was so small many of the wounded were being treated outside on the ground. Doctors scurried around trying to treat the wounded, their aprons dripping with blood.

As we moved along the side roads, the uniform color changed to blue, but the scene was much the same.

The smell was awful. The loud sounds of cannons I had heard yesterday had been replaced by the screams of dying men. It was like nothing I had ever seen or heard before. It is difficult for me to even describe it.

There were heaps of dead soldiers along the roads, in the fields, and in the woods. The soldiers lying here, there, and everywhere had horrible wounds on any and all parts of their bodies. Some were headless. Others had no faces. Bodies were missing arms and legs, sometimes both. Arms and legs were lying with no bodies nearby.

No matter where I looked, I saw sights I could not believe. There was a boot attached to a leg, not connected to anything above the knee. There were strange piles that probably once had been men. There was so little left of them I was not sure.

I saw dead and dying horses in every direction. Some had their riders still in the saddles. Men lay still with dead horses lying on top of them.

Several broken cannons stood silent, their barrels pointing to where men had stood yesterday. Trees were knocked down and fences were broken.

Fires burned everywhere. I had to watch carefully to drive the wagon around holes in the road. Buzzards by the hundreds looking for their next meal picked at the dead bodies.

A soldier hobbled around with a missing leg. Others were without one of their arms. Men were rifling through the dead men's pockets, and stealing the shoes from the dead and dying. Colored men were digging graves. It would probably take them months to bury all the dead.

Soldiers dressed in blue and gray lay piled together along a lane. There were so many bodies I couldn't even have begun to count them. Some looked like they were just in a peaceful sleep and would wake up in the morning. Others had looks of horror now frozen on their faces forever.

One young soldier held up his hand for us to stop. Mr. Newberry nodded and I reined in on the horse. "Please, I beg you sir. Shoot me," the soldier pleaded, as if he were asking for a ride home. "Put me out of my misery. I will be eternally grateful. I am about to meet my maker anyway. Could you please hurry the process?"

Mr. Newberry signaled me to go forward. He could or would not aid the helpless lad. We left him to die on his own.

I feared by the time the sun would set today, many more of the wounded would join the dead and the field would again be silent. We passed cornfields with rows and rows of bodies lying where corn would normally stand tall at this time of year. The corn stalks now lay alongside the fallen soldiers.

Several times Mr. Newberry ordered me to stop as he talked to people who were working to help the wounded soldiers. They asked him for bandages and medicine, but we had nothing to give. Mr. Newberry told them he did not know where to go to get what they needed.

I saw a small stone bridge over the creek. Bodies dressed in blue were piled three or four high on top of each other all along the little bridge. I could not imagine what it must have been like here during the fighting.

When we finally returned to the farm, I couldn't sleep, thinking of all the mothers who would never see their sons again. This was the war that I had read about. The articles in the newspapers had not prepared me for what I actually saw, smelled, and experienced.

I feared the horrors I had seen would haunt me for a long time. I wondered who the officers were in addition to General Lee who led their men into these battles. What good was it that so many men had died here? It was a day I will never forget.

September 19, 1862

I was tired this morning when I woke up. I was troubled by what happened at Antietam Creek. So this was the war I had heard and read about. It had sounded exciting and distant, with battles far away in the South. Today it did not seem exciting or distant.

Two wagons pulled into the farm lane this morning asking for a guide to drive them around. Mr. Newberry offered my help.

The men in the wagons were photographers. I was ordered to help them. After my trip yesterday, I did not want to drive through that mess again. As a slave, I didn't have any choice.

I boarded the first wagon with a man named Alexander Gardner. He and his assistant, James Gibson, who drove the other wagon, were from the Matthew Brady Studio. They were excited because no photographer had even been on the field of battle so soon after the fighting was finished.

I led them to the battle scene. It was worse than before.

We started by the little white church, standing broken, surrounded by what the battle had left behind. "The Dunkards normally worship there," Mr. Gardner said. The church seats were crowded now with the wounded, being cared for by doctors working to save as many as they could. Their job looked hopeless to me.

I was asked to stop often. The two men wanted me to help point out soldiers who were freshly dead for their photographs. I helped as best I could to unload the equipment and cameras.

At each stop, while the photographers worked, I sat on the ground, finding whatever shade I could. And I stared out onto the horror of the field.

There was no hurry in these men. Each photograph took a long time to set up. The photographers worked quietly. I wondered if they cared that a few days ago the men they were capturing in their photographs had been alive. When they were finished, we lifted the cameras back onto the wagons and moved further along the rows and rows of the dead and wounded.

Along the sunken road, bodies of the blue and gray soldiers were tangled together. The grass was blood red along both sides of the lane.

We drove to the little stone bridge across the creek someone said was the lower bridge. Bodies of soldiers dressed in blue were still lying on the bridge and floating in the water.

I saw a very small lady directing a group of women as they treated the wounded and comforted the near-dead. She was pointing here and there to others who needed help. Wherever we went on the field, she seemed to follow, with the wagon that carried her and her supplies taking the same route we were taking. She seemed to magically arrive with help where it was needed the most.

At the bridge, she reached down and gave water to a soldier who looked no older than a school boy. He slurped the water from the ladle, dribbling more down his chin than into his mouth. He thanked the lady with a small salute, and then slumped on the ground, laying dead silent.

I took the photographers back to the farm where Mr. Newberry fed them and let them stay overnight. He yelled out to me as I was hobbling back to the shanty, that the photographers wanted me to drive them back into the battle site again tomorrow. I had hoped I did not have to go back again.

September 20, 1862

This morning I returned to Sharpsburg with the photographers and their wagons. The smell today was much worse than I had remembered from yesterday. Mother had described hell to me once. I think this is as close to going through hell than anything I had ever seen.

At the little church, I saw dozens of bloody arms and legs piled high outside the window of the hospital. Nothing I had ever seen was as terrible as that sight to me. I heaved my breakfast, and probably the supper from last night, as I had to stop for several minutes before I was able to move on.

Mr. Gardner and Mr. Gibson worked throughout the day, keeping their comments to themselves. They were really good at just stepping over dead men as if the soldiers were not even there, to set up the photographs they wanted.

The sun shone brightly. The heat pounded down on the dead. Many bodies were gross and bloated. Other bodies were attacked by packs of hungry dogs.

Vultures seemed to multiply as the days went by, with a never ending source of nourishment piled higher than a church supper. The large, ugly looking birds continued to grab the flesh from the dead soldiers all along the way, not even moving when the wagon came close.

Several women walked through the piles of the dead, looking for a loved one. Their mission seemed impossible. Another woman wailed loudly, cradling a man in her arms who had already passed.

When my time with the photographers was finally over, I went home and cried for the thousands of lost souls I had seen at Antietam Creek.

In my days of working with the photography wagons, I saw that small lady who was helping the wounded numerous times. She was there when we arrived in the early morning and remained there when we left at the end of our long weary days. I finally asked someone who the lady was. They said the tireless helper was a nurse -- Clara Barton.

September 25, 1862

Today I returned to the blacksmith shop, hoping to forget the horrors of the war. It wasn't that easy. Even if I could push it out of my mind at the shop, in the evenings my brothers wanted me to tell them what I had seen.

They listened, not believing what I was telling them. But in truth, my stories were not close to what I had seen. I had trouble putting into words those horrible sights.

My brothers just wouldn't let go. All of a sudden, being a soldier wasn't looking so exciting to them. It wasn't looking much better than being a slave. They admitted finally that they would rather go out and tend the field instead of grabbing a musket and facing enemy shots fired right at them.

Each night the horrible sights and sounds and smells kept me awake. I was afraid the horrors of the battle field at Antietam Creek would never be gone from my head.

Photograph by Alexander Gardner
Battle at Antietam Creek
Library of Congress

Chapter 14
The President Visits Sharpsburg

October 3, 1862

Today Mr. Newberry ordered me to take him to the Grove farm on the western end of Sharpsburg on the way to Shepherdstown. He had been invited there to meet the president, Mr. Lincoln.

I drove the wagon through Sharpsburg and then back the lane to the farm. I watched him get down off the wagon at the tent in front of the Mr. Grove's house. Mr. Newberry said this was the Union headquarters. President Lincoln was visiting with General McClellan.

I drove the wagon between the house and the barn, and stopped. I tied the horse to a fence post. I sat in the grass and watched from there.

It seemed odd to me that two weeks after the big battle here at Antietam Creek, the Union General was still here. The rebel soldiers had already disappeared back into the South.

Soon after we arrived, a buggy approached the tent and two men got out. One was a very tall, thin, bearded man dressed in a black coat and with a tall black hat. I was sure that man was President Lincoln as I had seen drawings of him in the newspaper.

Several soldiers in blue saluted the two men who had just arrived and led them to the large tent. Mr. Newberry was standing by the tent, talking to a Union officer. Mr. Newberry and the officer both turned toward the men who had just arrived. The men from the buggy shook Mr. Newberry's hand.

I noticed the photographer Alexander Gardner was there, the man I had taken around the field of battle. He was setting up his big camera in front of the tent. He arranged many different groups of the men to be photographed. And then he ducked under the camera's drape each time to take the photographs.

Mr. Newberry stood aside. I don't think he was invited to be in the photographs.

It was strange for me to see Mr. Newberry with all the soldiers in blue. He had been such a friend just a few weeks before to the men in gray.

I expect Mr. Newberry knew to side with whichever one happened to be winning that particular day. It looked today like the boys in blue were winning.

When he was done, Mr. Newberry walked over to the wagon and asked me to take him back to the farm. As we passed the tent, Mr. Newberry pointed out the tall man from the buggy and said he was President Lincoln. It was the man I had picked out before.

Because I had never seen a president, I took a good long look over my shoulder. The president was not a happy looking fellow. I had been told he was a friend of the coloreds. I was delighted to have seen President Lincoln up-close.

October 5, 1862

After seeing President Lincoln, I thought of the sadness that showed in his face. Seemed to me he carried the burden of the whole country at war on his shoulders. It looked to be a heavy weight for him.

I wondered to myself how this white man had become so concerned about us coloreds. He was the second white man I had known about who wanted to help us — the other, of course, being John Brown.

I thought it strange using their names together because they seemed so different. One was the president, held in respect by the Union. The other, a common old man, who some thought was a criminal.

October 17, 1862

I was becoming more and more trusted by Mr. Newberry. On occasion, he would send me into town alone with his wagon to the general store, post office, and hardware store with a list of things that he needed me to pick up for him. I enjoyed my new-found freedom but was smart enough not to abuse it.

I continued to hear about the awful war whenever I went into town. They talked about how long the country would continue to be at war and how many would have to die before the fighting would stop.

I wondered if those in other towns not yet touched by battles would think like my brothers; that being a soldier was still something exciting. No one around here thought that now. You just had to pass all the new graves at the cemetery to know that war was a terrible thing for your town.

Perhaps Alexander Gardner's photographs of the horrible scenes of the dead and dying would help the people decide "enough is enough" and the killing would stop.

Lincoln at General McClellan's headquarters
Sharpsburg, Maryland   October 3, 1862
Photograph by Alexander Gardner
Library of Congress

Chapter 15
Hearing About the Underground Railroad

November 13, 1862

The colder weather was making my leg ache even more than usual. No matter how much I worked on the injured spot every evening and every morning, nothing seemed to help. I even worked with the liniment I use in softening saddle leather and kneading my thigh as if it were bread.

And deep down inside, because of my hatred for Mr. Newberry and how he had hurt me, I started seriously planning my escape.

Today in town I heard news from other slaves of the Underground Railroad that coloreds could ride to freedom. They whispered about Quakers and other groups helping fugitive slaves find refuge. They mentioned that Mrs. Ritner in Chambersburg, Pennsylvania helped runaway slaves from Maryland. I knew before long I would be riding that Underground Railroad and leaving old Mr. Newberry behind.

I wondered if the glorious railroad to freedom was like the one that passed by Colonel Washington's place at Beall Air.

All this time I was also plotting how to pay back Mr. Newberry for the eighty lashes and the crippling of my leg. I was determined that something awful was due him. I wanted to make sure that I got even with him on my way off the farm. It needed to be something very slow and very painful - - a gift I could leave similar to the one that had marked me for life. It would be my going away to freedom present to him so he would never forget old Catesby. I waited for the chance.

December 4, 1862

Winter was tough at the Newberry farm. The cold and snow stopped much of the work in the fields. Robert and Thom helped me some at the shop.

They were probably just as glad to stay close to the heat as anything because my fireplace was the warmest spot on the farm. My brothers were even able to help me fix the chimney that I had told Mr. Newberry needed to be repaired soon because it might fall down.

Mr. Newberry had purchased some new wagons replacing those he had sold to the rebel army. I now had fifteen wagons to keep in working condition. The wagons didn't go out much in the winter due to the muddy road, but I still needed to make sure they were ready.

My brothers continued to remind me of our need to get even with Mr. Newberry. Did they think I had forgotten? I assured them that of all people, I knew and remembered. It was one of my concerns too. The cold and my sore leg were not a good combination for me, so every minute during the winter I was thinking about Mr. Newberry's injury to my leg.

I kept telling them, "All in good time. We need to have a plan. But we have to wait before we do anything." It was a good thing that they trusted me. We waited.

Chapter 16
President Lincoln Frees All Slaves

January 5, 1863

When I was sent into town today, a man at the general store was reading aloud from something he said President Lincoln declared — that Negroes were now all free for eternity. I didn't know what to make of it, but I guess I needed to start planning a different life. It was hard to believe I really was free. I remembered my pledge to Billy to become a free black. I wrote down what the announcement was called from the newspaper -- the Emancipation Proclamation.

I looked up those big words in my dictionary too. I found that emancipation means "to set free from restraints like slavery" and proclamation means "a declaration or announcement."

My first thoughts on being free were that I would be able to travel back to Charlestown soon to visit my other brothers there and to see Colonel Washington. And to visit my mother's grave.

I couldn't wait to get back to the farm to tell the others. When I got back, the others said Mr. Newberry had heard the news too. He told them all to act like they always did. What the president said didn't apply to his slaves.

I was confused. Why didn't Mr. Newberry have to free his slaves? The man in town had said Mr. Lincoln freed all the slaves. I was mighty upset and even more determined than ever to be free.

I lay awake long into the night. What President Lincoln said and what Mr. Newberry said didn't fit together. One of them was not right. It had to be Mr. Newberry. I was sure that what President Lincoln said was the way it was supposed to be.

January 15, 1863

Every day I thought about President Lincoln. I was right. He was willing to take a risk, like John Brown, to free the slaves. It was not exactly the same kind of risk, but a risk each man took in his own way. Neither was right or wrong. They just had a different idea on how to free the slaves. From that day forth, when I finally started seeing the similarities, I decided John Brown had done good work for the slaves.

I tried to figure out why President Lincoln's idea didn't free Mr. Newberry's slaves. I thought that Mr. Newberry feared freeing his slaves and rightly so. After all, we all owed him. As long as he kept us bottled up here, he was getting free labor.

What my mother had said about slavery being mental chains was starting to make even more sense. She was right. Our real chains had been opened by President Lincoln but Mr. Newberry made us think they were still locked around our legs.

The others can think we are still captives, but Catesby will not believe that. I believe that I am free. Now it is up to me to break Mr. Newberry's chains and escape.

Chapter 17

My Escape to Freedom

January 20, 1863

I continued to drive Mrs. Newberry into town to get her supplies. With each trip, I was learning more and more about the Underground Railroad.

I knew I couldn't let the other slaves at the farm know my plans because I did not trust them. I could not afford to have anyone know what I was planning. Even my best friends on Mr. Newberry's farm would have to be surprised.

I had thought to take them along. But I needed to worry about myself and my own safety. I had the most determination. I could read and write. And I had the blacksmith skills. I thought I had the best chance to be a successful free black man. None of them had that. I knew I had to plan my escape on my own. They would all be upset that I didn't tell them, but would be praying for my successful escape.

January 25, 1863

My plan was to break free soon. I knew I could make it on my own to Chambersburg, Pennsylvania, which was about 30 miles to the north. I could follow the mountains to get there. I had been given directions to find Mrs. Ritner in Chambersburg.

Mrs. Ritner, a white woman, was a conductor on the Underground Railroad. I dreamed of meeting this angel, Mrs. Ritner. I knew she was a friend of President Lincoln and was helping him. And she would help me too.

I knew she would take me in and hide me, and then send me on my way to the next station on the Underground Railroad and to freedom.

February 5, 1863

Today I decided to make my escape. I was going to be free like President Lincoln said. And I could not wait another day. Who did Mr. Newberry think he was saying that what President Lincoln declared was not good enough for his slaves?

I went to the shop this morning, just like every other day. While I got the fire going and worked hard all day, I stuffed straw into my other shirt and pants. I was going to set up my clothes like a scarecrow when I left work that evening, making it look like I was still standing by the fire. If anyone looked in the window, it would seem like old Catesby was just standing there working away as usual.

When it was dark, instead of going to the shanty, I propped up the stuffed scarecrow in my place and limped into the woods with my small sack of treasures. All I had in the bag were my journal, my dictionary, several pencils, the coins I still had that Billy had given me, and the photograph of Colonel Washington. That was all I owned.

Knowing I would need to take some food with me, I had saved some bread from the last few meals. I grabbed it from my hiding place and threw it in my sack and over my shoulder. I stayed off the main road, limping along as quickly as I could. The darkness covered me for now.

Charlie Cosey, a man who I knew I could trust, had agreed to take me to Boonsboro by wagon. He met me behind the German Reformed Church in Keedysville.

I climbed onto his wagon. We traveled the road quietly to Boonsboro. We turned east and then went along the National Pike toward Frederick, Maryland, to the top of the mountain. I asked him to stop. I climbed down, thanked him, shook his hand and paid him a couple of coins Billy had given me.

Charlie said, "Good bye, my friend," and added, "Good luck, Catesby. You deserve to be a free man. The Lord is with you. I will never tell anyone where you have gone."

I knew Charlie wouldn't tell anyone.

I waited until his wagon had turned around and started down the mountain toward Boonsboro. I hobbled north along the ridge of South Mountain. My crutch wasn't much use here in the rocks as I stumbled and hobbled along.

I had not forgotten my vow to get even with Mr. Newberry before I left. It is just that the closer I got to my escape, the less important my revenge became. I feared facing Mr. Newberry would alert everyone else. I knew with my bad leg I couldn't make a quick escape. I had to have all the hours of darkness to get as far away from the farm as I could. Besides, mother's message, "Vengeance is mine, sayeth the Lord" had popped into my head.

It was more important that I escape with my life than to get even with Mr. Newberry. Mother would have been proud of my decision to seek freedom as my best revenge.

I stayed away from houses and the main crossing roads as I slowly limped along the mountain top. I was pretty sure no one would come looking for me until morning, so I got a pretty good head start. Now that I had such a badly injured leg, courtesy of Mr. Newberry, I had to just do the best I could. I had enough energy to limp along most all night, though I rested often. I knew I was safe for the time being.

The darkness slowed me down. I stumbled and fell. But I was real determined. And that gave me extra strength.

February 6, 1863

When the sun came up, I found an overhang in the rocks and sat down to rest. I could imagine when Mr. Newberry found me missing the other slaves would be beaten. He would try to get them to tell him where I had gone. That is why I had not told anyone. No matter how much he beat them, they would not be able to help him find me. I felt sorry for them, but in not telling them, I was actually helping them. They didn't have to lie for me about something they did not know.

I was sure Mr. Newberry would try real hard to bring me back. He might pay a slave catcher a reward to find me. Or he might go to court and have a warrant signed for my arrest. I knew Mrs. Newberry would have been sad to see me go. She would also be hopeful I would make it to freedom. I was sorry I didn't get to thank her again for being so kind to me.

I needed to be careful. Blacks were free in Pennsylvania, so it would not be unusual for a black man to be traveling by himself. But a large muscular colored man with burns on his arms, a bad leg and a metal crutch, would certainly not be forgotten by anyone who would see me. I might as well have had a sign hanging from my neck that said, "fugitive slave – wanted -- dead or alive."

Whenever I saw someone along the trail, I told them I was making my way to a new job in Chambersburg.

Near Mont Alto, Pennsylvania, I met a man. I told him I was hungry, but willing to work for a few days for food. His name was Jack Snyder. Mr. Snyder took me to his farm where I helped fix his barn. After a few days, I told him I was really a slave who had run away. It didn't seem to matter to him at all.

Mr. Snyder was willing to give me extra money in addition to food and shelter for work. It was obvious to him I was a good worker. I stayed with him for a whole week.

Chapter 18
Reaching Mrs. Ritner in Chambersburg

February 20, 1863

When I finished my work in Mont Alto, Mr. Snyder offered to give me a ride to Chambersburg. He said he was very thankful for the repair work I did on his barn. He was glad to be able to help me gain my freedom. He was tired of the war and didn't believe in slavery anyway.

Was he kidding? It was Catesby who was thankful to him for helping me.

My long difficult journey finally brought me to Chambersburg. I followed the directions I had been given to Mrs. Ritner's house. I knocked on her door. When she greeted me, I was as happy to see her as I had been to see anyone in my whole life.

The lady surprised me by saying that she had been expecting me. The day before a marshal had given her my description and asked if she had seen me. She told him the truth that she didn't know of me. She said he would not come back for a couple of days. I would be safe if I kept out of sight.

Mrs. Ritner was quite helpful. Her husband was the son of the former Governor of Pennsylvania and a fierce opponent of slavery. She said she felt God called her to help on the Underground Railroad.

Mrs. Ritner talked at length about her work. She asked about me and how I had known how to find her. I told her my story.

She felt certain I could get a job with a friend of hers in Cashtown, Pennsylvania. She would give me forged papers saying I had been a free black dated even before the president's recent announcement. That would allow me to get paid for my work. Cashtown sounded like heaven to me.

Mrs. Ritner said the part of Virginia where I had been born was familiar to her. She had worked with John Brown. She had helped some of his men before and after the raid at Harpers Ferry.

When I told her I had been held prisoner by John Brown and was present when he was captured, she became quiet. I added that it wasn't until recently that I had realized the old man had risked his life to free coloreds like me. I told her I was thankful for all his troubles.

A tear ran down her cheek. She said she was real sad that John Brown had been killed.

She quickly changed the subject. Mrs. Ritner fed me and hid me in a special passage below her house.

It was cold, dreary and dark in the cellar, but she promised it was also safe. I noticed a huge rat sharing the underground passage with me. The rat seemed to have been well fed, so it was not interested in bothering me.

February 21, 1863

Mrs. Ritner and I talked and talked. She had helped many coloreds escape to freedom over the years, sending some as far away as Canada.

I asked, "Where do I climb on board the Underground Railroad train?"

She laughed out loud. And then she said "Oh, I'm sorry, Catesby. I forget that many believe the Underground Railroad is like the railroad trains they have seen. Our Underground Railroad may be a boat, or a wagon, or a tunnel. It's whatever way we have for fugitive slaves to be hidden and passed from point to point."

I told her of my confusion over President Lincoln's freeing the slaves and Mr. Newberry saying his slaves were not free. She said because Mr. Newberry's farm was in the North, President Lincoln's freeing the slaves really did not apply to his slaves.

Mrs. Ritner said the president's announcement was not popular with everyone. It was going to take a long time before all the slaves would be freed. President Lincoln's declaration was just a first step. "Slave owners," Mrs. Ritner said, "are going to hold on to their slaves for as long as they can. Perhaps after the war, the slaves will finally all be free."

What Mrs. Ritner said helped me better understand. But I wasn't waiting around until the war was over. I was going to be free as soon as I got to Cashtown.

Mrs. Ritner's house today
East King Street
Chambersburg, Pennsylvania
(Private business)

Chapter 19
Arriving in Cashtown, Pennsylvania

February 22, 1863

Mrs. Ritner told me when I arrived in Cashtown, I needed to ask for Mr. Harold Quinn at the Willow Grove Hotel. She arranged for me to ride all the way in a wagon with Roger who was delivering messages for her. She said anyone at the Cashtown Hotel would be able to tell me where Mr. Quinn lived.

"Thank you, Mrs. Ritner. Some day I will repay you, I promise. And I will pray every day for your success on the Underground Railroad."

She touched my arm and said, "Be careful, Catesby. And God speed."

The trip was bumpy, but sure beat hobbling along on foot. The roads were rutted from the rain. I don't think Roger missed even one rut the whole trip, as he was quite friendly and talked all the way, paying close attention to our discussion, but ignoring the bumps in the road.

He was a man who often moved important packages for Mrs. Ritner. Usually the packages were hidden in a compartment under the wagon. Today, because I had papers, I didn't have to travel that way, even though I was his package.

Roger loved working for Mrs. Ritner. She paid well and was always helping the coloreds to freedom. Roger liked doing his little part in the Underground Railroad. He said, "I am called a baggage master for the Underground Railroad because I carry the packages."

I was delivered to the Cashtown Hotel. I paid Roger a coin and thanked him for helping me get to here. I was happy to have been brought here. He turned the wagon around, waving at me as he headed back toward Chambersburg.

A pretty colored woman sweeping the porch of the hotel knew of Harold Quinn. She sent me off with directions to his place.

I hobbled back toward Chambersburg, along the road we had just traveled. I found the tavern the lady said was at the corner of Bingaman Road and the Chambersburg Turnpike. There was a sign out front "The Willow Grove Hotel."

By the time I arrived at the hotel it was late afternoon. The hotel was a large, two story building with a long porch on two sides. I limped up the steps and knocked on the main door. I asked the colored man who answered if I could speak to Mr. Harold Quinn. He invited me inside and said he would fetch Mr. Quinn.

The place was quite noisy, filled to the brim with people eating and drinking. Several turned to look at me, probably wondering what I wanted.

A well-dressed, man appeared. He introduced himself. "I am Harold Quinn."

"My name is Catesby. I've been sent by Mrs. Ritner of Chambersburg," I said proudly as I handed him my papers. "She said you needed a good blacksmith."

"Come in, Mr. Catesby," he responded, motioning me into a room next to the bar. "Mrs. Ritner sent me a message that she had someone to help me out. I have been without a blacksmith for almost six months."

He welcomed me and shook my hand. And then he invited me to sit down. Mr. Quinn was probably about forty years old. He was a little taller than me. He had the strong weathered hands of a working man. He had a bushy mustache and a hairless forehead like Colonel Washington.

"I have been desperate to find a replacement blacksmith," Mr. Quinn continued. "My horses, wagons and equipment here need prompt attention. And I have lost valuable business from my neighbors who have been taking their smithing work all the way to York. I am delighted you are here."

96

"Thank you, sir," I responded. "But it is Catesby who is delighted to be here."

Mr. Quinn wanted to know all about me and how I learned the trade. I gave him much of the information about my life to that point, withholding some that I wasn't sure I needed to share. I feared my new-found freedom.

He was talkative and cheery. I liked him right away. He had a spark of energy about him that gave me hope for better times.

He told me that I would run the blacksmith shop for him. I would pay him a monthly fee that would include rent of the shop, a small house where I could stay, and an evening meal at the hotel. I could keep all the money beyond that and what my supplies cost. I told him that sounded wonderful.

"In spite of losing much of the area's blacksmithing business, I am sure as soon as you get set up and the word gets out, business will start coming back here," the man continued.

I heard a door open and close behind me. I turned to see who had come in. Mr. Quinn got up and greeted an attractive lady with an embrace.

"Catesby. Please meet my wife, Joanne. Joanne, this is Catesby, the blacksmith Mrs. Ritner has sent to us."

I stood and bowed slightly as she reached out and shook my hand.

"Welcome to our home, Mr. Catesby," she said with a very soft voice. "We are glad that you are here."

"Thank you, Mrs. Quinn. I am honored to be here."

Mrs. Quinn said that dinner would be served. She insisted I stay. I was excited to be asked to have dinner with them. I had forgotten how hungry I was.

She called a waiter. He returned shortly with three plates of ham and potatoes. I found it to be the best meal I had ever eaten. We talked into the night. They were surprised to hear I could read and write.

Mr. Quinn said that my education would help me run a successful blacksmith shop.

I explained to Mr. and Mrs. Quinn that even though President Lincoln freed the slaves, and in spite of my papers saying I was a free man, my owner had not freed me. I had run away. I needed for them to know that in case someone arrived to try to take me back to Maryland.

Both said they understood. They told me if Mrs. Ritner sent me, everything was all right by them too. They would stand up and defend me if anyone came looking.

I promised them I would be no trouble and the best blacksmith they ever had. But I admitted too, I would need their help in getting the business up and running again.

"You'll do fine here, Catesby," he assured me. "But I will help you get started."

Finally Mr. Quinn led me across the yard, showing me the blacksmith shop. And then he set me in a small house nearby. Shortly after that, I fell onto a fine soft bed.

I stayed awake, in spite of the grand old bed. I thought about tomorrow and the start of my new life -- my life as a free man. I promised myself I would not look over my shoulder and be fearful of the men who might be looking for me. I was determined to make the best of the place where God had delivered me. I thanked mother for her guidance and the Underground Railroad, run by Mrs. Ritner, for bringing me here.

The Cashtown Hotel today   (Inn and Restaurant)

The Willow Grove Hotel today
(Private residence)

Chapter 20
My First Day as a Free Man

February 23, 1863

My first morning at the Quinns, I limped just 15 yards or so to my new shop which was right behind the kitchen of the hotel.

As I entered, I thought about how special this day was — a day I would never forget. This was my first day I ever worked for pay. It didn't feel any different, except now I was free. How I liked the sound of that. In fact, I said it out loud to myself throughout the day when no one was around. "Catesby's free."

I was going to have to get used to that. In my mind I still owed Mr. Newberry eighty lashes and for injuring my leg. I hoped the other slaves back at Mr. Newberry's in Sharpsburg, Maryland who weren't so fortunate as I was, would someday punish him for my injury.

Mr. Quinn's blacksmith shop was bigger and better equipped than either Colonel Washington's or Mr. Newberry's. I had newer equipment and a better selection of tools.

The bellows was made of wood, with wooden paddles. All I had to do was turn a handle to keep the fire going. I had never seen anything like that. There was a tire bending machine, a wheel upsetting clamp, and a wagon tire annealing furnace. Mr. Quinn's shop even had a paint room upstairs, and a small lift with cables to operate it.

I wish Billy could have seen this shop.

I spent the early part of the day getting a fire going and touching every tool in the place. Anyone watching me would have thought I was a kid in a candy store trying to make up my mind what to purchase with my coins. Instead, I was a real blacksmith, new to the shop, and trying to see what was there to help me do my job.

Mr. Quinn came in around noon and said he had arranged for several of the neighbors to bring in some projects for me. He handed me a note with the projects written down.

Ruth Davis needed several hooks made for her fireplace. Tish and Peter asked me to make a set of candle holders for their daughter's birthday coming up next month. Ron Marcus asked Mr. Quinn if I could make a watering can for his wife, Robin. And Ed Smith requested an iron door decoration for his wife, Peggy, for their anniversary. Mr. Quinn asked me if I could start with those jobs while he brought in some more.

"Yes, boss," I offered with a little salute.

"Wait a minute, Catesby," he responded without missing a beat. "I'm not the boss here. You are."

"Sorry, sir. That's going to take me a bit of getting used to," I answered with some embarrassment.

He laughed and patted me on the back. And then he left to go back to the hotel.

I tacked the list of projects on the post and started scouring the shop for the materials and tools I needed. That afternoon I had already started all four.

I was excited and exhausted at the end of my first day on the job. When I got back to the house, there was a loaf of fresh bread, still warm, a flask of water and a hunk of ham on my table. It must have been delivered by an angel as I had given no thought at all to eating.

The bed looked very inviting at the end of a long day. But I lay awake, this time trying to think about how much better today had been than any day in my whole life.

Catesby was now a free black man. This was the day my mother and Billy had trained me for. This was the day John Brown, President Lincoln, and Mrs. Ritner had all helped me reach, in their own way.

I was thankful for every one of them. And I hoped someday, every one of my brothers at Beall Air and at Mr.

Newberry's and the ones at farms and plantations everywhere across this country, would also be free.

February 25, 1863

This morning I had been sent by Mr. Quinn to the Cashtown Hotel to pick up a package. The person at the counter was the colored woman who had given me directions the day I arrived here. She gave me Mr. Quinn's package and asked me to sign that I had received it.

The lady smiled at me. She looked down at the paper.

"Catesby," she said. I nodded that she was right.

"Hello, Mr. Catesby. My name is Marcia King. I am very pleased to meet you," she said with confidence. "Please stop by again when you are in town."

I was quite bothered by her. I have not been around ladies much, but I liked what happened today.

Marcia was mighty pretty. She had long black hair with a pink ribbon in it. Her long dress was green and brown. She was a little shorter than me. She had a fine shape and a smile that could light up the darkest room.

I thought a lot about her that evening when I was eating and getting ready for bed. That Marcia was a mighty fine lady, for sure.

March 5, 1863

Life was getting to be an exciting and wonderful routine for me. Mr. Quinn continued to bring me the list of jobs. I worked hard to complete them.

I repaired the hinge on the door of the Catholic Church, fixed the grill plate on Mrs. Sprinkle's fireplace, and replaced the latch on the White family's gate. I fixed several broken locks for Mr. and Mrs. Clowers of Gettysburg and fixed Mr. and Mrs. Reid's wagon. I even made a crude but useful wheel barrel for Mrs. Quinn's flower garden.

Mr. Quinn said he was happy that I was able to get the work done so quickly. He also said my work was of good quality. Billy's lessons on how to determine what to charge and showing me how to keep accurate records were coming in real handy.

Mr. Quinn told me today besides running the Willow Grove Hotel he was an elected member of the Pennsylvania House of Representatives. As a government official he explained, he was often in Harrisburg overnight. He wanted me to know the nights he would be gone so I could help keep an eye on Mrs. Quinn if she needed me. I told him that would be no problem at all. I would be happy to help him.

March 8, 1863

Mrs. Quinn asked me today to take her to the general store in the wagon. She said she would help me shop for food items I could keep in the little house.

When we were finished, I asked Mrs. Quinn if it would be all right if I stopped at the Cashtown Hotel to see my friend, Marcia. She said she would wait for me, but I should not be too long. I told her I would hurry.

Not only did I see Marcia there, but she talked to me again. I forget what we talked about. She made me very nervous. She has an amazing sparkle in her eyes. They twinkled like the stars in the night. Her smile could melt an iceberg. We didn't talk long. I had to return to the wagon to take Mrs. Quinn back home.

When finished with her chores and we returned home, Mrs. Quinn thanked me for taking her. "Your pleasant company today, Catesby, has made my trip delightful. I am pleased that you are part of our family."

March 11, 1863

I saw the February 28 issue of *Harpers Weekly* newspaper today. There was a drawing in the newspaper of colored troops of the First Louisiana Home Guards. They were helping President Lincoln in the Union Army.

I was surprised and pleased to read that the coloreds were allowed to be soldiers too.

March 12, 1863

This morning I traveled into town again with Mrs. Quinn, taking her to pick up some supplies. She asked if I wanted to stop to see Marcia. I said "Yes, I would like to do that."

While Mrs. Quinn was in the general store, I limped to the hotel to see Marcia. We talked some more. I wish I could remember what was said. I need to pay more attention to our little talks.

When Mrs. Quinn and I returned back to the hotel, and I limped to my little house, I thought about being there and talking to Marcia. I think I've got a liking for that girl.

March 16, 1863

Mrs. Quinn came to the shop today for the first time. She looked around and watched me work. "Catesby," she finally said. "There's a dance this weekend at the Murphy barn. Mr. Quinn and I are going. Would you like to ask Marcia and come along with us?"

"I don't dance, ma'am," I mumbled, dropping my head and trying to hide. The thought of asking Marcia to a dance was even scarier to me than the thought of trying to dance with my crippled leg.

"You don't have to dance to take a lady to a dance," she explained. "She knows you like her. I'll bet she's dying to go with you. So, Mr. Catesby, what are you going to do about it?"

"I will think on it, Mrs. Quinn," I told her. "I will let you know." The thoughts were already racing through my head. This was my big chance with Marcia. I wanted to be with her. I wanted to ask her to go. But right then, I was scared to death to ask.

Mrs. Quinn gave me a few minutes to think on it. And then she said, "Don't wait too long. Some other fellow might ask her first."

"Mrs. Quinn," I quickly announced. "No one is taking Marcia to any dance, except me. I will ask her."

"Good idea, Catesby," she finished with a curtsy. "Please save a dance for me."

Late that afternoon I asked Mr. Quinn if I could borrow the wagon to go into town. I wouldn't be gone long, I promised, because I just wanted to ask Marcia to the dance. He was excited. He thought it was a grand idea.

That wagon ride was the longest I had ever taken, though it probably was only about ten minutes in length. I was as nervous as if I had to convince St. Peter to let me through the pearly gates.

My hands were sweaty and cold. I was feeling like a scared little boy. I wanted Marcia to go to the dance so badly. What if she said no? What if someone else had already asked her and I had lost my chance? I couldn't bear those thoughts.

What finally gave me strength was thinking back to my mother and what she had taught me a long time ago. "God made you the best he could, Catesby," mother told me. "He walks with you every day. Give your troubles up to him. And be not afraid."

I said a little prayer to myself, "God, please help me get through this."

I was a bit calmer as I got closer to the Cashtown Hotel. I tied up the wagon and limped up the porch step and into the building. Marcia was not at the desk where she usually sat. I panicked. I fumbled around, finally spotting her coming across the road. I waited. My heart was pounding in my chest. She saw me and skipped over to where I was standing. "Catesby. How nice to see you. I didn't think you'd be in town this week."

"Hello, Marcia," I said, surprising myself that my nervous feelings had gone away. "I made a special trip just to see you. I was hoping you would be able to go to the dance at the Murphy Barn on Saturday night with Mr. and Mrs. Quinn and me."

"Catesby. I thought you would never ask," she shouted, loud enough for everyone in the hotel to hear. "I would love to go to the dance with you. In fact, I have been sewing a new dress just in case you asked me to go."

I was excited. I was also speechless. All I could think of to say was, "Thank you, Marcia. You have made this a great day."

Bowing slightly, I turned and limped out the door. Marcia followed right behind, and asked, "Catesby. Didn't you forget something?"

"What?" I asked, turning around, without any idea what I had forgotten.

"What time are you coming to fetch me?" she asked with a grin on her pretty face.

"Oh, sure," I added, as if I suddenly remembered I was suppose to tell her that. "Six o'clock."

"Catesby. I will be ready long before that," she admitted. "I am so excited that you asked me. Pick me up here at the hotel."

I don't remember anything on the wagon ride home except I was happy she was going to the dance with me.

March 18, 1863

Mr. Quinn said a stranger had come to the house last night looking for a runaway slave from Maryland. "He was looking for you, Catesby."

I was quite fearful I was going to be taken back to Mr. Newberry. But when Mr. Quinn put his hand on my shoulder and told me not to be afraid, I suddenly felt at ease.

"I showed him your papers, Catesby," Mr. Quinn assured me. "Your papers are all legal and proper. There was nothing he could do but go back empty handed. And I told him not to come back if he knew what was good for him."

"I have connections, Catesby, and the man was made aware," he went on. "He was told he was not welcomed in our area. He will not return."

A tear ran down my cheek. No white man had ever stood up for me and protected me. Now I owed Mr. Quinn too, but not the same way I still owed Mr. Newberry.

"Thank you, Mr. Quinn," I said, shaking his hand up and down. "I don't know how I can ever repay you."

"You are family here," Mr. Quinn announced proudly. "There is no need to even think about trying to repay me."

Both Mr. and Mrs. Quinn had said they considered me family. I was happy about that. Perhaps that was how Colonel Washington felt about my mother.

It was a moment of truth for me. It was a moment when I finally became Catesby, the man, and no longer Catesby, the colored man.

Drawing of First Louisiana Home Guards Colored Troops
February 28, 1863   <u>Harpers Weekly</u> newspaper

Chapter 21
The Dance

March 21, 1863

I worked throughout the day on Saturday. Mrs. Quinn told me to be sure to quit early so I could come to the hotel and take a bath. She said she bought me a new shirt. She wanted me to try it on so that she could make any needed changes before we went to the dance.

I had already finished Gary Fleming's project. I stopped work on the Tim Collins' rig right around four. I went to the Quinn's part of the hotel. I tried on the shirt. It needed to be let out at the arms a bit. Mrs. Quinn promised to have it ready by the time I got out of the bath tub.

She had filled the bath with sweet smelling salts and made it hot for me. I soaked in the bath for some time. It was the first real bath I ever had. I was used to just washing down in the evening with a pitcher of cold water from the spring or washing in the creek. The hot water felt good on my bad leg and on the burns along my arms. I didn't want to get out. But I decided I needed to.

I dried off with the towel she had left for me. I put on my pants, socks and shoes. I noticed my shoes had been dusted off. They had a shine that made them look almost new. Mrs. Quinn must have done that while I was in the bath too. I shaved.

She handed me my new shirt. It fit well. "Catesby. You look handsome. May I have this dance?" she teased.

"Thank you, Mrs. Quinn," I said. "Thank you for the shirt, the bath and for shining up my shoes. Most of all, thank you for inviting me to the dance and helping me get together with Marcia. I couldn't have done any of that without you."

"You would have asked her someday, Catesby," she insisted. "I'm just not sure when. I got tired of watching you two being nice to each other but never getting together."

With that she patted me on the back and said, "Marcia deserves a good man like you."

I brought the buggy around. Mr. and Mrs. Quinn got on board. And then I drove to the Cashtown Hotel to fetch Marcia.

Marcia was waiting on the porch when we arrived, looking prettier than I had ever seen her. Her dress was red with a big hoop skirt. My heart pounded as I got down from the buggy and limped over to greet her. I held out my hand, but she went straight past it. She put her arms around me in a warm embrace. I liked it.

"You look very handsome, Mr. Catesby," she offered.

"Marcia, you look really pretty tonight," I confessed. "Everyone at the dance is going to wish they were with you. But it is Catesby who is the lucky one."

I introduced Marcia to Mr. and Mrs. Quinn. Mrs. Quinn told her, "We have heard so many nice things about you, Marcia. We are happy you are going with us tonight."

Marcia curtsied, and blushed, saying, "Thank you, ma'am."

I helped Marcia into the buggy. I drove to the nearby Murphy barn dance. We could hear music coming from the barn even before we turned in the lane. There were a whole slew of folks there already.

Mr. and Mrs. Quinn and Marcia got down from the buggy. I pulled it into an open spot along the rail fence. I tied the horse and limped back toward them as they were waiting to go into the barn.

Marcia grabbed my hand. We followed the Quinns.

"You know with my lame leg, I cannot dance," I announced full of shame before the issue could come up for discussion.

"Do not fret, Catesby. We can still enjoy the dance," Marcia promised.

Mr. and Mrs. Quinn motioned for us to sit with them at a table near the back. We sat down. Marcia pulled her chair around next to me, reaching out again to take my hand in hers.

A band played with the fiddler leading, tapping his foot as he pulled the bow back and forth across the strings. A dozen or so couples were dancing some kind of dance I had never seen. I heard Marcia call it a jig.

Mr. Quinn tapped me on the shoulder and pointed out some of my customers who were there including Mr. and Mrs. Sprinkle and Mr. and Mrs. Reid. Mr. Quinn introduced us to Judge Wills and his wife from Gettysburg.

Mrs. Quinn showed us to the refreshment table where I picked up a cup of cider and filled a plate with fruit and cheese. Marcia carried my plate back to the table for me.

As I looked around the barn I saw it was as much a social gathering as a dance. Many folks like the Quinns seemed to be getting to know the neighbors they had not seen in a while. They walked around and talked with people at many of the other tables.

Marcia noticed some folks she knew from the Cashtown Hotel. She took me over to meet them. I got to meet Mr. Mickley, Marcia's boss, and Mrs. Vogel, the hotel's cook. They seemed quite friendly. I know particularly that Mr. Mickley treated Marcia with respect. Marcia said he was a good, honest and fair man, with no care that she was colored. She liked Mrs. Vogel. "She teaches me all kinds of cooking secrets," Marcia said.

Mrs. Quinn embarrassed me by insisting that I promised to dance with her. She had to drag me onto the dance floor. I just kind of stood there leaning on my crutch and swayed to the music while she danced around and made a big fuss. We laughed and carried on. Before I knew it, Marcia had taken Mrs. Quinn's place, "cutting in" as she called it.

"I thought you couldn't dance, Catesby," she hollered over the loud music. "Look at you now."

The band played on and on, featuring the harmonica on one song and the dulcimer on another. Each member of the band was sweating up a storm, and enjoying themselves almost as much as the people who were dancing. Many of those not dancing got involved by singing along or clapping to the music.

When it was time to close down, no one wanted to go home. I got the feeling perhaps they should have these affairs more often since so many people were having such a good time.

Mr. and Mrs. Quinn insisted I take them home first, and then take Marcia home. And so I did.

I admitted to Marcia that I had feared the idea of the dance, but had enjoyed myself totally. She admitted that it had been Mrs. Quinn's idea to get me to dance and then to have her take Mrs. Quinn's place. I told her I thought it had been a grand plan.

Marcia had me take her to her house after the dance instead of going to the hotel.

She had told me she lived with her mother, her father and her little sister, Bonnie.

She talked all the way home. This time I was alert and paying attention. Marcia talked about going to public school, being a good student and learning all she could. She got the job at the Cashtown Hotel right out of school.

She was 18, going on 19. Her sister was 12. Her father worked at the hardware store in Gettysburg. Her mother worked at home as a seamstress, making clothes for area ladies. She had helped Marcia make the dress she wore to the dance.

This was her second dance, she said. The first boy who took her was what her father called "a horse's arse." She was not allowed to see him again. That was quite all right with her, because she didn't like him anyway.

Before long, we arrived at her house. It was a tiny log home with a small porch just down the road from the Cashtown Hotel. She lived close enough to walk to work.

A lantern burned in the window. It looked like someone was waiting up for her.

I helped her down off the buggy, holding her hand tightly so she wouldn't fall. Marcia whispered to me, "Wait here, Catesby. I will be right back."

I tied up Mr. Quinn's horse and limped onto the porch. I sat down on the bench and waited.

Marcia returned and sat down on the bench, pushing real close to me. Within a few minutes the lantern went out in the window. The only light on the porch came from the moon high in the star-filled sky. It was a pretty night. I was with a pretty girl. I didn't want to go home. I don't remember when I ever felt better.

"That was some fine dance, Catesby. Thank you for inviting me to go with you."

"It certainly was a grand evening, Marcia. It is one I will never forget. Could we do this again sometime?" I added, surprising myself with my boldness.

"I like that idea a lot. In fact, mother said I could invite you to supper next week. It wouldn't be fancy or anything. Would you like to join us?"

"That would be mighty nice. I would like whatever she would be fixing as long as this pretty young girl will be sitting next to me at the table."

"Oh, Catesby. You say the nicest things to me."

"What night would you like me to come over?" I asked.

"How about Wednesday at six? Will that fit in your busy schedule?"

"That will be great. I will look forward to it."

Marcia grabbed my hand and held it tight. Her soft delicate skin tickled my worn hands. It felt wonderful. I didn't want to let go. We sat staring into the night, just enjoying each other and not saying anything at all. I could have stayed there forever, except for a loud knock on the door.

"My father wants me to come in now, so he can go to bed. You have a safe journey, Catesby. Thanks again for taking me to the dance."

With that Marcia jumped up, jerking my hand and helping me stand up. She pulled me towards the buggy. I untied the horse and prepared to leave.

But before I was able to climb into the buggy, she surrounded my waist with her arms and kissed me right on the lips. I was surprised and taken back. As quickly as it happened, she let go and ran into the house.

"Good night, Catesby. Sweet dreams," she shouted, as she disappeared through the door.

I was surprised but thrilled. I liked what she had done. "Why hadn't I thought of kissing her?" I wondered as I climbed on board the buggy and set out for home.

When I got back, I unhitched the horse and settled her in the barn. I limped over to the house, tired but happy from a long day. I was excited by what had happened with Marcia. I couldn't have planned it any better myself.

I did not have the sweet dreams Marcia asked me to have. That was mostly because I did not sleep. Instead, everything that happened from the time I arrived at the hotel to fetch her to the banging of the door when she went inside, I replayed over and over in my head. This Marcia, I decided, was very special.

March 24, 1863

I could not wait for Wednesday. I worked hard at the shop, fixing a wheel on Dennis Frye's wagon, making a large new hook for the Spellar fireplace, and fashioning a spring for neighbor Jim Smith's buggy. But no matter how busy I was, I was just marking time until Wednesday night's dinner.

Mrs. Quinn teased me about bringing the buggy home so late from the dance. She asked me if Marcia and I had a good time. She wanted to know all about us. I told her everything that happened except the kiss.

And I told her that I had been invited to Marcia's house for supper. Mrs. Quinn suggested I make something at the shop to take to Marcia's mother. I wish I had thought of that, because that was a terrific idea.

March 25, 1863

I decided to make a spoon Marcia's mother could use in the kitchen. Billy had showed me how to shape a big spoon with a looped handle. When finished it would be about three feet long. I worked on it all day on Wednesday and completed it just before time to leave.

I was nervous about meeting Marcia's mother and father. I borrowed the Quinn's wagon. Mrs. Quinn gave me a big red ribbon for me to tie on the spoon. I put the present under the wagon seat. I was quite proud I had made it all by myself in the shop. Billy would have been proud too.

I wore the same shirt Mrs. Quinn bought me for the dance. It looked new, but I have to admit, that's not why I wore it. It was the only good shirt I owned.

I arrived at Marcia's house about six. Marcia was already waiting for me on the porch. I pulled the wagon up to the hitching post and climbed down. I tied the horse. Marcia bounded down the steps toward me as I turned back to the wagon to fetch the spoon.

"Catesby," she said enthusiastically. "It's good to see you again." With that she threw her arms around my neck and gave me a big squeeze. I squeezed her back. She giggled. "You are so strong. I'll bet if you wanted to you could hold me here until I had to scream for help," she teased. That was true.

She broke free and ran onto the porch. "Hurry, Catesby. My family is dying to meet you."

I reached under the wagon seat and pulled out the spoon with the red ribbon attached. I limped toward the porch. Two women waited with Marcia in the doorway. "Catesby, this is Bonnie, my sister. And this is my mother."

I bowed slightly, reaching out to shake their hands. "I am very pleased to meet both of you. This is for you, ma'am," I added, passing her mother the gift.

"It's beautiful, but you didn't have to buy me anything."

"I didn't buy it, ma'am. I made it in my shop," I announced proudly. "I am a blacksmith."

"It is even more beautiful if you made this yourself. I will treasure it," her mother said.

"Come on in, Catesby," Marcia urged, grabbing my hand. She pulled me inside the house. "Supper is ready. I'll call father. Sit here," she said, pointing to a chair at the table.

Bonnie sat across from me, eyeing me with some doubt. "How come you are limping?" she asked.

"Bonnie, for God's sake. Mind your manners," her mother screamed.

"Oh, that's all right," I told her. "It's the first question I get asked. I really don't mind." I turned to Bonnie. "I got injured in my blacksmith shop in Maryland. It was very painful for a while, but doesn't hurt at all now. It's just a bother. Did your sister tell you I'm a very good dancer even with a bad leg?"

Marcia came back in the room, saving me from her sister, saying, "Catesby. This is my father. Father, this is my friend, Catesby."

I stood and shook his hand. "I am pleased to meet you, sir."

"The pleasure is mine, Mr. Catesby. Marcia has talked often of you," her father insisted. "I know Mr. and Mrs. Quinn are real good folk," her father continued. "I had heard you were a good blacksmith even before Marcia started bragging about you."

"Look what Catesby made for mother in his shop," Marcia announced, proudly showing off the big spoon to her father. He took it and examined it.

"That's a fine piece of work, young man," her father told me.

"Thank you, sir. I got good training from Billy when I was learning blacksmithing in Virginia. He said any woman who did cooking could always use a good spoon."

Marcia and I sat down. She reached over to squeeze my hand. Her mother and sister brought in biscuits, peas, potatoes, and roasted chicken. It all looked and smelled wonderful.

I started to reach out for the potatoes, and then stopped. Everyone around the table had their heads bowed. I bowed mine too.

"Heavenly Father," Marcia's father prayed. "Thank you for bringing Mr. Catesby into our area and into our daughter's life. May he be a frequent visitor to our humble house. Bless this food you have provided from your bountiful harvest. May it nourish our souls. In Jesus name we pray. Amen."

"Amen" echoed around the table — even from my humble mouth.

Now it was time to eat.

The food tasted even better than it looked and smelled. Except for meals at the Willow Grove Hotel, her mother's cooking was the best I had even eaten. And I told her so.

During supper I was asked about living in Virginia and Maryland and about learning how to read and write. Marcia had told them plenty, but I had to fill in the details. They were eager to listen. I was the night's entertainment, trying to answer all their questions without the awful sin my mother warned me about — talking with my mouth full of food.

Marcia's family seemed genuinely fond of me. Marcia beamed with pride as if I were her "show and tell" project for school. Bonnie wasn't too sure about me — but Marcia's mother and father were enjoying my company. And I was enjoying being with them.

I looked around to check out her family. Bonnie was just as pretty as her sister and seemed bright and cheery.

Marcia's mother was small and young looking for an older lady – about my mother's age. She wore a plain dress with a white panel overlay which she probably made herself. Her hands were delicate and smooth like Marcia's. The three ladies surely looked a lot alike.

Marcia's father was meek and mild appearing. His hands were quite soft, like he didn't do a lot of outdoor work. His handshake was strong and confident.

When it was time for me to go home, Marcia's parents said they enjoyed having me and would like to see me become a regular visitor to their home. I told them I liked being here and would come back, while at the same time ignoring the face her sister was making at me.

Marcia walked me to the wagon. We embraced. This time I joined in a wonderful kiss.

Marcia broke free, and ran onto the porch. And then she turned and waved to me. "Catesby, come back soon," she yelled before disappearing into the cabin.

If the Quinns would have seen me when I got home, they would have noticed that I was smiling.

March 30, 1863

Mr. Quinn was a fair and gracious man. He treated me right, helped me run the business, and became my friend. Tonight he invited me to the tavern for dinner with his whole family. I enjoyed beef and potatoes with Mr. and Mrs. Quinn and their two children, Craig and Kelli.

Kelli was about eight years old. She was both pretty and friendly, much like her mother. She was bubbly and real charming. She took to me with ease, wanting to be right next to me wherever I was.

Craig looked just a little older than his sister, maybe about 11 or 12. He was studious in appearance and acted real cheerful. Between his sister and his mother, he probably had to fight to get a word in with them. He was not too sure about me and kept his distance.

Tonight Mr. Quinn asked me for the first time about my injured leg. I wasn't really ready to tell him about Mr. Newberry, but figured I owed them the truth since they had been so good to me.

I explained I made a big mistake one day at the shop on Mr. Newberry's farm. I was receiving a beating and laughed at Mr. Newberry when it was over, because he hadn't hurt me any. He grabbed a hot poker from the fire and stabbed me in the thigh.

Mrs. Quinn flinched. I thought she was going to be ill.

"I am so sorry to distress you, Mrs. Quinn," I said. And I meant it. I didn't want to upset her.

"How awful of Mr. Newberry," she exclaimed. "What did you do to him?"

"Nothing, ma'am. I still owe him for that one."

Their children were not allowed to speak at the table, but my story had them listening. Both children grew up in a much different place than I did. It wasn't surprising that they were so interested in what I had to say. There were no slaves in Pennsylvania. Mrs. Quinn had told me I was the first colored man that had ever been invited as a dinner guest into the private part of the hotel where they lived.

The children watched as their parents treated me as their friend. That helped them to accept me. But it was another story to ask them to understand what I had gone through.

After supper the children questioned me and listened with interest. They wanted to try to understand. It was going to be hard for them to realize how different it was to be human like they were or to be property like I had been. Treating me as a human came natural to them. I was not a colored man to the Quinn children. I was a family friend.

They wanted to touch the burns on my arms and asked me if they hurt. When they heard what Mr. Newbery had done to me, they wanted to go back to Maryland to hurt him. They were not able to understand why he had hurt me on purpose. Most days I struggled with that myself.

Craig asked how I got from Maryland to Cashtown. I told him about hobbling along the mountain and riding on the Underground Railroad. He also wanted to know if the South was different than the North. I told him I didn't see many differences but I knew the two parts of the country believed in different things.

"Does your leg hurt when you walk?" Kelli asked.

"No, not anymore. But it sure hurt a lick when it was first injured," I said.

Craig asked why I was getting a beating in the first place. I explained to him that sometimes slaves were beaten for no reason at all. And that day had just been my turn. They said that was not fair. I explained according to the law, slave owners could do anything they wanted to slaves. The law allowed that. The Quinn children did not seem to understand. Deep down inside, I didn't understand that myself.

The children wore me out with their questions. I really didn't want to go home when they stopped asking. I felt like I was at home in their house. This must have been how mother felt some days at the Beall Air mansion.

When it was time to go, Mr. Quinn thanked me for all the good work I had been doing. Word was getting around that I was the best blacksmith in all of the Commonwealth of Pennsylvania. People with orders of work to be done were finding him without his having to look for them.

I thanked him for helping me and for being a good friend. I told him how proud I was to be working here.

Chapter 22
Courting Marcia

April 8, 1863

Whenever we were together, Marcia talked a lot about her job at the Cashtown Hotel. She told me the hotel had been built over a spring giving them a cold area in the basement for storage and fresh water all the time. They also had a bake oven in the fireplace. She especially liked helping bake apple pies. Apples were always plentiful in the area.

She said Mrs. Vogel's cooking was great, with the favorite food of the guests there being her chicken and waffles, though her chicken corn noodle soup, and ham and bean soup were also quite popular.

Marcia did most anything at the hotel that they asked her to do. She especially liked to check in the guests and find out where they were from. The hotel had guests from nearly everywhere.

Marcia cooked, made the beds, cleaned, did the laundry, and swept the large porch. Sometimes she did some sewing. Other times she took the sewing home and her mother helped her with the more difficult jobs.

She said she often heard strange sounds at various times inside the hotel. Several guests thought the sounds were from ghosts. Marcia had really never seen any ghosts herself, but wasn't afraid to look for them.

April 10, 1863

Marcia asked me often about my life before Cashtown. Since she had grown up here, Maryland and Virginia were places she had only heard about or read about. She listened because she was real interested. And I wanted to hear about her life in Cashtown too.

She told me her grandmother, Miss Sheryl, lived with them and had taken Marcia under her wing. "Miss Sheryl always told me to decide what I wanted and go after it. That's how I got the job at the Cashtown Hotel," she proudly admitted. "I have missed her so much since she has passed."

"Miss Sheryl had been in an accident when she was younger and walked with a cane, limping like you do. I am surprised it didn't slow her down or get in her way," Marcia explained. "Like you, Catesby. Your leg doesn't get in your way either."

"When I asked Miss Sheryl about her leg, she acted like she didn't know what I was talking about," Marcia continued. "It wasn't any big deal for her. She taught me that every one of us has things we have to overcome. Overcoming those make us who we are. And that God doesn't give us anything we cannot handle."

Marcia said she thought Miss Sheryl was less restricted than most people even with her limp. "There wasn't anything she wouldn't try or couldn't do," Marcia insisted. "That's why she was such a wonderful grandmother."

I kind of wished I had got to meet Miss Sheryl. I know we would have become good friends.

Mrs. Quinn insisted I bring Marcia to supper so they could get to know her too. She suggested a week night when the hotel wasn't so crowded and noisy. We picked the date, April 14. I asked Marcia. Marcia was thrilled with the idea.

April 14, 1863

I borrowed Mr. Quinn's buggy to fetch Marcia tonight to bring her to the hotel. The Quinn children had picked daffodils for the table from their garden to make the evening a little more festive. Both children promised to be on their best behavior, I think due to a lecture on the topic from their mother. They greeted Marcia as if she were an old friend on a return visit.

Eileen, the hotel cook, prepared a pork roast with apple slices and yams especially for us. It wasn't on the hotel's menu that evening. It was delicious.

The four adults talked and laughed during the meal. After the dishes were cleared, the children grabbed Marcia and took her to play some games. Marcia waved a quick goodbye as she was kidnapped to another part of the inn. I feared they would wear her out before too long.

Mr. and Mrs. Quinn asked about Marcia and me. I explained I was really enjoying her being with me but did not know what the future held. They politely smiled and steered the conversation to the shop.

Mr. Quinn told me, "I am very happy with the business at your shop, Catesby. In your second month here, the amount of jobs you finished surpassed any month since the shop was built. That's due to the great work you have been doing. Your shop has a fine reputation. You should be proud. I think after the war is over, business will be even better."

I was happy to hear the praise. I thanked him.

When Marcia returned, the Quinn children had indeed run her ragged. She was tired, but happy as a lark on a spring day.

"Your children are wonderful, Mr. and Mrs. Quinn," she offered.

"Marcia. You are welcome in our house any time. We will expect that Catesby invite you here often," Mrs. Quinn suggested.

"Yes, ma'am," I said, jumping up and answering before she even had a chance to turn and give me the idea. "I hear you."

I took Marcia down the road to her house. We enjoyed several kisses before I had to go back home. On the return trip, I got a few moments to myself to think about just how good Marcia and the Quinns were to me. And thanked God for allowing me to be here in Cashtown with them.

May 5, 1863

I continued to see Marcia often. We sat by the stream. We talked for hours on the bench at her house.

We spent time talking about our whole lives and even talked about what kind of life might be waiting for each of us in the future. She asked me if I was courting her. I said yes, without being real sure what that meant. She seemed happy about that.

We kissed and held hands and touched. We laughed and laughed. The more time we spent together, the harder it was to be apart. The more time we spent at her house, the more of a pest her sister became. Bonnie didn't like me spending so much time with Marcia, because it was taking away time she would normally spend with her sister. She never gave us even a minute alone.

And when I got home Mrs. Quinn always asked me plenty of questions about Marcia and me. She wanted to know everything. "Was I going to ask Marcia to another dance? When was I bringing her to the hotel again for supper? What did we talk about when we were alone? Did her parents like me? Had I kissed her yet? Were Marcia and I falling in love?" I answered most of her questions.

Her last comment puzzled me when she added, "Catesby, you aren't getting any younger, you know."

May 22, 1863

Marcia was such a regular part of my life. I couldn't think of her not being there. She was my best friend, which surprised me. That spot had always been taken by my brothers.

It seemed alright because Mr. Quinn said Mrs. Quinn was his best friend. He said he would rather be with her than anyone he had ever known. I was starting to feel that way about Marcia too.

June 20, 1863

I spoke to Mrs. Quinn tonight after dinner to see if she needed anything. Mr. Quinn was in Harrisburg at some important meeting and wouldn't be home for a couple more days. She said everything was going well but she was thankful that I asked.

And then she asked about me and Marcia.

"Well, Mrs. Quinn, if you want to know the truth, I have been seriously considering asking her to become Mrs. Catesby," I answered, surprising myself at how good my idea sounded now that I heard it spoken out loud. "I have thought a lot about it. We are best of friends. We are good together, better in fact than either of us is separately. And besides, as you said, I'm not getting any younger."

I was not expecting her reaction. After the shock wore off, she lunged at me, almost knocking me over and ending up with her arms around me. "Oh Catesby," she screamed. "That's the best idea anyone has had around here in a long time. Wait until Mr. Quinn hears this. He will be very happy for you. In fact, he and I have actually talked about this very thing."

I was pleasantly surprised.

She let go of me and continued. "Catesby. Mr. Quinn and I own a large section of land. We would like to sell you a parcel behind the barn and help you and Marcia build your own house there. You could pay us some each month and live right there beside the blacksmith shop."

"That's a mighty fine plan, Mrs. Quinn. Do you think Marcia will want to be Mrs. Catesby and live there?" I asked.

"Catesby. I'm as sure as I am about the sun coming up in the morning. Now you hurry up and go ask her," she suggested.

And I did. Mrs. Quinn was right. Marcia was quite happy to be asked to be Mrs. Catesby. We talked about a wedding in the fall.

Chapter 23

The War Comes to Cashtown

June 30, 1863

This morning Mr. Quinn informed me that I needed to be prepared as soldiers were coming into the area and might need my blacksmith services. The Army of Northern Virginia had been in Chambersburg and was marching our way along the Chambersburg Turnpike.

July 1, 1863

In the morning, Mr. Quinn invited me out on the porch to watch the soldiers as they passed the hotel and marched toward Cashtown. Long columns of gray clad soldiers were marching by, packing the road with eight or ten men marching side by side. It reminded me of Sharpsburg, Maryland all over again. But this time there were many more soldiers.

These soldiers seemed even more rag-tag than the ones I had watched before. Their gray uniforms were muddied and torn. Some had wrapped rags around their feet but quite a few were just barefoot.

We offered them water. The men drank it down as if they had not had any in some time. They looked undernourished and tired. I did not envy their lives as soldiers.

Thousands marched by continuously for several hours.

Many of the people fled toward Chambersburg and passed the troops, going in the opposite direction. They were fleeing on foot, in buggies, and in wagons. They weren't carrying any cargo except their children, leaving as quickly as possible to get out of the way of the troops.

The soldiers brought in their wagons for repair. I worked hard to fix them. They complained of long marches all the way from the Shenandoah Valley near Winchester, Virginia during the past few days.

And just like in Sharpsburg, their gray clad officers came to me to shoe their horses. Shoeing horses was pretty easy for me, but there were long lines of horses needed to be shod. I was not sure I would ever get them all finished.

Their horses seemed to be as weary as the men were. Mr. Quinn brought a special officer to have his horse shod. When I looked up, I recognized him as General Robert E. Lee. The general looked weary but neat and well outfitted. His long gray jacket showed wear and tear, with three stars on the collar.

The general looked at me kind of funny. I hobbled over to give his horse an apple when I was finished. He laughed and told me he had a feeling that his horse already knew me.

"Yes sir. I put shoes on your horse in Sharpsburg."

"Traveler," General Lee responded.

"I'm sorry, sir. I did not understand what you said."

"Traveler," he repeated. "My horse's name is Traveler. I remember you. You are a fine blacksmith."

"General Lee, sir," I inquired. "If I could be so bold. Are you the same Colonel Robert E. Lee from the John Brown raid at Harpers Ferry?"

He acted surprised at the question. "Yes, that was me," he admitted. "How did you know that?"

"I was one of Colonel Lewis Washington's slaves and was a prisoner there. Your men rescued me when they captured old John Brown," I added. "I never got to thank you for that."

He continued on. "For a colored man, you sure get around. What is your name?"

"Catesby, sir. Just plain Catesby."

"Well, just plain Catesby. I thank you for treating Traveler so well and for being so grateful for the work I did in Harpers Ferry some years back."

The general bowed slightly and reached up for Traveler's reins. He mounted, gave me a little salute, and then left to catch up with the others.

Mr. Quinn said he asked General Lee to have lunch at the hotel, but the general refused, saying he did not want to get Mr. Quinn in trouble.

July 4, 1863

I've been busy for the last three days shoeing horses and fixing the army wagons. I could hear cannon fire throughout the days, off in the distance. Mr. Quinn shared with me that fierce fighting was taking place. He said thousands from both sides were dying along the roads and on the hills surrounding the nearby town of Gettysburg.

July 5, 1863

Today Mr. Quinn asked me to take him to Millerstown to Squire Miller's Inn to drop off a package. We sloshed through a severe rain storm complete with lightning and thunder, trying to avoid huge water-filled holes in the road.

We delivered the package. I turned the wagon around to go back to Cashtown. We couldn't get back on the road because a long line of army wagons carrying the gray-clad soldiers wounded at Gettysburg were passing through Millerstown on their way back to the South.

We watched in horror. The soldiers were in pitiful shape. They were the most defeated bunch I had even seen. As the wagons hit bumps on the water-filled road, soldiers cried in awful pain -- some even begging to be shot to ease their troubles.

Other soldiers limped alongside the wagons. Some were missing arms or legs. Many were bandaged and bleeding. Several dropped in the puddle-filled street, exhausted and unable to go any further. I wondered if another wagon would pick them up and take them along or if they were destined to end their lives in Millerstown.

We watched for what seemed like hours as the long wagon train continued past where we sat. It seemed like there was no end to the line of rebel wagons.

When we finally started toward home, Mr. Quinn and I were quite shaken, as I had been at Antietam Creek. The images, sounds and smells were almost the same.

When we finally got back to Cashtown, another Confederate wagon train carrying wounded from Gettysburg was passing by the hotel and moving toward Chambersburg.

The terrible war, it seemed, was following me wherever I went.

July 7, 1863

The photographers came in their wagons today, looking for a man they would pay to drive them into Gettysburg. Mr. Quinn asked me to do it. I told him my story of driving the wagons for the photographers around the battle field at Antietam Creek. I explained how horrible that job had been. As his friend, I certainly would do the job again. But if he didn't insist, I would rather not go. He said he understood and would find someone else.

Mr. Quinn said the three-day battle here produced even more dead than at Antietam Creek. I was glad I didn't see it this time. I had seen enough.

The battle was the talk of Cashtown and the Willow Grove Hotel. The Cashtown Hotel and other buildings in the area had become hospitals.

July 21, 1863

The next few times I took Mrs. Quinn to the market, the battle at Gettysburg was all anyone talked about. They described the same things I had seen at Antietam Creek — the piles of bodies, men slowly dying in the fields, the horrors of the battle grounds, the efforts of the doctors trying to help and the unending job of burying the dead. If anyone knew what they were talking about, it was me. I could shut my eyes and see just what they were describing. I had been there. I didn't want to go there again.

Men said that thousands of Confederate soldiers crossed a large field to attack the center of the Union lines. The Union soldiers and their cannons had chopped them to pieces. Very few rebels lived to retreat. It was said that both the blue and the gray armies lost thousands and thousands of men.

Men talked at the Willow Grove Hotel about a great Union victory here. The men said the Confederates had thrown everything they had at the men in blue. They insisted the Union men had taken the best rebel charge and stood tall. Others argued that both sides lost so many men it was hard to determine if there was a winner here at Gettysburg.

I was troubled that the war was continuing long after Antietam Creek. It didn't make much sense to me why so many thousands had to keep dying. Did anyone really know why? Did anyone care?

Were they really fighting over the slavery issue that folks in town had said was the reason? If so, why were the whites fighting for us and the coloreds sitting at home and waiting for it to end? Shouldn't the coloreds be fighting too?

I wished I could have asked those questions of General Lee. He certainly seemed to be a decent man.

I asked Mr. Quinn but he didn't know the answers.

I read in the newspaper about the dead and wounded. I wondered when all this killing would end. Would any mother see her son alive again?

Before too long, business got back to normal. But the battle was still talked about everywhere I went. The war had gone somewhere else. It became someone else's problem. It was out of sight but not out of mind.

July 23, 1863

It took me several weeks to find the time to scout out the battle grounds with Mr. Quinn. I was avoiding the trip on purpose. But after asking me a couple times, I agreed to go.

We spent the day driving the fields of battle at Gettysburg in his wagon.

The town itself had survived the fierce fighting, though buildings south of the square were visibly damaged.

There were holes in the ground and in the road. There was rubble all around. The ground in places had been burned. I was happy that bodies of the dead and wounded I had seen at the fields of Antietam Creek were gone from the ground here. There were mounds of dirt I suspected were graves all over the area. Hospitals set up in homes, schools and churches were still crowded with the wounded.

We traveled slowly around the fields, torn up and in some cases still smoldering. A stench, like at Antietam Creek, was present. Mr. Quinn said farmers from the area had been paid to cart off the dead for burial. He said the casualties at this battle were over 35,000.

September 5, 1863

News of the war I read in the newspapers made it sound further and further away. I wondered if it had touched Charlestown and Shepherdstown like it had touched Sharpsburg and Gettysburg. I had already read that part of Harpers Ferry had been destroyed by the Confederate army early in the war.

Mr. Quinn told me, "Catesby. I hate this dreadful war. Joanne and I are blessed that Craig is not old enough to be a soldier."

"Sir. What do you think about colored soldiers helping in the war for the North?"

"That, Catesby, is certainly an interesting idea," he said.

September 10, 1863

Mr. Quinn brought a deed into the shop today. The paper was to sell Marcia and me a parcel of land beyond the barn. We were very excited to have our own property. But that wasn't all.

Mr. Quinn had arranged for some Amish neighbors to come by next weekend and build us a little house.

Marcia and I both cried as we signed the papers while enjoying supper with Mr. and Mrs. Quinn. They congratulated us. They were quite excited about our new house. And so were we.

We were as happy as any two people we knew, with such good friends like the Quinns. They were always helping us.

September 25, 1863

Today all the Amish neighbors pitched in and built our house. It was amazing to watch them work, like bees in a bee hive. They started at sun up and had our little house finished before the sun went down.

Marcia and I walked through, touching everything in our beautiful new home. We both cried tears of joy. The cabin wasn't big or fancy, but it looked like a castle to us. And it was ours. We were so proud. In another week, when we are Mr. and Mrs. Catesby, we will move in. It was like a dream come true. We owned land. We owned our own house. And soon we would be married. It didn't seem possible.

Mr. Quinn helped me pick out a horse and wagon on my own today at a sale in Carlisle. I had saved money myself, just like he had showed me. I was proud to be the new owner even though the wagon was used by someone else for a time.

I named my horse Billy, in honor of the man most responsible for me being a real blacksmith. Every time I called to Billy, my horse, I thought of Billy, the blacksmith, at Beall Air. The wagon was not fancy but it was mine. I bought it fair and square. It was my property, just like I had been Mr. Newberry's and Colonel Washington's property.

When we got back to Cashtown, I thanked Mr. Quinn for helping me buy my horse and wagon today. He said he was proud to have watched me buy them with my own money.

Chapter 24
Marcia Becomes Mrs. Catesby

October 1, 1863

Today is my wedding day. Mr. Quinn helped me pick out one of his suits and Mrs. Quinn made it fit me.

I took a long, hot bath, thinking as I bathed, of my feelings of joy, excitement and even a little fear, all mixed together. It reminded me of my first day as a free man. This too would be a day I would remember for a long time.

I shaved and dressed. I put on a new pair of boots the Quinn children had given to me as a wedding present. I looked and smelled better than any other day of my life. If only Colonel and Mrs. Washington, Sam, Jim, Mason, Billy, Robert, Thom and my mother could see me now.

Mrs. Quinn said she had never seen such a handsome colored man as me. She asked me to look in the mirror. I didn't even know who that man was staring back at me in the glass.

The Quinns wouldn't let me see Marcia before the wedding saying that was some kind of bad luck. I didn't want any bad luck today.

Mr. Quinn drove me to the church in his best buggy. He parked the buggy and tied up the horse behind the church. We went inside the rear door behind the altar. There we were met by Father Brian Owens and two young altar servers. Father gave me my instructions and asked me if I had brought the rings I made in the shop. I had them in my pocket.

When I finally saw Marcia on her father's arm, she was walking up the aisle toward me. I don't think I had ever seen anyone more beautiful. Mrs. Quinn had helped fix her hair in some kind of braid and then tied live daises through the braids. Marcia's mother had made her a fine long sleeve white wedding gown.

Marcia walked down the aisle like she was the queen of Pennsylvania. All eyes in the whole church were on her.

She cried, I cried, Mrs. Quinn cried, and Marcia's mother cried. I thought this was supposed to be a joyous event, yet everyone was crying.

Marcia's father was not crying. He looked real pleased to be walking his daughter down the aisle. When they got to me, her father reached out his hand and shook mine. "Take good care of her, Catesby," he insisted. "Make me proud of you, son."

"I will, sir. I will," I stammered, my heart pounding like a hammer from the shop.

Marcia reached out and took my hand. We turned toward Father Brian to begin. She held my hand tightly. I don't know whose hand was shaking more, hers or mine, but between the two of us, we were not able to hold our hands still. Marcia was holding me up on one side and my crutch was holding me up on the other side.

Father Brian started with the "dearly beloved" and proceeded right through the ceremony. I did not hear much, as I was just trying to get some looks in toward the pretty lady who stood beside me holding my hand and wishing to become my wife. But I didn't miss out on the "I, Catesby, do take thee Marcia, to be my lawfully wedded wife. To have and to hold, in sickness and in health, as long as we both shall live. So help me God."

And I listened too while Marcia looked me in the eye and pledged the same back to me.

The pastor blessed the rings and showed us how to present them to each other. Marcia hadn't seen her ring that I made in the shop as I had sized it with another old ring. She looked at the ring closely as I slipped it on her finger.

We were finally told to turn to the people. Father Brian announced that we were now man and wife. He introduced us by saying, "May I present Mr. and Mrs. Catesby."

Next to President Lincoln's announcing of the freeing of the slaves and Mr. and Mrs. Quinn saying I was part of their family, it was the nicest thing anyone had every said.

I thought this was another moment I wish Alexander Gardner, the Antietam Creek photographer, could have captured with his fancy camera.

We were told we could now kiss. And we did. This time the kiss was not a surprise, as she had surprised me with that first kiss when we went to the dance. I was willing, ready and eager to kiss my new wife. The people cheered for us. And then Father Brian invited us all into the church basement for refreshments.

The wedding party was the best party I have ever been to. We sang and ate and traded embraces with every man, woman and child in the room. We opened presents. Everyone toasted our upcoming life together. And Marcia and I danced as best we could with my lame leg. As expected, Mrs. Quinn insisted on dancing with me too.

When the party broke up, I helped my beautiful bride into the buggy Mr. Quinn had left for us to use. We headed to our new house. Marcia, my new wife, held my hand the entire ride, without saying a word.

When we got home, I tied up the buggy and lifted her down to the ground. We kissed gently and I started to take care of the horse. "Don't be long, my dearest husband," she whispered.

I took Mr. Quinn's horse and buggy into the stable. I moved as quickly as my bad leg allowed, unhitching the wagon and settling the horse in the stall. I finally limped back toward my new wife. I don't think she had moved at all except to turn around and watch me walk toward her.

We walked hand in hand. I stopped at the door and told her I wanted to carry her into our new house. And she let me. I pushed open the door and threw my crutch inside. I didn't have enough hands to hold the crutch and my wife too. I lifted Mrs. Catesby slowly into my arms, desperately trying to maintain my balance, and carried her into the house. I set her down right inside the door, afraid I might drop her.

The lamp in the house had been lit (probably by Mrs. Quinn). There was an open bottle of wine and two glasses on the table. A note propped up against the bottle read "Mr. and Mrs. Catesby. May you love happily ever after. Harold and Joanne Quinn."

Marcia started crying. I took the lamp and led her into the bedroom. We had just purchased the bed that filled most of the small room. No one had ever slept in it. I put the lamp on the table. Marcia sat down on the bed and pulled me close, encircling my waist with her arms as I stood in front of her.

"My loving husband. I must tell you a secret," she said very shyly.

I stepped back out of her embrace and thought, "What possible secret could she need to tell me now?" I feared the answer.

"From the moment I saw you limping up to the Cashtown Hotel the day you were looking for Mr. Quinn, I have known someday you would be my loving husband. I had prayed to God for him to bring you here to me. That is my secret. This is a dream come true for Mrs. Catesby." And with that, the tears flowed even faster down her face.

"Oh, my darling, Marcia. While it has taken me a bit longer to discover you, I am quite sure that you have it backwards. It is God who has brought you to me."

We both laughed. She laid down, still wearing that beautiful dress, and motioned for me to lie down beside her. We laid there together, in each other's arms, just getting used to the feeling. I was excited, but worried about what to do next.

I spent the rest of the long night learning how to be loving with my new wife.

October 2, 1863

I admitted as grand as the loving had been, I had absolutely no idea what I was doing because it was the first time for me.

Marcia said not to worry. It was her first time too. And she promised that practice makes perfect. We just needed to practice often.

October 25, 1863

We practiced often for the next several weeks. And she was right about it getting better and better with practice.

October 30, 1863

I continued to work at the shop. Marcia still worked at the Cashtown Hotel. I took the wagon and drove her to work in the morning. She was usually finished before I did, so she got a ride to the shop to watch me work.

As the days went by, she spent more and more late afternoons here in the shop. At first she just watched me work. "You are such a master at what you do, Catesby," she commented. "I enjoy watching you." And then after a while she started getting involved at the blacksmith shop because she wanted to help me.

Chapter 25
The President Visits Gettysburg

November 18, 1863

Mr. Quinn and his wife invited us to go into town tomorrow to hear President Lincoln speak in Gettysburg. The president was going to dedicate the cemetery to all the Union men who died there during the awful battle in July. We were both happy to go and see President Lincoln.

November 19, 1863

I got the horse and buggy ready. I helped Marcia on board and then drove the buggy to pick up Mr. and Mrs. Quinn at the front porch of the hotel.

We headed to Gettysburg. It was a pleasant day to travel except that the roads were packed with people going our same direction.

Mr. Quinn directed me to Judge David Wills' house which was right in the middle of the town. I was quite surprised to hear that President Lincoln was there.

Mr. Quinn said Judge Wills had set up the cemetery dedication and had invited the president to speak. I stopped and the Quinns got out of the buggy. Mr. Quinn told me to keep the buggy close as they would only be a few minutes.

There were a couple dozen other buggies tied to the hitching posts around two sides of the house. I pulled in beside one and got down to brush Mr. Quinn's horse while I waited. The center of town was quite crowded with people. There were fancy buggies and groups of soldiers and others waiting for the parade. Bands were playing. It was a grand affair.

The Quinns returned shortly and gave me directions to the cemetery. Mr. Quinn told me they had talked to President

Lincoln. I wished I could have talked to the president too. I would have thanked him for freeing me and my enslaved brothers and sisters.

The Quinns boarded the buggy. I drove through town following a long line of other buggies going to listen to the president speak.

I hitched the buggy outside the cemetery. Mr. Quinn told us they had reserved seats near the platform. He said we should stay close to the buggy, but to also enjoy ourselves as he felt certain we could watch from here. But he encouraged us to move forward if our view was blocked or we couldn't see or hear what was going on.

A long procession of soldiers and officials marched down the street from town.

It wasn't too long after the marchers entered the gate that I heard a commotion behind me. It was President Lincoln who I recognized from Sharpsburg.

I am not trying to be disrespectful, but he certainly did look uncomfortable on that horse. His long legs hung down to the ground. It looked like they should have found him a taller horse.

The president got off his horse right next to Mr. Quinn's buggy. A colored man took his horse to tie it to the post. The president looked our way and smiled. He tipped his hat, and then took long strides into the cemetery. I wondered if he really did tip his hat toward us or I just wished he had. I asked Marcia what she thought. She thought he had done that for us.

Marcia and I found a spot on the grass where we could see all the people on the stage. We thought we were close enough to hear.

There was some fine music playing while everyone gathered. A minister said a long prayer. The band played some more. And then an old white haired man talked on and on and on.

I slept through part of it. Marcia woke me before the man was finished. I was thankful I had not missed the president's talk.

Everyone was mighty happy when the speaker finally stopped and sat down. The crowd cheered loudly, perhaps because he was finally finished. I did not think the people came to listen to him.

President Lincoln was introduced next. There was loud clapping as the president stood to speak. As quickly as he started speaking, he was finished.

I was surprised President Lincoln spoke such a short time. All I remember was that he said, "All men are created equal." I was certain he meant colored men too.

The Quinns came out from the ceremony. I helped Marcia and them up into the buggy. When we got back home, I told Mr. Quinn I had a crazy thought. "I think the president tipped his hat to us."

"That's likely, Catesby," Mr. Quinn said with a grin. "I described you to him at the judge's house. I asked him to look for you at the cemetery next to my buggy. I told him that you and Marcia were very grateful for what he had done for your people."

Oh, to be able to tell my brothers back in Sharpsburg that not only did I see President Lincoln again, but that he tipped his hat to me. They would have never believed me.

That night I promised God if I got the chance, I would try to repay the president for freeing the slaves. I didn't rightly know what I was promising, but I was sure I would do something.

Chapter 26
Returning to Beall Air

November 25, 1863

As our wedding present, Mr. and Mrs. Quinn paid for us to travel back to Charlestown including staying overnight at inns both going there and coming back. Mr. Quinn agreed to drive the buggy and go with us, since we would be traveling into the South. He had received a pass so we could get through the lines safely.

I talked the whole way there, telling Marcia and Mr. Quinn about my life at Beall Air. They knew about Colonel Washington as I had shown them the photograph he had given me.

I was excited that they would finally meet my family, including Colonel Washington and his new wife, Ella, and my brothers Billy, Sam and Mason. I told them about each one of my friends. And I talked about my mother.

By the time we got close, I had described the mansion house, the shanties and the blacksmith shop.

As we rounded the last bend in the road, there in front of us was the mansion house of Beall Air. The house I remembered as being so big and beautiful had fallen apart. Marcia and Mr. Quinn must have been surprised to see it because it certainly wasn't the mansion house I had described to them. But it was still home.

I motioned for Mr. Quinn to drive the buggy around back, nearest the slave shanties where I had lived. I was shocked. The place looked deserted. The shanties were empty. Even the mansion house looked to be closed.

Mr. Quinn stopped the buggy and hitched it to the post. I climbed down and helped Marcia get out of the buggy. A man who I did not recognize came toward us. He asked if he could help.

"I am Catesby. This is my wife, Marcia, and my friend, Mr. Quinn," I told him. "I was one of Colonel Washington's slaves before I was sold. I have come home to visit. Is anyone here?"

"I am John Earnest. I am the only one who lives here," he said. "I was appointed overseer to Beall Air when Colonel Washington took assignment in France."

"Where are Mrs. Washington and the slaves?" I asked.

"Mrs. Washington has moved back to Clover Lea," he told us. "The slaves were all sold to pay off the mounting debt on the plantation."

"What about Billy, the blacksmith?" I asked.

"He was a free black man. He chose to go to upstate New York to set up a blacksmith shop near where his brother lives," he explained.

It took me a while for all this news to sink in. What had felt like home was suddenly feeling like somewhere I didn't belong. Marcia must have felt my discomfort, because she moved nearer and took hold of my hand.

"My mother is buried in the cemetery. Do you mind if I visit her grave and wander around a bit to show them where I grew up?" I asked.

"No. Stay as long as you like. I have work to do. I hope you don't mind if I attend to it," the man replied, as he started to walk away.

"We will see ourselves out. Thank you, sir," I called out.

I limped back to my mother's grave with Marcia and Mr. Quinn following close behind. I spent a few minutes in silent prayer and then told them about my mother. We pulled weeds around the sign Billy and I had made.

We walked to the blacksmith shop. It too had seen better days. The building had been neglected and stood like an old weary stool on its last leg. I gave them a quick tour.

I told Marcia and Mr. Quinn I was feeling very sad, because I thought they would be meeting my friends.

I was shocked at the condition of the place. I wondered to myself where I would be today if I had stayed here.

We went back to the buggy. I snatched the box I had brought along and asked Marcia and Mr. Quinn to hide it in the barn over yonder for safe keeping. If something happened to me, I wanted the box with my journal to be here at my home at Beall Air.

Looking for Catesby

Catesby's life obviously continued on from that point, even though the journal of his life story ended with his visit back to Beall Air.

I was determined to continue to pursue him, with just a few clues. He had become someone I felt I had known from long ago. I wanted to find out what happened to him. He had piqued my interest. I didn't want to let him go just yet. If the rest of his life had been as intriguing as the first part, it would be of great interest.

All the clues I really had to go on were Catesby; blacksmith; Marcia Catesby; and Harold Quinn of Cashtown, Pennsylvania. I was hoping that was enough.

I had never been to Cashtown previously. My only introduction had been a famous Mort Künstler painting called "Distant Thunder" of General Robert E. Lee leading the Confederate army past the Cashtown Hotel prior to the battle of Gettysburg.

Cashtown wasn't that hard to find. Finding Harold Quinn, Catesby, and Marcia Catesby proved to be much more difficult.

An 1883 map showed the Willow Grove Hotel. I headed for that sector of the Pennsylvania countryside. The area was exceedingly charming, with rolling hills, lots of orchards, fruit stands and the Knouse and Musselman processing plants. The economy of the area for many years has relied on the production of the fruit trees. It seemed that they were still producing today.

I found the old Willow Grove Hotel at the corner of the Chambersburg Pike and Bingaman Road. The property, however, had changed hands many times over the years. The current owner, Mr. Norwich, showed me where the blacksmith shop once stood behind the former hotel. Mr.

Norwich was friendly and easy to talk to, but had no information on the people I was looking for.

I tried several sources in the area of Cashtown including the Adams County Historical Society and the local public library. The Quinn name was still around.

Catching up with someone named Quinn wasn't as hard as finding someone who was familiar with Catesby.

The first stop of my search brought me to the Barry Quinn place. The house was quite large, on an elaborate parcel of ground near the old hotel.

I approached the farmhouse with great expectations. A boy about twelve answered my knock on the door. He was very polite. I told him I came to see Barry Quinn. The young boy wanted to know who was calling. I gave him my card, telling him my name was Bob O'Connor and that I was an author. The lad invited me into the foyer and pointed for me to have a seat. "I will be back shortly," he said, scooting up the stairway two steps at a time.

It wasn't but a few minutes later that a well-dressed man of about forty-five descended the stairway heading toward me. I rose from the chair and was greeted by the man with an outstretched hand. As we shook hands he offered, "Mr. O'Connor, welcome. I am Barry Quinn. How can I help you?"

I explained my trip to Cashtown and my research on Catesby, the blacksmith, his wife Marcia, and Harold Quinn. I told him they lived in this area during the Civil War.

"Those names do not ring a bell for me," he offered. "There are several Quinn families in this immediate area, but the families are not related. My kin settled here in the 1890s, which is quite a bit after the time period you are researching. Perhaps you might try Dexter Quinn over on the west side of town."

He provided me directions to the Dexter Quinn home. I thanked him for his help. We shook hands. I headed out the door toward stop number three.

Dexter Quinn's place was small. It was only a one-story cottage with a tiny barn out back.

My knock on the door brought a delightfully cheery, middle-aged woman out onto the porch. "May I help you?" she asked.

I told her my name, explained my search and how I had been sent here by Barry Quinn. "Do you or your husband know any of the people I am looking for?"

"The names aren't familiar to me, but Dexter may know. They would be his blood relatives, not mine. Let me fetch him for you to talk to." With that she turned and went back into the house.

I looked around. Several cats by now had found my pant leg and were rubbing against me for attention. What is it about cats, which I don't particularly like, being attracted to my leg? I tried as best I could to ignore the feline creatures.

Mrs. Quinn returned, bringing along her husband. "This is Dexter," she announced. "Tell me again what your name is."

"O'Connor. Bob O'Connor. Nice to meet you, Mr. Quinn."

"It's Dexter, please. Mr. Quinn is what you would call my great grandfather. I'm Dexter," he said, almost as cheerfully as his wife had been. "Tell me who you are looking for."

"I am searching for information on a man named Catesby who was a blacksmith at the Willow Grove Hotel during the Civil War. His wife's name was Marcia."

"Hmmmmm. Seems to me there was a blacksmith around here by that name. He was a black man with a limp, if I'm not mistaken."

"That's him," I said excitedly. "That's who I am looking for."

"Let me think," the man said, trying to retrieve some more information from his memory. "I remember hearing my grandfather mentioning him, though I don't think he was related to this Quinn family. I heard tell he went off to war as a blacksmith in one of the colored regiments. I don't know much beyond that."

"Dexter," his wife jumped in. "Do you suppose they would know over where John Quinn and his wife run the Blue and Gray Bed and Breakfast on Old Route 30?"

"Honey, you may be right."

"I appreciate the information. How do I find their house?" I asked.

Dexter Quinn provided me with directions to the bed and breakfast. As I left, I felt at least I was making some progress. By the process of elimination, I was getting closer to the people I was looking for.

He had provided me with information I had not known, that Catesby had been a blacksmith with the colored troops. I was buoyed along with new enthusiasm.

I found the Blue and Gray Bed and Breakfast on Old Route 30. The house, belonging to John Quinn, was an elaborate two-story Victorian building reminiscent of the Civil War era. There was a small sign out front advertising accommodations. I knocked on the door and was greeted by a pleasant looking, well-dressed woman with fiery red hair.

The "fifty something" lady welcomed me like an old friend. She obviously thought I was a potential customer of her fine establishment, but offered no apparent disappointment when I told her what I was looking for instead.

"My name is Judy Quinn," she explained. "My late husband John, was a relative of Harold Quinn."

Mrs. Quinn said she had no information about Catesby but had heard John's mother speak of him. His mother was old, pushing 90, she offered, and was of sound mind even though it was perched atop a very frail body. She was sure John's mother had spoken of Marcia Catesby too.

She walked me next door and introduced me to her mother-in-law, Carri Quinn. And then Judy said goodbye and walked away, leaving me with her aged mother-in-law.

Mrs. Quinn was sitting in her rocking chair on the front porch. Her purple smock covered her frail figure and reminded me when I get her age, I need to wear more purple.

Her worn shoes pushed off with each cycle of the rocking chair, keeping it in constant motion. I'd have bet this was the most strenuous activity in her life for the last several years.

"So, Mr. O'Connor," Mrs. Quinn began. "You're new around here. I ain't never seen the likes of you. Why would you be visiting this old lady today?"

I was about to respond when she continued. I guess she had just stopped to take a breath.

"This better be good whatever it is, 'cause I'm a busy lady," she continued. "Men come around to see me all the time. They usually bring flowers, thinking that will get them on my good side. I noticed you didn't bring any flowers for me. So you have no chance to get on my good side today."

"Well, ma'am. I'm a bit embarrassed about not bringing flowers," I stammered, not knowing how to react to this feisty lady. "Rest assured that I will bring two bunches next time I stop by."

"If there is a next time," the lady quickly retorted. "Don't be so sure you will be invited back, young man."

Whew. This was not going well. I needed to take control and find out if she had any information that I was seeking. I was not sure I was up to the challenge.

"I am an author," I stated, trying to get this conversation back on track. "I am looking for information about some people I think you might know. The man's name was Catesby. He was the blacksmith for Harold Quinn back in the Civil War. And I am also looking for information about Marcia Catesby, his wife. Do you remember telling your daughter-in-law that you had heard about Catesby and Marcia Catesby?"

"Catesby, the colored blacksmith with the bad leg?" she asked. "And Marcia was his wife?"

"That's them," I said excitedly, finally getting somewhere. "What do you remember about them?"

"Let me see," Miss Carri pondered. "It's been a while. But my memory is strong, especially about the good old days. Sit here beside me and I will tell you about Catesby and his wife."

I pulled a nearby chair closer to her, took out my notebook and pen and waited. She started with a story that would have delighted most anyone listening, except maybe for me. It took me almost no time to determine that as she talked about the Quinn family and the Civil War days, it was as if she had been there herself. Everything was in first person. She knew Catesby personally. He was a blacksmith. She helped his wife, Marcia, at the hotel.

From there she started talking about Mr. and Mrs. Quinn, the Willow Grove Hotel, the Civil War in Gettysburg, and on and on and on.

She said Harold Quinn was some kind of a politician, a Republican, she thought, or perhaps a Whig. And he was a friend to many people, including President Abraham Lincoln. Mr. Quinn's hotel was a thriving business and a popular local attraction. He had two children. Miss Carri had also helped Mrs. Quinn with those children, who were quite a handful.

There was some new information in her story. I was fired up, taking notes on each new revelation. But neither Marcia nor Catesby's names ever emerged again. When I asked, Miss Carri was ill equipped to answer any of my questions about them and what she really did know. Instead, she insisted I was interrupting as she continued to wind her tale *ad infinitum* with the information she was determined to tell me, regardless of what I might be seeking.

No matter how many times I asked about Catesby, the blacksmith, and his wife, the old story teller was not distracted at all. If there was anything about the two of them in her tale, I had to wait until she was good and ready to tell me about them.

Three hours into the story, which by now had repeated itself several times with no Catesby or Marcia in sight, I stood up, thanked her and started to leave. She said she thought I was being quite rude, and continued on with her story, telling it to the empty chair I had just vacated. I walked back dejectedly to my car.

Old Mrs. Quinn had been right with her prediction. I doubt if there was going to be a next visit from me, so I was not going to be bringing her two bouquets of flowers.

Judy Quinn saw me leaving and headed my way, signaling for me to wait. She asked me about her mother-in-law's information.

"If she did know anything, she was not capable of telling me today," I gently explained, not wanting to insult her mother-in-law.

"She comes and goes," Judy admitted. "I was hopeful she would be ready today to help out. Perhaps Uncle Bob in Gettysburg can tell you what you need. That's Miss Carri's older brother. Here. Let me write out the directions to his place."

I thanked her for her assistance and took the directions to where I might find Uncle Bob. At this point I was not hopeful Miss Carri's brother would be any more helpful. He would be over ninety years old.

In fact, I thought the trip to Gettysburg would certainly be just another waste of time.

The last time I had been in Gettysburg my water pump had gone out in my car. Mr. Brown of Excalibur Towing Service had to take me and my car all the way back to West Virginia. I wasn't optimistic about returning to Gettysburg today.

The address Judy gave me turned out to be an assisted living home on Baltimore Street in Gettysburg. I parked along the street in front of the home, walked up the sidewalk, and climbed the steps to the house. Obviously one day someone with means had lived here.

The large Victorian house had a long porch with a line of rocking chairs reminding me of the entrance to a Cracker Barrel Restaurant. The grounds were immaculately trimmed.

Upon reaching the door, I knocked, as commanded by a little sign "Knock for Entrance" and waited. An elderly man opened the door and cheerfully announced, "Welcome to

Paradise Home of Gettysburg. I'm Jim Teague. How can I assist you?"

I told Mr. Teague I had been sent here by Judy Quinn from Cashtown to see Uncle Bob Quinn.

"Yes, I am familiar with Mrs. Quinn. The man we call Uncle Bob is probably out back working in the garden," the man muttered. "I will take you to him," he added, surprising me with his offer.

I followed him through the massive lobby of the home, passing several lovely stained glass windows and a wonderfully fashioned hand-carved wooden staircase. We went out through a large door in the back. He stopped on another huge porch and pointed into the garden. "There he is. Wait here. Who shall I tell him is visiting?"

"My name is Bob O'Connor," I advised him. "Tell him I am a friend of Judy Quinn's."

He approached a very elderly man who was seated on a stool, meticulously working in what this spring would be the flower garden. Mr. Teague said something, causing the man to stop what he was doing and look my way. Uncle Bob stood up, took off his gloves and put down whatever tool he was using. Mr. Teague led him toward me and up the steps of the porch.

I shook hands and introduced myself to the tall, slender old man. He sported a white goatee and a head of white hair. His face reminded me enough of Colonel Sanders of chicken fame that he could have won a look-alike contest at the local fair.

He was quite a dapper chap. His jacket was thread bare at the elbows. He wore a button-down collared shirt and pleated trousers.

His boots were low cut and needed some polish. He wasn't as frail looking as his younger sister. He looked more alert, which gave me hope.

We sat down on the wicker chairs on the porch. I told him of my interest in the Harold Quinn family of the Civil War era. In particular, I was looking for a man named

Catesby, who was a blacksmith at the Willow Grove Hotel, and, his wife, Marcia.

I explained that my research had brought me to this area following their trail. I accounted for my finding of his journal about the life of Catesby. I rambled, talking about my upcoming book and the missing portion of Catesby's life I was seeking.

Uncle Bob looked at me quizzically. He listened politely but said not a word. He reminded me too much of his sister, Carri. I was not sure he was there with me. He watched me closely as I talked, but he didn't react, smile or anything. When I finished, he got up and walked inside. There was no "thanks," "have a nice day," or anything. He just vanished.

Not being sure if I was to follow him or stay put, I stayed seated on the porch. Had he gotten angry and left or just forgotten what I asked him? Was he coming back? Your guess was as good as mine.

Mr. Teague returned shortly, bringing with him two large glasses of pink lemonade. I thanked him and asked about Uncle Bob.

"Did he abandon you here?" Mr. Teague asked with a little laugh. "He does that. One minute he's here. The next minute he's gone. His M.O. is he usually returns. It may be a while though."

"Thanks for explaining," I muttered, thinking "Oh great. Uncle Bob is the Paradise Home of Gettysburg's 'resident nut.' I'll be here all day. I might as well enjoy the quiet time and drink my lemonade. Perhaps I will drink his too, like Uncle Bob would notice."

I checked my watch. It was a quarter to four. I didn't need to be anywhere in particular. I would give Uncle Bob a little time. I wasn't sure just how long I would wait, but I would wait a while.

I don't know how long I waited. I was kind of in "la la" land, enjoying the rare stress-free environment, and an opportunity for once to just "chill out." Perhaps I even snoozed a moment or two. I've been known to do that.

When I looked up, there was Uncle Bob, standing in front of my chair. I wasn't sure he remembered why I was there. I wondered if I needed to start at square one with him and tell him my story again.

Before I responded, he held out a photograph. It was one from the Civil War era. I took it in my hand to examine it. The man in the old photograph was dressed in a suit and tie, and sported a nifty mustache. I asked "Do you know this man?"

"Mr. Quinn," he said. "Mr. Harold Quinn. My great grandfather."

I jumped up and hugged Uncle Bob, to his and my surprise. "I have another one," he said gleefully.

With that announcement, he held out a second photograph. I looked at it, eager to see who it was. It was a man about twenty years old, looking like a younger version of the other photo, with a slightly different, even larger mustache.

"Who is this?" I asked.

"Mr. Craig Quinn," he announced quite proudly. "My grandfather."

By now I knew that Uncle Bob really had been paying attention. He evidentially had gone to his room and rooted through his things to come up with these two photographs. I felt like I had just been given a wonderful gift. Regardless of what happened the rest of the day, my trip to Gettysburg had proven valuable even amidst my skepticism.

"I have to go to my car to bring something to show you," I told Uncle Bob enthusiastically. "Please, don't go away," I begged.

He nodded, like he understood. I knew I needed to hurry because I was not sure he did understand. I doubted he would be here when I returned, no matter how fast I ran to my car.

I bounded down the porch steps, taking two at a time, ran around the side of the house and over to my car. I pulled my box out of the trunk -- my prized box. The one I had found at Beall Air. I raced to the back yard, fearing Uncle

Bob would be gone. Instead, he was sitting quietly on the chair, sipping peacefully on his lemonade.

He seemed glad to see me. I was certainly glad to see he had not disappeared. He smiled as I hopped up the porch steps.

I set the box down on the pink lace tablecloth of the round table and opened it. I took out my photograph and laid it in front of him. "This is Colonel Lewis Washington, Catesby's original owner," I told him.

Without saying another word, he got up from his chair and walked back inside the house again.

What had Mr. Teague told me about Uncle Bob? "One minute he's here. The next minute he's gone. His M.O. is he usually returns. It may be a while though."

This time I was determined to wait. And in about ten minutes he did return. He was clutching a box to his chest. The hair stood up on the back of my neck as he set it on the table. "Same as mine," he professed. And he was absolutely right. We had identical boxes.

"Where did you get this box?" I asked.

"My grandfather's attic right before they tore down his old house," Uncle Bob explained.

He handed me his box and motioned for me to look inside.

My heart fluttered with excitement. I remembered back to finding my treasure box and anxiously wondering what was inside. With his box, my anxiety level was pegging the excitement needle — my expectations sky high though deep down inside, I feared a big disappointment might be coming my way. "Be not afraid," I reminded myself, remembering that is what Catesby's mother would have told him.

Would I find the rest of Catesby's life inside this box?

I opened the box slowly. I found a small stack of old battered envelopes tied with a faded red ribbon instead of the journal I had been hoping for.

In reading the top envelope, I saw that it was addressed to Marcia Catesby, in Cashtown, Pennsylvania. "Wow," I shouted excitedly. "Perhaps this is an original letter from

Catesby to his wife." That would definitely be an amazing discovery.

Uncle Bob placed his finger on the ribbon and motioned for me to untie it and look some more. I carefully slipped the ribbon off. I quickly shuffled through a dozen more envelopes. They were all addressed to Marcia Catesby, over a time period from January, 1864 to April, 1865. The envelopes had various postmarks, including New York, Florida, Georgia, Virginia, West Virginia and Mississippi. There were another 6 without envelopes but dated from Anderson, Georgia.

"Open them," Uncle Bob insisted. I opened them one by one.

They were indeed from Catesby. This certainly would provide me valuable information on what happened to him from the time I had lost track.

"From Catesby," I explained, "to his wife. Thank you for saving these. I hope you will let me read them. They will be valuable in my research."

"Sure," he quickly responded.

I touched his box again and carefully examined it with my fingers. I'll be darn if it didn't look like it had a false bottom too.

I set it down. I picked up my treasure chest to show Uncle Bob. I opened the lid while he curiously watched. I showed him the false bottom. Then I carefully opened the inside lid where I had preciously kept the journal, "The Life of Catesby." I showed it to him.

He watched very intently. And then I held up his little box to show him I thought his had a false bottom too. Did he understand what I was showing him?

"Something hiding inside?" he asked with a smile. "Will you open it?"

"May I?" I asked.

"Please," Uncle Bob pleaded, "but don't hurt my box."

The man of just a few words did understand. He had the same concerns we had in trying to open my precious box.

Open it if you must, we had agreed, but please be careful not to injure the container.

I gave him an assuring nod, adding "Absolutely. I will handle it with great care."

I asked him if he had a knife. He nodded yes, got up and walked back toward the garden. I was hoping he was getting a knife, and not abandoning me again at this important moment.

He walked into the garden to where he had been sitting. He reached down and picked something up. And then he walked back my way with a smile. In his hand was a long serrated knife.

He set the knife down on the table and signaled for me to proceed.

My hand trembled as I carefully worked the knife along the sides of the box. I slowly and deliberately cut along the edges, trying to ignore the thumping of my heart. My anticipation was killing me. Perspiration ran down my forehead and into my eyes. I could barely see.

The inner lid of the box finally gave way. I looked at the old man beside me and explained, "It's your box, Uncle Bob. You get to open it."

"Me? Are you sure?" he wondered. A huge smile covered his weathered face.

"I am real sure of this, Uncle Bob," I answered. "Please go ahead."

He was nervous as a school kid with his first report card. But he was calm compared to me. You could have walked up behind me right then and said "boo" and I would have had a heart attack. I was a jumbled mass of nerves. Think positive, my friend would say. I thought positive and tried to "be not afraid."

Uncle Bob took his time. He carefully lifted out the lid. I almost couldn't look. He reached inside and pulled out a pile of old papers and what looked like two battered diaries. The papers were falling apart, all tattered and torn. The diaries looked like Catesby's first journal, though not in as good of shape. He seemed disappointed.

155

I got closer to take a look. Tears ran down my face. The top sheet of the pile was all I needed to see. On that page was the title, "The Life of Catesby," just like the cover of the journal I had found before.

I cried as I hugged Uncle Bob. He thought I was disappointed. He could not have been more wrong. He had no idea what he had shown me here on the porch of Paradise Home of Gettysburg. If he had given me a million dollars, he could not have given me anything more valuable.

I told Uncle Bob to sit tight. I found Mr. Teague. He took me to the pay phone. I called the Blue and Gray Bed and Breakfast and talked to Judy. I needed her to come over to the home right away. I would wait on the back porch with Uncle Bob. I invited Mr. Teague to join us too.

When she arrived, Mr. Teague and Judy helped me explain to Uncle Bob what we had found here. I needed his approval to make copies of the letters and journals.

"Go ahead," he insisted. "I want you to read them. But I would like to read them too."

"Absolutely. They belong to you," I assured him.

The frail old man stood by and watched as I made copies of every single letter and every single page on the copy machine in the office. That way Uncle Bob could keep the original journals and letters he had guarded all these years.

Mr. Teague counted the copies and presented me with a bill. I would have paid a lot more than ten cents per page for what I received.

Uncle Bob had stood watch over these valuable documents for years not ever knowing what was in his treasure box. It was as if he was waiting for me to help him unlock the secrets that it held inside.

What you and Uncle Bob are about to read is the rest of Catesby's story. And this time there's no need to ask, "So who's Catesby?"

Harold Quinn (left) and Craig Quinn

Part II

Chapter 1
Starting My Second Journal

December 11, 1863

Today I start another journal. I am older and wiser. I am a married, free black man. I am a real blacksmith. Mother would be quite proud of me today. I am proud of who I have become. I could not have predicted where I would be today or what is in store for me tomorrow. I have led an interesting life so far.

Being a free black man has been challenging. I gave the use of my leg to get here, but it was worth the pain.

My mother's valuable lessons of life have helped make me the man I am, just as Billy's important teachings have helped me develop into what Mr. Quinn calls "the best blacksmith in the Commonwealth of Pennsylvania."

Marcia and I are happy and prosperous. Life here in Cashtown, Pennsylvania is good.

Marcia has left the Cashtown Hotel and is now working right here at the Willow Grove Hotel for Mrs. Quinn. That saves me from having to take her into Cashtown each morning. The Willow Grove Hotel continues to be the place where families dine and travelers find a quiet place to stay over.

The blacksmith shop has enough work for two blacksmiths. Mr. Quinn has posted a handbill that we were looking to hire an apprentice. I looked forward to passing what Billy taught me on to someone else.

Three white lads applied for the position. Mr. Quinn and I showed each one around and talked to them about their experience and dreams. After a half day with them, Mr. Quinn and I talked about all three boys so we could decide which one to hire.

"The decision is yours, Catesby," Mr. Quinn insisted. "You need to be comfortable with who you hire. But I will help you make the decision. What are your thoughts on the three?"

"Brian is my first choice. He is married, has two small children and lives just east of here near Caledonia. He is a big muscular man with a strong handshake and hardened hands. Brian has helped at one of the furnaces in the area. He has some idea of the workings of a shop and the energy it requires. He had a colored friend at the furnace he said was as good a friend as any man could have."

"Neither of the two others, Steve and Ralph, is as good as Brian."

Ralph, I thought, had some discomfort around me, perhaps because I was colored or because of my limp. He didn't say, either way, but I could sense it. His hands were soft, like a girl's. I was not sure he had done any hard work. Seemed like if he worked here he would want to be the boss, and that wasn't going to happen.

I told Mr. Quinn I didn't think Steve had any respect for me. He could not look me in the eye when he was talking to me. I thought that meant we would have problems. He acted like he didn't think I'd have much to teach him. That attitude wasn't going to work here in my shop.

Mr. Quinn agreed on my selection. He said Brian had been his first choice too. He told me to send a message to Brian and let him start work tomorrow morning. John, who helped Eileen in the kitchen, rode over to Brian's house just after he finished with supper and let Brian know to come to work in the morning.

I lay awake excitedly all night long, wanting to remember my first day in the shop with Billy. I tried to figure out what he had taught me that first day so I would know what to teach Brian first. I decided I would start with the tools and go from there. I wanted Brian to be a real blacksmith someday, and to give him the same lessons Billy had given me.

December 12, 1863

Brian was already at the shop when I arrived in the morning, ready and eager to get started. At least a dozen times today he said "I just want to thank you, Catesby, for the chance to learn from you. You will not be disappointed that you chose me."

As Billy had done, I invited Brian to watch as I worked. I showed him each tool and explained what each was used for. He repeated the name back to me. And then when I asked him to get me a particular tool, he would know which one it was. I explained why I was using that tool and what I was trying to do with each one.

Brian was smart and willing to learn. And I wanted to tell him everything I had learned from Billy. I just wasn't very patient. I wanted to tell him and show him everything today.

I knew Billy had been smart showing me rather than telling me — so that's how I thought I could best teach Brian.

The tools were just one part. The fire was much more complicated. It was going to take a longer time to have Brian learn the fire, just as it had taken me a long time to learn it.

December 16, 1863

Winter in Cashtown was harder than the last winter in Sharpsburg. There was more snow and more cold here. I was grateful for our cozy house with a strong roof the Amish had built for us. I was plenty warm during the day as my fireplace in the shop was the warmest place in the whole area.

It snowed about a foot today. I watched the Quinn children throwing balls of snow in the morning and making a snowman in the afternoon. I gave them some of my old clothes to put on the snowman. They added a branch under the snowman's right arm that looked a lot like my crutch. If the snowman hadn't been all white, someone might have actually thought he was Catesby.

Brian and I took the wheels off the Quinn's wagon today and put on the sled runners to get them through the deep snow. It wasn't a task I had ever done before, but between the two of us, we learned as we went along.

December 20, 1863

I liked Brian more and more as the days went by. I was sure Mr. Quinn and I had made the right choice. Brian was quick at learning, and as smart as anyone I had known. He seemed real sure of himself and happy that he was learning from a good blacksmith.

Brian questioned everything I did, asking why I did something a particular way. He didn't need to ask the same question twice. He learned the first time around. He was strong as an ox, stronger in fact than I was on two good legs. He asked about the burns on my arms. I told him what Billy had told me. They were the trademarks that came with the job. I hadn't even remembered I had burns on my arms.

December 25, 1863

We celebrated Christmas at the hotel today with the Quinn family. Eileen prepared roasted turkey that I could smell all the way over to my little house. It tasted even better than it smelled.

I presented the Quinn children with a checker game. I gave Mrs. Quinn a long spoon like the one I had made for Marcia's mother. Mr. Quinn got a new rake. I gave Marcia a set of candle holders. I made all the gifts in my shop.

Marcia presented me a new hammer. Mr. Quinn had helped her order it from a New York forge. And she gave me another journal, to use when I filled this one.

The Quinns gave me a beautiful new sign with "Catesby's Blacksmith Shop" on it. I was proud. Mr. Quinn helped me hang the sign right out front, at the corner of Bingaman Road and the Chambersburg Turnpike.

The Quinns got candles for Marcia that fit nicely in the candle holders I had made.

December 26, 1863

Before long Brian and I were talking about other things besides blacksmithing. He asked about being a slave and, of course, wanted to have me answer everyone's favorite question, "What happened to your leg?" He told me about his life too.

Brian had been born in Carlisle. He had been working since he was old enough to have a job. He had worked at a furnace in nearby Mont Alto for a couple of years. He didn't like the owner, feeling that he was dishonest and cheating his customers. Brian said he couldn't stand to see that happen.

He had always enjoyed metal objects and wondered how they were made. He liked the feel of the metal on his skin. He had seen the handbill for the job at the blacksmith shop and had prayed that he would be chosen.

Brian was a natural with the shop. Once I showed him, he soaked the lessons in like a big sponge. He helped cut the time in half it took me to complete my projects by just giving me a hand. By the end of the day, he had me pretty much tuckered out.

Marcia liked Brian too. She pointed out how respectful he was of me as his boss and of the equipment that belonged to Mr. Quinn. She said something could be said about how good he was around her, Mrs. Quinn and the Quinn children.

"You are a good teacher, Catesby," Marcia told me one night. "You explain things very easily for someone to understand, making it easy for Brian to learn. I am very proud of you, my husband." Along with the praise came her embrace.

December 28, 1863

Marcia visited the shop every day. She watched me work. She was curious, always wanting to know what this tool did, or how that one worked. Or how I knew it was the right time to pull the metal out of the fire to shape it. Her favorite job was to run the bellows for me.

Marcia delivered the finished projects so the customers got the item before they were promised delivery. She said that was good business to give folks more than they expected.

As a wife, she certainly was more than I expected. She was loving and supportive. On days when she could, she packed me a lunch. She always walked slowly so even with my limp, I could keep up with her.

I finally told her about my bad leg and how the nasty Mr. Newberry crippled me for life. She had told me several times that out of respect for me, she would never ask what happened.

When she heard the story, she cried and cried. And then she spent the next several hours exploring every inch of my skin around the wound, caressing it and loving it. I think it was her way of saying that she loved that leg too. And she did.

"Thank you for telling me, Catesby," she said later that evening. "You are a great man for carrying that leg along behind you every single day without ever complaining. My grandmother never complained about her leg either." And then she added, "I know Miss Sheryl would have admired you, my husband."

If I hadn't already loved the wonderful Mrs. Marcia Catesby, that night would have gotten me to that point. I don't think I could have loved her any more than I did then.

Chapter 2
Meeting Dr. Martin Delany

January 3, 1864

Today Mr. Quinn said a doctor's wagon had a broken wheel near Gettysburg. I was the closest blacksmith. He asked me to go to see if I could help get the doctor on his way.

I left Brian to watch the shop. I assigned him several simple projects I thought he could do without my help.

I filled the wagon with the tools I thought I would need and some extra wheels. And then I drove the wagon toward Gettysburg. I traveled until I found a broken down wagon and a well-dressed black man sitting along the road next to it. I stopped, got down off my wagon, and went to meet him. I told him my name. "Are you the doctor?" I asked.

"Yes. I'm Dr. Martin Delany."

I was surprised that he was a colored doctor. I was not expecting that.

I said I was there to fix his wagon if I could. He told me he was on his way home to Wilberforce, Ohio. He said he would really appreciate it if I could help him.

Dr. Delany was perhaps the blackest man I had ever seen. He had a fine wagon. The wheel was broken beyond anything I could fix. I told him I would need to sell him a new wheel. He said that was all right with him.

I looked for some rocks nearby and carried them into the road. I stacked them up to use as a fulcrum, to lift the load off the wheel so I could remove it. I had a long pole in my wagon I used to get the leverage I needed. As I pushed down on the lever, I was able to lift up the axle.

The doctor talked to me as I worked.

He asked about my status as a colored man and I asked his. We had both been born slaves but gained our freedom. We had both learned to read and write. I told him how my mother had taught me.

The doctor explained, "I was not allowed in school, so I sat outside the open window and repeated all the lessons the white children were reciting out loud inside the building. When the authorities found out I was learning, they tried to arrest my mother because it was against the law for coloreds to learn to read and write in Virginia. Instead, my mother loaded us in a wagon with provisions as if we were going to a picnic. But there was no picnic. Instead, we escaped to Chambersburg, Pennsylvania. Much later I studied at Harvard College to become a doctor. It was one of the only schools that would teach the coloreds."

As we talked, I worked to pull the wheel. I had done it many times, but this one was a bit fancier than I was used to. It took me a little longer. When I finally got it off, I examined the wheel. I found the hole for the axle a bit larger than the wheels I brought.

I got a wheel off the back of my wagon and started working on the hole with my file. I needed to make the hole bigger to get it over the axle. I was sweating even though it was a cold winter day.

Several times I tried the wheel on the axle, but it still did not fit. I filed all the way around the hole again and again, until finally, with some grease, it slid onto the axle. I locked it in with the lynch pin, and used the lever to lower the wheel onto the ground. The wheel held. Even though the new wheel was a bit smaller than the one I had taken off, I told him I was sure it would hold to get him home.

Dr. Delany thanked me and paid me cash. And then he invited me to join him for supper. I was honored to break bread with him. He got aboard his wagon and told me to follow. We stopped at a nearby inn, tied up our horses and wagons out front, and went inside.

An older woman told us she was serving roast beef and potatoes. That sounded real good to us. We continued to talk as if we were friends who hadn't seen each other for years.

Dr. Delany was interesting to listen to. He told me he was always pleased to find coloreds who were educated.

He asked about my leg. I told him the story of Mr. Newberry. He said he had heard similar stories of cruelty. My situation didn't surprise him but he said it was going to have to stop.

No colored man I ever met was as smart as Dr. Delany. Seems like he was not only proud to be a free man, but he was proud to be a black man. I never got that impression from any other colored man I had ever talked to or listened to. I could have listened to this educated man all night long. He impressed me with his attitude toward himself and the coloreds in general.

"There is nothing you cannot do, Catesby. Nothing at all," Dr. Delany insisted. "You just have to believe in yourself."

I asked if he was talking about the mental bonds my mother had told me about.

"You are exactly right, Catesby. That is it. Very few coloreds understand the idea," he added. "Obviously your mother knew."

Our meals came. I dug in as I was mighty hungry. As we ate, we continued to talk.

He asked "How did you become a free blacksmith, Catesby?"

"A free black man, Billy, taught me everything I needed to learn for my trade. When I was a good blacksmith, I was sold into Maryland. After I was injured, I ran away to Mrs. Ritner who helped me with the Underground Railroad. And then I was sent to work with Mr. Quinn in Cashtown. Now I am able to have my own blacksmith shop, keep my money and even own my own house."

He nodded and seemed pleased. "Mrs. Ritner is one of our best operators of the Underground Railroad in Pennsylvania. You were lucky to have hooked up with her."

The man from Ohio said the future for coloreds after the war was very bright. He told me since President Lincoln's proclamation freeing the slaves, many coloreds were joining the Union army to help win the war.

I told him how happy I was about the president's freeing us. I wondered out loud if the president would let me be in his army to help out as a blacksmith, even with my bad leg.

Dr. Delany said the army certainly needed good blacksmiths to keep the horses and wagons moving. And he didn't think my bad leg and hobbling would keep me out of the army. In fact, he said, he was recruiting colored troops. He could help me get enlisted. It would mean that I would get paid the same as being a soldier.

"Dr. Delany," I asked. "Could I have some time to think about this? I need to talk to Mr. Quinn and my wife."

"Certainly, Catesby," the doctor assured me. "In fact, I'm in this area a couple more days to finish up. And then I am going back to Ohio. I have to pass through Cashtown on my way home. May I stop by the hotel sometime on Friday to meet and talk to you again?"

"Yes, sir," I offered with excitement. "That would give me time to talk to Marcia and Mr. Quinn first. Can you come around noon?"

We shook hands and agreed to meet at my blacksmith shop on Friday. I told him we would serve him a meal at the hotel before he left for home.

I climbed onto my wagon and made my way back to Cashtown. I thought about what might be possible, but was not sure whether Mr. Quinn and Marcia would be as happy about me joining the Union's colored troops.

When I got home, I boarded the horse and wearily limped to the house. Marcia, as always, was waiting with a loving embrace. I couldn't wait to tell her about Dr. Delany, although I decided to talk about the colored troops later.

Marcia was interested in hearing about Dr. Delany and his ideas. I talked with her for a long time, sharing my admiration of the man. I told her how I fixed his wagon and dined with him. Marcia wanted to know how a black man could become a doctor, where he had studied and where he lived.

I slowly turned our discussion to his recruiting activities of colored troops. I told her how important both Dr. Delany and I thought colored troops were to winning the war. And how many colored men were enlisting to pay the president back for freeing them from slavery.

Marcia was not as excited hearing about the colored troops as she had been about Dr. Delany himself. "Do you think President Lincoln would want a man with a bad leg as a colored soldier?"

"Absolutely not," I responded with no hesitation at all. "But he may need a few good blacksmiths. Even one who has a limp."

Marcia looked me right in the eye. She was real good at seeing right into my soul. A tear ran down her cheek. "I hadn't thought of that, Catesby. But you are probably right."

January 4, 1864

Today I met with Mr. Quinn and told him of Dr. Delany. I told him I was considering the idea of becoming a blacksmith in the colored troops. He was very supportive.

"You know, Catesby," Mr. Quinn said, "I will support whatever you do. I do not think the war will go on much longer. Brian can tend the shop. I can hire a striker to assist him. In the last month, he has learned much from you. I can certainly take my wagons up the road for repair if he is unable to fix them. That's what I did before you came here." Mr. Quinn added that he would keep an eye on Marcia if I left to go into the army.

January 8, 1864

Doctor Delany arrived just about noon. We greeted like old friends. We walked toward the hotel. We met Marcia and Mr. Quinn in the dining room.

Mr. Quinn shook Dr. Delany's hand. Marcia bowed slightly. I could tell they liked him already. Lunch was served. As we ate, Marcia asked him about being a doctor.

"I attended Harvard College and worked with leeches, something I studied early in my career," he explained to her. "I am certain leeching is important because it cleanses the blood."

When the talk finally came around to the colored troops, Doctor Delany was speaking generally about all troops. "The Union army is winning. The colored troops will help win the war. I think as many as 200,000 coloreds will enlist," he said.

He talked of the good points and bad points for someone who enlisted. "Soldiers are well paid. They get a uniform, a rifle and bayonet, a blanket, and other supplies. Soldiers are ordered to travel often, sometimes in the heat of summer and the cold of winter. The battles are indescribable with as many men dying from wounds and disease as from being killed in action."

I mentioned that I had seen first-hand what happened at Antietam Creek. I knew the dreadful truth about the battles themselves.

Marcia asked what role a blacksmith would have in the Union army. Dr. Delany explained, "The blacksmith stays off the field of battle during the fighting and follows the soldiers. Most of his work would be putting the wagons back together after the battle and keeping the wagons and horses ready."

Then Marcia surprised me and asked, "Would you allow Catesby to enlist, even with his bad leg?"

"Absolutely, Mrs. Catesby," Dr. Delany answered. "I think your husband would be a fine addition to the colored troops, bad leg and all. I would be proud to enlist him."

"As a recruiter for colored troops," he said, "I will not pressure Catesby to join. It is totally up to him. I can sign him up and take care of his enlistment. Or I can travel back to Ohio without his enlistment. There will be no hard feelings."

Dr. Delany agreed to go outside and let us discuss it further. When he left, Mr. Quinn stood up and shook my hand. "You know where I stand, my friend," he told me. "I will leave so you and Marcia can talk."

We were quiet for a few minutes, when Marcia started talking without waiting for me. "Catesby, you are my man," Marcia offered. "I will be with you whether you are here or not. I love you with everything I have. Go, my husband. Go help President Lincoln win this war. And then hurry home to me. I will wait as long as it takes. Just stay away from those battles. You're hobbling enough." With that she squeezed me tight, like she didn't want me to go.

When she let go of the embrace, I went out to talk to Dr. Delany. We came back into the hotel. He set the enlistment papers out on the table and explained them to me. I grabbed his pencil and filled them out. I wrote my name, Catesby, my place of birth, Beall Air, Charlestown, Virginia and signed the paper. I left the birthday and age blank, explaining to the doctor that I did not know when I was born.

He looked at the paper and asked, "Catesby. Were you one of Colonel Lewis Washington's slaves?"

I was stunned. "Yes, sir. How did you know that?"

"I know Beall Air," Dr. Delany laughed. "I grew up just a few miles down the road in Charlestown. We were practically neighbors."

We talked for a few minutes about Colonel Washington, who he had visited several times as a youngan.

"Is it true old John Brown took Colonel Washington prisoner at the raid on Harpers Ferry?" Dr. Delany asked.

"Yes, sir," I admitted. "And he captured me too. Colonel Washington and all his slaves were held prisoner until the soldiers came to free us."

"Well, I'll be," Dr. Delany added. "I'll bet you didn't know that I met John Brown in Canada when I was living there. I helped him run his convention in May of 1858. I was surprised he caused so much commotion in Harpers Ferry, though I know he was determined to free the slaves. He told me of those plans but didn't mention where he was going."

He asked if I knew of John Avis, the jailor in Charlestown. I told him I did not know of him.

Dr. Delany said John Avis and he had been best friends during their childhood, before Delany's family fled when he was around ten years old. He and Avis, one a colored man and the other a white man, had exchanged letters frequently over the years.

"Avis took good care of John Brown while he was in jail in Charlestown," Dr. Delany explained. "I suspect that may have had something to do with the fact that Avis knew I was a friend of old John Brown."

Dr. Delany swore me into the army that night before he left. He gave me directions as to how to find the Fifty-Fourth Massachusetts Volunteers, a letter introducing me, and another recommending me as a blacksmith. He wished me well. And then he told me to stay out of the action and come back safely. He said he was proud that he could be the one who enlisted me.

January 9, 1864

Next morning early, Marcia fixed me a big breakfast, and gave me some extra provisions for my trip while I hitched up Billy and prepared the wagon.

I told Brian I would be leaving for a while and that Mr. Quinn would help him run the blacksmith shop until I returned. I told him Mr. Quinn would hire a striker for him if they thought he needed the extra help. Brian said he wasn't ready to run the shop by himself. "I need more training."

I told him he was right. But I also told him he could learn by doing. That would help him get through.

I only took my journal, a few pencils, my enlistment papers, a little bit of money and my letter of introduction from Dr. Delany in my duffel.

And then Marcia handed me a small parcel. "Don't lose this. Keep it close to your heart," she insisted.

I opened it slowly, unwrapping the paper carefully that surrounded the present. Inside was a photograph of Marcia.

My eyes filled with tears as I thanked her for the precious gift.

"Oh, come on, Catesby," Marcia laughed. "You didn't think I was going to let you forget what I looked like while you were gone, did you? Mrs. Quinn and I both got those little photographs taken in Gettysburg. I was going to give it to you at a special time. I think this is a special time. Hurry back, Catesby. I will be waiting for the next dance."

I gave Marcia a huge embrace and walked away, not knowing when or if I would return. It was a tough time for me, even though I was certain I was doing what I was supposed to do. It was time for me to help President Lincoln.

Mr. and Mrs. Quinn and their two children stood on the porch and waved as I went past. "God speed," Mr. Quinn shouted.

The roads were full of ruts and rocks. Travel was slow and difficult. But I was committed, so I pushed forward.

I chomped slowly on the beef jerky and apple Marcia had put in my duffel. I was not sure how long they were going to have to last me.

Marcia Catesby

Dr. Martin R. Delany

Chapter 3
Joining the Fifth-Fourth Massachusetts Volunteers

January 13, 1864

Dr. Delany said the Fifty-Fourth Massachusetts Volunteers in Boston were accepting colored enlistments from all over the area. He had signed up recruits from Ohio, Pennsylvania and the District of Columbia on his recent trips. He said I would have to travel to New York to join them as they had left Boston in May and were now in the South. A ship at the New York harbor would take me and the other recruits to the army's camp.

The trip took four days of hard travel. I was quite tired when I arrived in New York City. I took my horse and wagon to the livery and sold them for twenty dollars. I hated to sell Billy and my wagon. They were the only wagon and horse I had ever owned.

I stopped at the Fifty-Fourth Massachusetts Volunteers' office on the docks in New York and was assigned the steamship *Maple Leaf*. The ship was sailing the next morning.

I was not told where we were going. I only knew that we were going to find my unit in the South.

The man at the office said the Fifty-Fourth Massachusetts Volunteers had already seen action in July at James Island and Fort Wagner in South Carolina. They had lost many men, but had also accounted for themselves quite ably. Whereas coloreds weren't thought to be good and trusted fighters, now they were called patriotic and brave soldiers. He said they would be accepted in the major battles. And the enlistment numbers were growing almost every day.

I boarded at a tavern, mostly listening to the tales of the war being told by bar flies who had no more seen action in the war than I had. The more they drank, the more horrible their stories became.

Since I had actually been on a fields of battle at Antietam Creek and Gettysburg, their descriptions were inaccurate as to what one might actually have seen on the battle grounds. I let them have their fun without comment. While waiting, I wrote to Marcia.

New York City
January 13, 1864

Dearest Marcia

I arrived in New York to take the steamship *Maple Leaf* south to catch up with my regiment. I don't know where I am going, but was told we would only be traveling a couple of days.

My trip to New York was difficult, as the recent rains have made a mess of the roads. But I am anxious to join the Fifty-Fourth Massachusetts Volunteers and to help President Lincoln win this war.

I have very mixed thoughts about being here. I know on the one hand that I am doing my honorable duty. But I am already missing your smile and tender touches.

Your photograph soothes my lonesome heart. I already miss the feeling of your hands passing gently through my hair. I miss hearing your sweet voice in my ear. I miss your laughter and your tears. I miss your toes entwined in mine. I miss your smell after you take your bath.

We are being told the war won't last much longer. I expect to be home within a few months. Soon we will have those rebel lads on the run.

I promise I will take great care and come home when the war is over. You can count on that.

Your loving husband,
Catesby

January 14, 1864

Seventeen colored men boarded the steamship *Maple Leaf* heading for the Fifty-Fourth Massachusetts Volunteers' camp.

The sailing was pretty rough. We were hit by a bad storm. The steamship rolled back and forth from side to side. I hung on so I would not fall into the angry sea and die even before reaching the Fifty-Fourth Massachusetts Volunteers.

I heaved time and time again over the side of the rail. I have never been so sick and frightened in my entire life. This was worse than being shot at while a prisoner at Harpers Ferry or driving the wagons for the photographers through the dead and wounded at Antietam Creek. I never thought the storm would let up. When it did, they took roll call and found everyone was accounted for. We were thankful that the sea was finally calm again.

January 19, 1864

Today we sailed into Jacksonville harbor in Florida. When we finally landed, we couldn't get off the ship fast enough. Several kissed the ground. I swore I would never leave land again. I had barely survived the storm. We were given directions to the Union camp. Our small group caught up with the Fifty-fourth Massachusetts Volunteers just outside of town.

As new recruits we were cheered as we entered camp. The soldiers had been told we were on our way. We were shown to the Union command on a hill overlooking the tent city. An officer led us to the main tent where we were asked to produce our enlistment papers. Colonel Edward N. Hallowell, the white officer who was the commanding officer, issued a general welcome.

"We appreciate your enlistment in the Fifty-Fourth Massachusetts Volunteers," he announced. "In just a minute you will be assigned to your unit. In the meantime, I want you to think about this. The Fifty-Fourth Massachusetts Volunteers are a proud and brave fighting force of colored soldiers from twenty-four different states. I would pit my men against any in the Confederate Army. Remember, as you become a member of this unit, it is up to you to maintain that high level of courage and responsibility."

He called out the men's names and assigned each to a company. And then he saluted and dismissed us.

I waited until the others had left as my name had not been called. I limped up to his table. He looked up at me with some question in his mind and said, "I appreciate your enthusiasm in enlisting son, but with that bad leg, I cannot use you as a soldier."

"I know that, sir," I answered quickly. "I am not here to be a fighting soldier. My name is Catesby. Dr. Delany said you needed blacksmiths. I am one of the best blacksmiths in Pennsylvania." With that I handed him Dr. Delany's letter of recommendation.

He read the letter quickly, and then looked up. "That's different, son," he responded. "Of course, we can use a good blacksmith to keep this army rolling. In fact, this regiment has been without a blacksmith for some time. Please report to Captain Bill Jordan with the supply wagon train. The wagons are located at the south end of the camp."

I saluted and went outside. I asked a sentry to tell me where I could find the supply wagons. He pointed to the right. I limped off in that direction. A soldier helped me find Captain Jordan.

Captain Jordan had that same look in his eye as I approached him, hobbling along as fast as I could go. He wondered of what use a crippled soldier could be. I introduced myself and told him of my mission with his wagon train.

The captain was excited when he found out. Soldiers had been assigned to the blacksmith wagon, but none were blacksmiths, the captain admitted.

"Catesby, sir," he shouted. "You are a God send."

The first night in camp, the captain walked around with me. I inspected the army wagons. Many were patched together just so they could move out with the rest. He showed me the blacksmith wagon, which was poorly equipped. I wished I could have brought my own tools from my shop in Cashtown.

The wagons needed lots of attention right away. Captain Jordan said he would try to fetch me some help.

January 20, 1863

Repairing all the wagons seemed like an impossible task. But as Billy had taught me, I had to put them in order and do just one at a time. I made a note, numbering each wagon, and listing just what I needed to do to get it up and running.

It was going to take time and some very hard work. Even with my fire and all my tools back at the shop, the job would take a long time. I could only go one day at a time and I had to start today. I started with the worst one first. That wagon was all busted up. I decided it was beyond repair. Instead, I took it all apart so I could use the parts that were still good on another wagon. That took all day.

January 21, 1863

The second wagon was in bad shape too. But now at least I had some good pieces of the first wagon I could fit onto the second one. The day passed quickly. I actually finished the second wagon and started on the third one.

January 22, 1864

In general, the men of the Fifty-Fourth Massachusetts Volunteers were in good spirits and were proud of their actions.

There was, however, plenty of grumbling about the pay differences between the white soldiers and the coloreds. The white soldiers got $13 per month plus $3 for clothing allowance. The colored soldiers got only $10, with $3 subtracted from that pay to cover the costs of the uniforms. I was told colored troops were being paid as laborers not soldiers.

It didn't make any sense to our men that the colored soldiers were paid less. They were fighting the same enemy and risking their lives as much as the whites.

All the colored men had families back home too. I think if a representative of the war office in Washington City had come around, the troops here would have tarred and feathered him for the total unfairness of the pay rates.

Two young lads had arrived in camp and were sent to me, assigned as aides. They were Bill and Tom. They were both around 13 or 14 years old, and too young to enlist. They tried lying at the recruiting office following their relatives into camp.

After several weeks in camp the two lads had been annoying most of the men, trying to find a place to land so they would not be sent home.

The officers of the Fifty-Fourth Massachusetts Volunteers got tired of chasing the two youngsters out of camp, only to have them come back. When Bill and Tom were caught this last time, they were assigned to me as their punishment. I laughed, wondering who they were actually punishing, Tom and Bill or Catesby.

Captain Jordan told me he hoped I would work them so hard they would want to run back home. But that didn't happen. After a while, I found their help quite valuable. And Bill and Tom actually liked working for me. The three of us could tackle a job much easier than I could by myself.

Jacksonville, Florida
January 25, 1864

My dearest Marcia

I found the Fifty-Fourth Massachusetts Volunteers in Jacksonville, Florida. They were quite happy to have a blacksmith.

The trip aboard the steamship was frightful. We ran into a terrible storm. I was seasick the entire trip. Remind me to remain on land forevermore.

We will be at camp for a few more weeks, and then we will move out to points unknown. I will try to keep you informed with my letters.

I miss you most when the work of the day is done and I lie restless in the tent. I feel empty as a dry coffee cup without you, my dear.

I am torn by my love for you and my desire to help President Lincoln because he freed the slaves. I hope I have made the right decision.

Your loving husband,
Catesby

January 30, 1864

Bill and Tom were having the time of their lives. Even though they could not be real soldiers, they had the chance to be in the camp every night just like the real Union army. They got to eat and sleep with the soldiers, and to "play" soldier when the men let them carry their rifles around the camp. They were sometimes allowed to drill with the soldiers so that when they were old enough, they would already know how to do that.

They were cousins, from Dixon in northern Illinois. Their one uncle, Jerry, was a soldier in the regiment and their other uncle, Jim, was the regimental chaplain.

Bill was tall with long shaggy black hair. He had an army cap, but his hair hung out all around the bottom.

He was quiet. It wasn't because he didn't have anything good to say. He only talked when spoken to. If you asked, he answered. His answers were quick and to the point. He wasted no words on anyone.

Bill looked and acted older than Tom. He even had some gray hair. He was strong and muscular, so working around the fire and lifting heavy objects didn't bother him any. He had the start of a mustache. He could read a bit, explaining he knew just enough to get by. The lad's only bad points were that he was curious and often was missing if there was something more interesting to do around the camp.

Tom was short and skinny as a rail. It looked like a good strong wind would knock him down. He was always happy, humming or tapping his fingers. He laughed at just about anything anyone said. And he made faces whenever I talked to him. Tom was real likable and a joy to be around. He could brighten the dullest day.

Tom acted less mature than his cousin. He was always eating something, but it didn't show on him. There was not an ounce of fat on him anywhere. He had skinny arms, skinny legs, skinny hands, and skinny ankles. His clothes were baggy, because the army had nothing that small for him to wear.

He wore small wire framed glasses that made him look real smart, like perhaps a professor. He did know how to read and write. He had a good sense about him that he likely was born with. Tom liked working with me and watching me work. He said someday he was going to be a blacksmith too, just like Catesby. I don't think he was strong enough to be a real blacksmith.

Tom loved to work the bellows and keep my fire going strong throughout the day and into the night. He was real good at fetching too. But he was also a practical joker. He would go fetch my tools, coming back with a hammer when I asked for pliers. He did that knowing full well he fetched the wrong tool. And then he'd laugh and laugh as if I had told him some grand joke. He liked to put the tools back in the wrong place too, so when I couldn't find them, he would get them for me. I think that made him feel useful.

Bill was always out watching the soldiers drill. He wanted real badly to be one of them, not one of us. When they let him, he got to carry a rifle and march in step behind them. Whenever it came time to find Bill, Tom knew to look where the men were drilling.

182

Here I had skinny Tom always around, yet not strong enough to lift the bigger hammers, and muscular Bill, who could lift the hammer like it was a feather, but often missing when I needed him.

Of course, neither lad knew anything about blacksmithing. I reminded myself that on my first day at Beall Air, I didn't know anything about blacksmithing either. Tom and Bill would just have to be quick learners because this army was close to moving out. We had much work to do to get the wagons repaired.

February 2, 1864

The wagons had broken springs, busted wheels, and fractured axles. Not having much equipment, we had to piece things together as best we could. Tom and Bill learned quickly how to build me a strong fire from the charcoal we had on the blacksmith wagon. Just having that tended by one of them all the time assured me that my fire would not go out.

The captain checked in on us and found that I was really a hard worker. What he seemed to like best was that I was keeping those two youngans out of trouble. It was two less things he had to worry about.

I proudly wore the blue uniform of a Union private. Bill and Tom had grabbed parts of uniforms off dead Union men, and if you weren't looking real close, they actually looked like soldiers too. They were both looking to find a real small dead Union soldier someday so that Tom could find a better fitting uniform.

February 7, 1864

The blacksmith wagon was low on equipment. We had a bellows, an anvil, a large supply of charcoal for the fire, several hammers of different sizes, pinchers, pliers, a plane, nails, a chisel, forceps, a wood block and lots of horse shoes. We had scrap wood and metal in boxes on the wagon. We had a few extra wagon wheels, hitches and hinges.

Men waited in line with their wagons and horses. We worked all through many long nights, finally making some good progress. We were least active during the day, and most busy late into the night and early each morning. We would not have been much help to the regiment if the horses and wagons were not fit to move out. Often we got no sleep at all there was so much work. I shoed horses, fixed wagon wheels, and even repaired rifles and muskets.

Sometime when the work load was lessened, our business changed to helping the soldiers fix personal items such as a locket holding a photograph of a loved one.

We even repaired a pipe, a candle holder, a tin cup, a canteen, and a broken belt buckle. We worked on flag poles, buckets, forks, a crucifix, holsters, bugles, drums, chains, oil lamps, saddles, harnesses, and spatulas.

We tried to patch up anything brought to our wagon. Amongst our biggest challenges was repairing a harmonica, a watch, and a pair of binoculars.

Jacksonville, Florida
February 7, 1864

Marcia, my love

Each night Bill, Tom (the youngans assigned to me) and I wait for the wagons and men to return to camp to see what additional repairs we have to make before morning. As the men rest, weary from the day's activities, it is time for us to go to work.

When I fall into my pile of straw at the end of my work, my thoughts return to the sparkle in your eyes and your smile. It comforts me in my loneliness. You have become part of my insides — living and breathing with me — not separate in any way.

As I breathe, you breathe. I think of your embraces and caresses. I do not know when I will be enjoying them again. I wonder when your wonderful tender lips will be brought close to mine. Thoughts of your wonderful healing hands bring a smile to my face. I long for the warmth of your skin against mine.

I am keeping back out of the war as promised.

Be patient. I will return. Maybe the next battle will turn the tide. Believe that you will not have to wait long to see me.

Your loving husband,
Catesby

February 14, 1864

Our Union wagons were always falling apart. Looked to me like whoever the army purchased wagons from gave them the worst of the lot.

Between the ruts in the road and the weight on the wagons, the wheels and axles got battered around all day long.

We were also assigned to taking care of all the horses of the Fortieth Massachusetts Mounted Infantry and the Independent Massachusetts Cavalry Battery. That certainly kept us busy. Bridles were torn and worn, and had to be repaired. The horse's shoes needed work. But for the most part, the horses were in better shape than the wagons.

Our blacksmith wagon was enclosed with sides and had a roof, much like the photography wagon I had driven at Antietam Creek. Many nights when the rain pelted down upon the soldiers, Tom, Bill and I stayed dry in the wagon.

Old Blue, our work horse, pulled the wagon without complaint. She was steady and as reliable as most of the men in our unit.

Tom hid my crutch today and I had to hobble around without it. He was laughing the whole time and hobbling too, just to try to get under my skin. It worked. I was angry as a hornet at him, though I knew it was just his nature to play.

February 15, 1864

Our regiment's men were itching for battle. Our soldiers did much more marching and drilling than fighting. I heard the officers say the colored troops were being held in reserve, and not allowed to go onto the field. Our men were real tired of the Union's white officers not trusting to put them into the fight.

Jacksonville, Florida
February 15, 1864

My darling Marcia

Life in camp is not bad. I have much to eat, a bed of straw to sleep on, and plenty of work to keep me busy.

Bill and Tom are learning and have been very helpful. They work beside me at night. During the day we sleep while the soldiers are marching in formation and learning the drills.

Our army has trained and trained and are ready to go to battle. But for some reason the white officers are not very willing to put them into the fight. I am too busy to worry about that.

Tonight I miss your playful spirit and your beautiful sparkling black eyes. I miss talking to you — watching you form every word with your lips. And I miss hearing you say "I love you, Catesby."

The last thing I look at before I go to sleep is your photograph. I can almost taste your kisses. I miss having you lay close to me as I sleep.

As promised, I will stay back and out of the way, far behind any of the fighting.

Until the war is over, I remain,

Your loving husband,
Catesby

The three of us got real friendly with Wally, the cook, and the men who work the mess wagon. They stay back from the action too. The better friends we are with Wally, the more food we get on our plates.

It has taken us almost a month of hard work to fix the wagons we could fix. Those that are beyond hope of fixing, we stacked by the road, to get pieces from them for other wagons as needed. Tom, with his unusual sense of humor, calls it the "wagon cemetery."

February 17, 1864

We got word today we are moving out soon. My two boys are itching to watch a battle close up. Captain Jordan ordered us to stay back and out of the way. I am mighty happy to do what I am ordered to do, even though Tom and Bill are disappointed.

Being the army's blacksmith was hard work for me. Still, I was helping President Lincoln and that was important to me. I did not have to remind myself why I volunteered to be here.

A soldier's life was a little bit like being a slave. You are "owned" by the officers. They order us around. Men here think twice about not following orders. I think those of the Fifty-Fourth Massachusetts Volunteers who were former slaves will tell you being a soldier is much better than being a slave.

Jacksonville, Florida
February 18, 1864

Marcia dearest

I continue to work in the camp in Jacksonville. We are moving out tomorrow, but have not been told where we are going.

Even if our men go to battle, do not worry about me. We will stay a long ways back from the battle, at the end of the supply train. There is no danger back there.

Each night you come by and lay with me in my dreams. I hold you close and feel your warmth. I miss your kindness. I miss how you can cast yourself to me, reel me in, and bring me up when I am feeling down and discouraged. I miss the smell of your perfumes and the clean smell of your clothes.

My heart feels bare as an empty old army canteen. My shoulders and neck miss your wonderful hands touching them.

I look forward to the day when the war is over and I can hold you in my old and tired arms again.

I will write more next time.

Your loving husband,
Catesby

Chapter 4
Regiment Moves Out

February 19, 1864

Today we were ordered to march to Barber's Station.

Two other colored units marched with us. They are the Eighth U. S. Colored Troops, led by Colonel Fribley, part of the Haley's brigade, and the Thirty-Fifth U. S. Colored Troops commanded by Lt. Colonel William Reed, part of the Montgomery Brigade.

Unlike the Fifty-Fourth Massachusetts Volunteers, the Thirty-Fifth U.S. Colored troops have not seen any action. One of their men talked to me at length one evening, telling me most of their men had been slaves from the Virginia and the North Carolina area. About twenty-five percent of the Fifty-Fourth Massachusetts Volunteers' men had been slaves. Over half know how to read and write.

The commanding officer over all our troops, around 6,000 men, is Brigadier General Truman Seymour. About 600 of those are from the Fifty-Fourth Massachusetts Volunteers.

February 20, 1864

We left from Barber's Station at half past eight this morning and marched toward Lake City. Our troops now include three brigades of infantry, the Independent Massachusetts Cavalry Battery, the Fortieth Massachusetts Mounted Infantry and the artillery.

Our men marched in three columns along the railroad tracks, led by the cavalry. We reached Sanderson by noon and stopped to eat. An angry southern woman told several of our officers, "You will come back faster than you go." We laughed at her comments.

I heard gunfire shortly after the men resumed the march. Reports came back to us that the Union cavalry was chasing the rebel cavalry toward the railroad station at Olustee, Florida.

Not much later, the soldiers began marching forward in double time. Our men dropped their bedrolls and knapsacks, littering the roads, as they moved quickly into battle. Bill, Tom and I followed the lead of the other supply wagons by pulling off the road and stopping. We gathered up as much of the equipment we could carry in the wagon. Now all we could do was to wait here until further orders.

We listened. There was nothing to see. We were too far to the rear. When the cannons started booming, the air filled with smoke.

Later in the day, a steady stream of our soldiers, battered, bruised and wounded, retreated past our position. The supply wagons were ordered to pull back to the rear.

That night we got back to Barber's Station after midnight. The troops were exhausted, having marched many miles today in addition to fighting a tough battle.

February 21, 1864

Today we returned to camp at Jacksonville.

Captain James Taylor of the Fifty-Fourth Massachusetts Volunteers talked about yesterday's battle to those near our supply wagons.

"The rebels chose their ground well. We chased them right into a position where they had already built trenches and fortifications. We found ourselves between two swamps and attacking amongst pine trees with almost no cover at all," Taylor added.

"They routed us, killing a whole slew of our men before the retreat was sounded. But I will tell you this. The colored troops went in grandly. We fought like devils," he said proudly.

"Besides the dead," the captain said, "we had to abandon many of our cannons."

Reports going around camp said our casualties included 203 killed, 1,152 wounded and 506 missing in action.

Estimates were that the Fifty-Fourth Massachusetts Volunteers had 13 killed, 63 wounded and 8 missing in action. We had lost almost thirty percent of our total army.

February 22, 1864

The hospital wagon was busy today, because of all the wounded soldiers. The nights at camp are no longer silent. Now we hear the screams of those who are in pain. After the battle, when they dug graves to bury the soldiers, they dug an additional grave to bury the extra arms and legs that had been cut off.

Jacksonville, Florida
February 23, 1864

My dearest Marcia

Our men fought in the battle of Olustee (also called the battle of Ocean Pond), Florida. I am disappointed we didn't win this battle. Our men fought bravely, but many were injured or killed. Each victory brings us closer to ending this dreadful war and letting me come home. There was no victory here today.

With everything I have seen about war, I am not only sure that war is hell, but that it never goes away. I cannot shut out the sounds of war even after the battle. The screaming of the wounded fills the night. I shudder when I hear the awful sounds of the saws against bone as doctors cut off arms and legs.

Tom, Bill and I are busy repairing all the wagons that were battered by the long trip and broken from the fighting. We are tired. And as promised, we kept a safe distance back and were never in any danger.

Your embrace tonight would be very comforting. I look at your photograph instead.

I hope I will see you soon.

Your loving husband,
Catesby

March 10, 1864

For several weeks, the troops rested up. The doctors patched up the men who had been wounded. We fixed up many broken wagons and tried to get them ready to move out when needed.

We stayed in camp. The officers said our orders are to stay put for now, but to disrupt the Confederate supply lines when possible.

April 25, 1864

Today we were ordered to follow a wagon train to fetch supplies in the Gainesville area. The supplies are important. The captain sent us to make sure all wagons would make it back.

A wagon broke down along the road. We stopped along side to fix it. The rest of the wagon train went on without us. The captain left a guard of twenty soldiers to protect us as we worked. Bill, Tom and I worked hard for about an hour, replacing a broken wheel. And then we moved out to try to catch up with the others.

Going up over a small hill, we were suddenly under attack. I pulled the wagon off the road as our soldiers fought the enemy. Bill, Tom and I huddled down in the wagon trying to stay out of danger. I was frightened, but not nearly as frightened as my two young friends, who were suddenly finding out that war is hell.

The fighting continued for only a few minutes. When the smoke cleared, our soldiers threw down their guns. They surrendered to a much larger Confederate force. Rebel soldiers rounded us up and took our wagon. They marched us several miles to where we were joined by a large number of other Union prisoners at a railroad depot.

We had to count off. There were eighty-seven men and two boys now in our group. We were shoved into a box car. When the door slammed shut behind us, we were in the dark. I had no idea where we were or where they were taking us.

The two youngans were frightened and huddled close to me. I heard some crying, but in the darkness, I was not sure if it were my boys or someone else.

In the train car we were packed together like pickles in a barrel. Counting the three of us, thirteen were from my regiment. There were others, all Union, of course, but from other units. The box car was hot. There was not much air. The smell was awful.

We traveled on the train for a couple of days. I slept a few minutes here and there. Tom and Bill huddled closer as the time passed. Several soldiers talked loudly, telling all around them what they were going to do to the rebels who captured us as soon as the train car door opened. Problem was, the rebel soldiers were armed, and we were not. Mostly it was quiet. I swear I could smell fear in the air.

The train finally stopped. I wondered where we were. The car door was jerked open. I was blinded by the sun for a few seconds. It was nice to see the sun. The stench in the train car had choked my air passages, blocking my breathing with a strangle hold. I drank in the fresh air.

We were lined up by twos and ordered to march toward the engine of the train. Bill paired up with me while Tom found a mate and stepped along just a few feet behind us. We didn't march quickly so even with my crutch and my limp, I was able to keep up.

There were long rows of Union soldiers forming up in lines as they jumped down from the train cars ahead of us. There must have been five or six hundred altogether. I spotted a sign at the depot, "Anderson Station." I still did not know where we were.

We were marching along a heavily forested area. There were armed rebels all along the line. Their soldiers looked real young to me, with their gray uniforms all tattered and torn. They were a scraggly looking crew, hardly the Confederate army's finest men.

It was certainly a pleasant place on the eyes. If the Confederate soldiers had not been there, I might have thought it was just another Union march to the next encampment. It was a grand day. Being outside was much better than being all cooped up in that train car.

After about ten minutes, the men in front of me started to talk excitedly about something. The rebels tried to quiet them down. There was something up ahead that was creating the fuss. I could not see what they were talking about.

Bill poked me in the arm and pointed up ahead. There was a huge wooden fortress, with a log fence about twenty feet high. Along the fence were dozens of platforms with armed rebel guards on each one. The men passed the word down the line. This was Anderson, Georgia.

The lines of men got quieter the closer we got to the fortress. I think we were all surprised at the large size of the fort. And the men were finally realizing that we were headed into a large prison. Suddenly the fear of the unknown became the fear of the known. And as comforting as it was to know where we were going, the fortress was still an enemy camp.

We were stopped at the gate. The soldier in charge announced that we would be let inside twenty or thirty at a time. Since we were toward the back of the line, we just had to wait.

I listened to see if I could hear anything. It was quiet enough to hear birds chirping in the trees, but the birds were strangely silent. The place looked tolerable from here. It could not be that bad. Besides, we had always been told if we were captured it would not be long before there would be a prisoner exchange. We could get right back to our unit.

When it was our turn to enter, we were taken in through a large gate, only to be confronted by another fortress gate. I looked around but could not see anything.

The guard closed the big gate behind us. He walked around us. He opened the gate in the front. That opened into another chamber.

We were herded forward about twenty yards. The gate behind us closed again. The guard walked around us for a second time. He opened the inner gate.

Chapter 5
Welcome to Camp Sumter

I was not prepared at all for what I saw when the inner gate opened. In front of me were thousands of Union soldiers. Some looked fresh and healthy, but others were just skin and bones, with barely any clothes covering them at all. Their rib cages were exposed. The men looked sickly and pathetic. Many just looked like living skeletons. This prison had more men than I had ever seen in one place.

The worst of the men were pitiful, more like piles of bones than living, breathing men. They seemed alive on some level -- some more than others. None of our group wanted to enter into that mass of men. But we couldn't turn back either. The last gate had closed behind us. The men inside watched us enter. Some reached out as if to touch us or ask for our help.

The place was so large when I turned my head in any direction, all I could see were more prisoners. There were bodies lying in every available space and in every possible position. Some were covered with filthy rags and bandages. Most had no shoes or shirts. A great many were sunburned while others were covered from head to toe with sores.

If I didn't know any better I would have thought I had stepped directly into hell as my mother had often described it from readings of the Bible. I was alive, at least for now. I was not sure how many of the men I had just seen could be listed as truly being alive.

Bill and Tom latched on to me, frightened to death as to what they were seeing around them. All they wanted was for me to hang on to them and take care of them. At their age they were likely the youngest here, two boys among a mob of men.

When all of the new prisoners had entered the main enclosure, a rebel soldier told us roll would be called. He said we were to find our own place amongst those who were already here.

And then he announced in a cheerful, but very sarcastic voice, "Welcome to Camp Sumter also called Andersonville Prison. I hope your stay here is a pleasant one."

Roll was called. We counted off. We were part of a group of 456 new prisoners. That was a small number compared to those already inside the fence.

I looked around but did not see even one inch where I could find room for myself and two lads. I could not imagine where they were going to put 456 new men. We walked around, moving down long rows of men who just stared. No one said a word.

The prisoners were mostly white. There were a few coloreds sprinkled in here and there. Several of the black soldiers nodded to me as we passed.

No one on the ground moved. There was no space for any of us. I thought we might have to walk around for days to find a place to sit. I was not sure a white man would share his space with three colored prisoners even though we were all Union soldiers.

I looked around. This was the most pitiful place I had ever seen in my whole life. It reminded me of the scenes after the battle of Antietam Creek except that most of the men here were still alive.

We walked down what looked like a street, wide enough for a wagon to pass, with men lining both sides. We walked for what seemed like a couple of hours. Finally a young white man pushed his things aside and gestured for us to sit there with him. He stuck out his hand. I shook it, thanking him for allowing us to be in his space. I introduced myself, Tom and Bill. He said his name was Aaron Putnam.

Camp Sumter, Andersonville Prison
Anderson, Georgia
Library of Congress photo

Chapter 6
Introduction to Prison Life

We had enough space for about one and a half small men, but we had to make it work for the three of us. There was going to be no stretching out or getting comfortable. There was hardly enough room for my crutch. I said a silent prayer, thanking God for Aaron who allowed us to share his ground.

Aaron told us, "You look like my friend, Todd, a free black man on my father's farm. That was why I reached out to you. I am from the Twenty-First Ohio, Company C. I got captured at Chickamauga in September and was taken to Belle Island Prison near Richmond, Virginia. The prisoners there were moved here when Andersonville Prison opened earlier this month."

"I was one of the first to arrive. There was plenty of grass then, and lots of room to spread out on the ground. We even had clean water those first weeks. With each day, more and more Union prisoners are brought in. The prison has become over-crowded. The conditions get worse and worse each day."

We listened, not quite believing we were here, but wanting to know what to expect. Aaron continued. "Since my capture, I have seen thousands of Union soldiers brought in. There are around nine thousand here now. Here you are no longer in the Union army. Here you are all alone. It is each prisoner for himself. And many soldiers are not going to make it."

He pointed to another gate at the other end of the fort and said, "That's the south gate. It's the only way you can leave here. The cemetery is the next stop past that gate. The men who leave through that gate are cold and stiff."

I promised myself at that moment and I promised both Marcia and my mother in heaven, that Catesby was not going to leave by the south gate.

Aaron continued. "The water here is too dirty to drink. Men stand along the stream that runs through the fort and do their business right there. I have seen turds floating in the water. Find somewhere else to relieve yourself," Aaron warned, "because we need to keep the water in the stream clean."

"There is not much medicine. Food comes some days but not every day. Whatever you get to eat, you have to save and eat slowly, because you are never sure how long it is going to have to last you."

Aaron was sure there were already more men here than the camp had been built to hold. There was no place for anyone else, but new prisoners kept coming in the gate.

I had my journal and a short pencil in my duffel. I started to write about the prison. Tom and Bill had seen me do this so they were not surprised. Aaron laughed and said, "I hope you are not wasting your time writing a letter because there is no reliable mail delivery to or from this hole."

"No," I explained, "I am writing in my journal. It is something I do often."

Anderson, Georgia
April 1864

My dearest Marcia

I know you will never receive this letter but I am determined to keep writing to you as much as anything to help me believe I will see you again. There is no mail service at this stockade. I will continue to scribble these letters amongst my papers here to let you know when I return home, how much I have missed you.

Bill, Tom and I were captured in Florida. We were taken to Camp Sumter, officially called Andersonville Prison.

I would be lying, darling, if I told you everything was going well. That is not the case at all. Things are so bad, in fact, I cannot be certain of anyone's future including my own.

We have little food, not much medicine, and no clean water. The place is terribly overcrowded. Men are dying all around us.

I can only pray that you will feel in your bones that I am still alive. You must continue to believe I will return to your loving embrace. Please keep the faith, even though you do not receive letters from me. I am determined, until my dying breath, to keep my promise, and return.

I cling to your photograph for strength. I pray to God that I will be able to see you again.

Your loving husband,
Catesby

The ground where we sit is as hard as a rock. There is no getting settled in. Whenever one of us moves, the others have to move too. There are men right behind us and others right in front of us. Men huddle together as close as they can.

The smell of the place is like the privy smell behind the hotel, only it was more like hundreds of privies side by side. Aaron said the smell is from the human waste of thousands of men with no sanitary facilities at all. I looked around and saw no place for anyone to go. Aaron said there is no place for that.

I noticed along the wall there was plenty of open space. I asked Aaron about it. "The director of prisons has made 'no man's land' along the inside of the stockade walls. They call it *the deadline*. It takes up about ten yards of space we could use as spots for more prisoners," Aaron explained. "Cross *the deadline* and the rebels on the platforms will shoot you, no questions asked. In fact, we have heard that guards who shoot someone get a thirty day furlough. Some men get so desperate they go insane and end up wandering right out into *the deadline*. It is like they were daring the guards to shoot them and put them out of their misery."

"And," Aaron added, "the way things work around here, as soon as a prisoner dies, the other prisoners are already fighting over the space he left behind."

Tom was already sleeping when the darkness came to the prison. I tried to find a position where I could relax.

The first night I was more interested in watching what was going to happen during the night. I did not have to wait long.

I could hear the frogs and crickets chirping. They sounded happy probably because they were hopping around outside the big fence. Inside I heard screaming of sick and wounded soldiers crying out for help. Aaron said there was no help to give them.

Aaron told us men were prowling around those who were asleep, looking to steal something of value. I dared them to come my way. I had nothing to give up. I was also not willing to give in to some other soldier just because I was colored, or just because I was the new man in the camp. I was willing to fight for my space and my rights. My debt to old Mr. Newberry could certainly be taken out of the hide of some not too smart thief.

Aaron and I made a pack that first night to protect and defend each other, and the two youngans at all costs. In order to live through this, we must work together.

I made several promises to myself that first night too. One was that I was going to survive even if everyone around me did not. Two, I was not going to go looking for trouble. But if trouble came looking for me, I was going to defend myself with everything I had.

Aaron was wrong. We were an army — the four of us. We were a small army but we were a force that others would need to worry about.

Chapter 7
Learning the Routine

Day two found us walking to roll call in the late morning. The main gate where we had entered (called the north gate) opened. Several wagons were brought in. Aaron said anyone in the group misbehaving or failing to follow orders during the roll call could cause our whole group to be denied rations. That was how they kept the men under control.

Roll call meant every one of the prisoners had to stand in line. Aaron urged me to take my journal, pencil and my duffel, my three worldly possessions, with me. Since everyone else was at roll call too, the first ones done could also go through and steal anything left on your spot on the ground. We were assigned a group of 90 men, with each man having a number. That number was our roll call number each and every day.

Following roll call, rations were handed out. There was not much to today's rations, but I was thankful for anything. I got an apple, and something that looked like bacon, only it was green. I told Bill and Tom to eat slowly, reminding them we did not know when our next meal would be coming. Being just kids, they did not listen to me. Within minutes their rations were gone.

When roll call was finished in our group, we went back to our space.

When we walked back I suggested we try to move some dirt around to make it just a bit more comfortable. Aaron had a spoon. I used it to dig around and loosen the dirt. I removed a small rock that had been cutting into my good leg.

Looking around I saw every kind of make shift lean-to imaginable. Men were being creative to find ways to get some shelter. Aaron said the shelters were called *shebangs*.

A few men had tents. Others had pieces of cloth held up by sticks. We had no covering at all.

I wondered why the rebels would build such a large prison without building barracks inside to house the men. The fortress was just a big open field surrounded by walls. On some days I imagined the heat of the sun fried the prisoners. In the winter, the cold would be awful. Most of the prisoners had nothing at all to protect them from the sun or the cold.

I was not worried as much for me. I had always been determined to be free. I was more worried for the other three.

Chapter 8
Getting Assigned a Nickname

Aaron said the men in the stockade all had nicknames. And he was already working on names for us. Aaron thought Bill looked like a bird with his long black hair. Aaron dubbed him *Raven*, which Bill kind of liked. Tom was named *Beanpole* because he was so skinny. I ended up being called *Hobble* because of my bad leg. I did not much care for the name at first. I guess he could have called me *Crutch* or *Limpy*.

I was curious so I asked Aaron what his nickname was. I should have known. They called him *Smiley* after his very large grin.

I thought a bit about the name *Hobble*. *Hobble* wasn't so much who I was but it certainly was what I did. People could identify me from a distance, so it made sense as my prison nickname. Calling me *Blacksmith* didn't work here because I was not able to be a blacksmith in the prison.

Actually *Hobble* wasn't as bad as other names I have been called in my life. My bad leg was an identification mark and a handicap for sure. My handicap was just more noticeable than some men's handicaps. I was not ashamed of my limp. It was just an inconvenience, nothing more. The name *Hobble* for me became a badge I wore with honor.

I looked in all directions. The men to the left of us were frail. They looked to be sixty or so years old, though they were probably much younger. Aaron said the older looking man (they called him *Stickman*) had been wasting away to nothing each day. He probably weighed about 70 pounds. We could count his ribs because they stuck out. *Stickman* could barely lift up his arm to hold his food.

At roll call others had to hold him up. His teeth had fallen out, probably from scurvy. His gums and lips were so parched they look like they would crack if he spoke.

Stickman looked to me like he did not have enough strength to swat a fly.

His mate was not much heavier. He was white as a ghost, with white hair, white eyebrows and a white beard. Aaron said they called him *Whitey*. That made sense to me. His legs and arms were covered had many open and runny sores. He wore short pants and nothing else. All day long he just stared out toward the wall as if in a trance.

The men on the other side of us were a bit healthier looking. Aaron said they arrived shortly after he did. He said *Pirate* was the one with the eye patch. *Pirate* had been wounded in the leg at Gettysburg. It had been amputated at the knee. He had a wooden stump. He had gone back to his unit after he got his strength back. All *Pirate* needed was a parrot on his shoulder and he would have totally fit his nickname.

The prisoner next to him was known as *Whistler*. Almost any time day or night he was whistling some tune. It irritated some of the men. He often got hit by dirt clods and rocks. I liked his whistling.

Aaron talked about his friends in camp being named *Peanut*, and *Blackie*. I could not wait to see if I could pick them out without having *Smiley* tell me in advance who they were.

I found *Peanut* the very next day, walking by in the afternoon. He was the smallest soldier I had ever seen. He could have been what my mother used to call a dwarf. He stopped over to talk to *Smiley*. We all got to meet him.

I liked the guy immediately. He laughed and joked about everything, whether it was about his friends and family back home, his fellow prisoners, or the hated rebel guards. No one was left out of his playfulness. How anyone could remain so cheerful in a place like this was beyond my imagination.

Aaron said *Peanut* was just like that every single day. He was a breath of fresh air. It was the highlight of Aaron's day to see *Peanut*.

Peanut said he was one of three in his family in the Union army. One brother had been killed at Winchester.

The other was critically wounded at Antietam Creek and was sent home.

It took me three tries to spot *Blackie*. I was not expecting him to be a white man. Aaron said many men were blackened from the soot of the fires they lit around the prison. And this man certainly had dark skin. *Blackie* was from the Thirteenth Tennessee Cavalry. He had been separated from the others when they were captured during the battle of Fort Pillow. He told me he had fought proudly beside many courageous colored troops during that battle.

Blackie said he had killed more than his fair share of rebels. He was just wishing he could find a musket so he could take a little target practice to knock those Johnny Rebs off the platforms on top of the wall. I would have liked to have seen that too.

Chapter 9
Meeting Other U.S. Colored Troops

I asked Aaron how many coloreds were in the camp here. He said he thought around one hundred or so. He knew some of them. The colored troops had voted Major Archibald Bogle their leader. We went to see Major Bogle today.

The major, like many of our officers, was a white man. He was from the Thirty-Fifth U.S. Colored Regiment. His assistant was Lt. Colonel George French, also a white officer, with the Eighth U.S. Colored Troops. Both had been captured while helping our troops at Olustee, Florida.

Major Bogle asked if I would help them. He did not have to ask me twice. I was certainly willing to join up with my colored brothers in whatever they needed.

"Can you read and write, sir?" the officer asked.

"Yes, I can," I admitted proudly.

"I am in need of someone who can compile a list of all the colored soldiers here so we will have a record. List their name, what unit they are from, date of death, and what ever else you think is needed. Make two copies. One for each of us. That way if either of us makes it out of here, people will know the names of the colored soldiers who were here."

"I would be happy to, sir," I said. "I think that it is a very good job for me."

Major Bogle told me he had been wounded at Olustee. He had been taken to the hospital at Andersonville Prison twice. Both times he was refused treatment because he was a white officer of a colored unit.

"Lt. Col. French has been refused medical help here for the same reason," he said angrily. "He is in bad need of help. The Confederate doctors also refused to treat the sick and injured colored soldiers."

That didn't surprise me. It was just like it was at Beall Air. I bet old Dr. Harnish and nurse Clara Barton would have treated the coloreds here.

When I asked him why he was imprisoned here with the enlisted men, he said, "The rebels don't think too kindly of white officers leading colored units against them. I don't know where they took the other officers."

Major Bogle said, "There are a half dozen colored units here but most of the colored prisoners are from the Fifty-Fourth Massachusetts Volunteers. They include some who had been captured during the battle of Olustee and others who had been captured in the summer of 1863 at Fort Wagner and James Island. They were transferred here from Belle Island Prison."

"Rebel soldiers in general," the major explained, "kill the colored soldiers rather than taking them prisoner. Maybe that's why there are less than 100 colored soldiers here."

The major said many of the colored soldiers were allowed to leave the prison on various details. Their primary job was digging the graves in the cemetery, which was a daily chore.

The major had met James Gooding, Charles Rensellear, Charles August, and William Smith also of the Fifty-Fourth Massachusetts Volunteers. They had not been captured with us. I wanted to find them anyway. He pointed out about where their spot in the prison was. I promised him I would visit them soon.

We had been told at camp if we were ever captured, we would be exchanged. The rebel and Union officials had worked out a system where they would trade even, one Union general for one rebel General, with officers being exchanged for an equal number from both the North and the South. An officer might be traded for fifty or more enlisted men. The major had heard rumors that even if an exchange was in the works, colored troops were not eligible. I thought that made sense since the Confederates had no colored troops to exchange.

Chapter 10

Gangs in the Stockade

Aaron told us to watch out for gangs, because they would steal anything we had. Gangs operated mostly at night when he first arrived. Now they beat people up and stole things from the sickly and infirmed, right in front of everyone else even in the daylight. No one said anything. The other prisoners all feared the gangs.

Recently gangs had taken shoes right off a prisoner while he was sitting there watching them do it. There was not anything he could do about it, because he was unable to fight back. Aaron said, "Those who are strong steal from those who are weak. It is survival of the fittest. Only the fittest survive."

Aaron said he thought because I was such a big man, with muscles, the gangs probably would not mess with me. He worried about the two youngans, Bill and Tom, as they were easy prey. He told me not to let them out of my sight even for a minute. Aaron and I realized how fortunate it was for Bill and Tom that they had us looking after them. If they had come in here on their own, they would probably have not survived. The gangs would have attacked them.

One day a gang walked by where we were sitting. Aaron saw them coming and warned me that they might be up to no good.

Sure enough, before the first man in the group was past me, a glob of tobacco had dropped out of his mouth and onto my crippled leg. I am sure he did it on purpose to see what I would do.

I surprised the man by grabbing his leg and pulling him to the ground faster than he could say "good afternoon." And then I picked up the glob of stinking tobacco and pushed it back into his mouth. "Drop something?" I asked.

He jumped up and wanted to lash out at me. Fortunately for him, he thought better of it. Instead, he walked away without looking back.

Aaron was the first of our group to react. "What a sight to behold. We call that bully *Mosby*. He has been pushing people around the whole time I have been here. The men with him are called *Mosby's Raiders*. They are a bunch of thugs. No one has ever fought him back until now."

That was my baptism under fire. At least I came out on top this time. Word coming back to us was that the colored man they called *Hobble* was mighty quick and tough for a guy who had just one good leg.

Another gang walked by a few days later. They watched us. Perhaps they wanted to check out the new colored man who dared challenge *Mosby*. This gang was a sorry looking bunch. If I had the chance to name them, I would have thought *Moron*, *Ugly Puss*, *Brutus*, *Grizzly*, *Monk*, and *Red Coat* would have been appropriate.

Peanut pointed out that *One-Eyed Jack* was their leader. He got his name from the fact he read cards to tell men's fortunes and had an eye patch. He had been a threat to all the men in camp. As long as *Grizzly* and *Brutus* were walking along side him, he was probably one of the bravest men in the prison. I didn't think *One-Eyed Jack* would be quite as brave without his bodyguards.

I was mighty tuckered out. After dark I nibbled at my food. I was so hungry by then that anything would have tasted good. And it felt good just to have my teeth and gums working once again.

I slept a bit. Still, I kept one eye open to guard the others.

It occurred to me that nine thousand men was certainly a much larger number than the number of rebel guards around the outside of the fort. "Has anyone ever thought of organizing an escape?" I boldly asked.

I got the "shhhh" sign for that comment. Aaron answered, "Most men here are so demoralized and downtrodden, they could not organize a church picnic. We fight for food and space on the ground. The sun and rain beat down on us. The gangs attack us when we are not looking."

"We trust no one. If we spent as much time thinking of ways to overpower the guards as we did in trying to protect our ground space and valuables from the gangs, we would have been able to break out a long time ago. Instead, we are disorganized and all working as individuals, rather than as an army."

I thought about that and realized Aaron was right. The system was working against our organizing any escape.

The ration wagons showed up in the afternoon today. We lined up again for roll call. This time our rations included a potato, a carrot, and a chicken leg. One of the men from our group dropped his chicken leg walking back to his spot. Half a dozen men rolled around the ground fighting over it. The soldier who lost his food fell down and started crying. I felt so sorry for the frail lad that I gave him my piece of chicken.

Back at our space on the ground Aaron thanked me for giving my chicken leg to the man they called *The Town Crier*. He said no one else would have helped that soldier but me.

We all watched tonight as they carried a few men from our section toward that dreaded south gate. That gate was the one where the dead were piled high to take their final journey. *Stickman* was one who didn't make it today. That didn't surprise anyone as he had been barely alive all this past week.

Aaron was right. *Stickman's* spot on the ground was already taken within seconds of his body being lifted and carried out.

I was surprised to hear a train whistle today. Aaron said that meant more prisoners were on their way. The north gate opened and a new group of Union soldiers got their first look at this hell-hole. The gate opened five different times. "Move over men," I thought. "We need to make room for a hundred fifty more soldiers."

Tonight I think I actually slept a couple of hours. I was beginning to get used to the sounds of the prison as my body learned how to fit into my little space.

Bill cried out in the night, I am guessing from a bad dream. I touched his shoulder and he calmed down a bit. He was probably homesick and worried about his future in this God-forsaken place.

Peanut came by this morning for another visit. For his size, he was probably pound-for-pound the bravest man in the fort. He walked around anywhere he wanted. No one bothered him. Knowing how bullies usually pick on the smallest man around, I was surprised that he was so strong.

He said his regiment was the Twentieth Michigan. They were cornered at Cold Harbor. The rebels overpowered them. He faked death in hopes that they would go away. Instead, they rummaged through the pockets of the victims and captured six of them who were wounded and still alive. He told me he was very determined to survive this awful place, so he could exact his revenge on enough rebels to make it worth his while. *Peanut* said he was hoping he could start with the guard at Post 17 who had gunned down his pal when the soldier accidentally fell into *the deadline*.

While Aaron guarded our sacred ground and my things, *Peanut* took us down the hill to see the stream. Aaron was right. Men who had spots nearby were making water and having bowel movements so near the stream that their feces were floating in the water. Others were washing and shaving in the same stream.

It made sense to me that the guards needed to block off that area so at least the water was drinkable. When I suggested it to the inner guard near the north gate, he roared with laughter as if I had passed him the best joke of the year. Nothing will ever be done, *Peanut* said, though he thought it was a workable idea. Best thing I thought we could do was get some kind of container that we could catch water in if it ever rained.

Anderson, Georgia
May 1864

Marcia my beloved

I remain in prison. Each day here is worse than the day before. We watch as more and more dead Union prisoners are carried and piled at the south gate, the last stop before the cemetery.

We have little to eat, no clean water or medicine, and terrible living conditions. Almost everyone around us is infected with some disease. More and more prisoners are crowded into a space no bigger than the field behind the Cashtown Hotel. Gangs steal food and belongings from helpless prisoners.

I pray each day that God will deliver me out of this hell-hole and back home safely. I cannot even imagine when that will be. We might be here until the end of this dreadful war.

Promises are made that we will be exchanged. I have been told that the coloreds will not be exchanged. The Rebel army has no colored troops to trade for us.

May God keep you, and Mr. and Mrs. Quinn safe. My love and faith carries me. I am determined more than anyone here to survive and return home. Your photograph was a grand gift, allowing me to look at you when I am lonely and fearful.

Until we meet again, I remain,

Your loving husband,
Catesby

Today as we walked, *Peanut* pointed out *One-Eyed Jack's* gang and their little corner of the stockade. His gang had done well. They had a tarp covering their spots held up by various sticks and poles. It was almost like a tent. They were well-stocked with shoes and shirts, pots and pans and containers full of water. That was because *One-Eyed Jack* and his boys had stolen all those items from others prisoners, other Union men, *Peanut* explained. All those items were for sale. They had opened a store for the prisoners.

The gang leader looked up as I limped past, but did not say anything to me. He knew who I was, and that was fine with me. If he came by to bother me, he would regret it. I was not afraid of him or his guards *Grizzly* and *Brutus*.

I looked for the men of the Fifty-Fourth Massachusetts Volunteers. Major Bogle's directions took us right to their spot. They had been captured in the battle at Olustee. Goodling and August were happy to see men of their own regiment. We traded stories of how we had gotten captured. We all promised to keep an eye on each other inside the prison. Two of the men, Rensellear and Smith, looked in very bad shape already.

As we headed back to our ground, I saw more and more horrible conditions around the camp. Spoiled food was being guarded as if it were gold. Men with open sores lay so close to other men I feared their body fluids were dripping on them. Prisoners having coughing fits were spitting on everyone around them.

I wanted to run away, or to wake up from this nightmare and find myself lying next to Marcia in my own bed. I prayed hard each night that someday this would just be a bad memory. For today, the horrible sight, sounds, and smells brought me back to the moment. This was Andersonville Prison. *Hobble* was going to come out the north gate in one piece, someday. There was not any rebel prison bad enough to break me.

I looked closely at a couple of the guards on the platform today. They looked young and scared. It looked to me like the sentry duty was being performed by men not fit enough to be fighting the battles for the Confederacy. This prison seemed to be a place even the rebels avoided. The guards looked thin and hungry too. I wondered if they were getting the same small amount of rations we were getting.

Chapter 11
The Deal of a Lifetime

One day they brought in the ration wagons in the early morning. The officer in charge said for the next twenty-four hours, the commandant was offering a deal. He read from a handbill saying that any prisoner who pledged allegiance to the Confederacy could leave the prison and take up arms for the South, with no penalty. If any soldier agreed to the deal, he would be given a uniform, a rifle and ammunition, monthly pay, transportation to the battle front and a piece of land he would own at the end of the war.

The official called it "the deal of a lifetime" though it was only available until roll call the following day. Anyone interested was to notify the guard nearest the north gate. Then he posted the handbill on the gate.

The prisoners booed and hissed at the rebel making the announcement. He was asking Union men to become traitors.

It did not seem to me that a rebel soldier's life was much better than ours. All the rebel soldiers I had ever seen looked hungry too. Many were shoeless. Their uniforms were in sad shape. I did not know of anyone who would have wanted land in the South.

Yet in the desperation at this horrible place, I thought there might be some prisoners here who would decide to take the offer. When they got their new gun and freedom, they could always go home.

I really would not have blamed Union prisoners who accept the offer as much as I blamed the conditions here. Men with families back home might be willing to sell their souls for freedom. I was not that desperate though I did understand the appeal of the offer the rebels had made.

I decided to watch the north gate tonight after dark, because that's most likely when someone would sneak off and try to get their freedom.

I did not think anyone would try it in the daylight, for fear their friends would think they were turncoats. The other prisoners might even kill them before they got to the north gate.

One of the Union prisoners from another ration group bolted the line during roll call today and climbed aboard the wagon. He threw vegetables into the crowd. The other prisoners cheered for the first minute, until the guards fired from every direction and brutally killed the man on the wagon. His section was returned to their ground without rations for that day. That was the rule. If anyone in your group got into trouble, your whole group went without rations.

The food for the day was a small chunk of well-cooked beef, a potato and an onion. Too bad we did not have a cooking pot. We could have made stew. As always, I saved my food until after dark.

When night arrived, Aaron and I watched the north gate. No one had made a move toward the gate since the morning announcement. From where we were sitting the torches around the gate would give us a good view. We continued to watch.

Sure enough during the night seven Union soldiers sneaked over and took the offer. The gate opened and closed quietly as each man, one at a time, left the fort. It was no one Aaron and I recognized. Still we were a little upset by their decisions.

Chapter 12
The Rains Came Thundering Down

It got so my injured leg was a barometer of telling changes in the weather. I could predict rain a day before it came because of the stiffness that would set in. My old leg cried out before all storms. It was crying out today.

My useless leg was a constant reminder of old Mr. Newberry. Even though my mother said, "Vengeance is mine, sayeth the Lord," I still dreamed about sneaking up behind old Mr. Newberry with a hot poker in my hand and doing some paying back. I would like to see the fear in his eyes as he turned around and saw me coming. I would love to hear some of his screams so I could laugh at him. I have been waiting a long time for that particular moment to take place.

The rains did come, as the stiffness in my leg had predicted. The storm thundered through the prison. We had no shelter, so we got totally soaked. The plan was to catch as much rainwater as possible in whatever container you had, because it was clean and drinkable. On every plot men scrambled to cup their hands or use whatever they could find to gather the fresh water.

The hard rain flowed under our spots and washed away everything we had not tied down. Suddenly the prison space shrunk. Flooding was moving the men off the low spots near the stream. The soldiers had nowhere to go. They had to move closer together to make room for the others.

My lips and gums were dry and cracked. They especially enjoyed the soothing rain. I had not wanted to drink from the stream, though I did wet my lips from that dirty water. The rainwater was refreshing and cleaned us. We all needed a bath. The rain was washing all the filth from our bodies and it was all flowing down the hill and into our little stream.

I worked daily to make sure my journals and letters were secure and dry in my duffel.

It rained parts of twenty days in a row. The miserable conditions became even worse. The stockade became a large mud hole. Prisoners drowned in their spots. Others washed down the hill and into the flooded stream, dying when they did not have the energy to save themselves.

Ration wagons came less often. We were told the wagons could not get through on the muddied roads.

Tom brought some laughter to our ground mates by taking my crutch and moving it like he was using it as an oar. *Peanut* jumped in to help with the joke by acting as the sea captain, pointing the direction he wanted Tom to steer the imaginary boat. "This way, matey," he yelled, as we all roared with laughter.

I licked at the rain drops as they pounded down upon us. We were at the mercy of Mother Nature for days as the rain continued to beat down on us. What originally was refreshing got to be down right annoying after the third or fourth day of the storm.

The rain finally let up and stopped. The camp was flooded and muddy. Men trying to walk fell in the slop. It was like wading in quicksand.

For a few days the rain brought high water levels in the stream and the current kept the water clean. It was actually possible to get a drink, though the lines waiting to take a sip were usually too long to even bother. This time when men tried to relieve themselves along the stream they got hit with dirt and rocks. Men told them to go somewhere else. Clean drinking water was becoming important with most of the prisoners.

When the sun came out and started drying things off, we all gave thanks. The rain had brought relief. But enough was enough. The rain also loosened the ground. Once again we could push it around to try to make it fit better to our body shapes. After several weeks, the sun became so hot it baked the ground making it even painful to walk.

My latest problem was paper and pencils. My journal was completely full. My pencil was an inch long stub which I could barely hold. Some around me laughed at my writing. I guess they thought I did not know how to write because of my skin color. How wrong they were.

I asked Aaron what to do. He said I could probably barter with the guard taking roll call. If I would give up some of my rations, he could probably be bribed to bring me paper, pencils and a small box to keep everything dry.

I asked a guard whose name was Allen. He said he would trade me my next two rations for paper and pencils. Several days later a package was handed to me at roll call. It contained three pencils, and a pad of paper inside a cigar box. I went hungry, but it was worth it.

I dug a hole under where I sat and kept the box there so no one would mess with it. Only my three partners knew where it was hidden.

Anderson, Georgia
June 1864

Dearest Marcia

The rains have dampened the spirits of the thousands of prisoners in the stockade. The storms have muddied the waters, drowned the unfortunate, and made a cesspool out of our already horrible situation. However, the rain has provided us with fresh clean water which we have been without for several months.

Life here is worse than when I last wrote. I doubt in returning home, I will ever be able to wash the awful smell off me. The sights and sounds haunt me. I beg God to deliver me from this hell on earth. I question why I am here. When will these horrors end?

Only the strong survive. Two dozen dead men a day are carried off to the south gate. I vow to never join them.

Tom, Bill, Aaron and I try to keep our faith by working together. It is difficult on some days with all the disease, depression, filth, and despair on all sides. I have not had enough food, and have lost weight. My uniform hangs loosely on my body.

Every night I lay awake looking at the sky, wondering if I was mistaken to leave you to help President Lincoln win the war. I don't think I am helping him much being here. The same could be said for the 20,000 other Union prisoners who are here with me.

I know I must make the best of the situation, as bad as it is. I will be free again some day. That continues to be my goal. I expect some day to hold you in my arms and comfort you again. I will make up for these months that I have been missing from your life. I will need those tender moments to help me forget the nightmares of Andersonville Prison.

Each day away from you, my dearest Marcia, makes life more difficult. But I will not give up. Ever.

This rebel prison will not break me, just like Mr. Newberry could not break me. I will return home as I have promised.

Until we meet again.

Your loving husband,
Catesby

Because Bill and Tom were so young, they seemed to have a different view of the war and the prison. Tom saw the goodness in men on both sides of the stockade. He noticed men sharing their rations and helping their sick neighbors. He pointed out the good work of guards like Allen and the colored troops. They worked to bury the dead, a job no one else wanted. He saw God's hand in many situations here.

Tom remained positive every day. He said his faith came from his mother. He felt sure that God would save us from this hell on earth.

Bill was real quiet. He was a keen observer with great vision and hearing.

He often pointed out raiders approaching, spotting them long before we had noticed. *Raven*, as everyone was now calling him, could even hear the train and ration wagons long before anyone else knew they were coming.

The lads were doing better with their rations than they had been when we first arrived. They were starting to realize that Aaron was right when he told them to guard their rations and eat them slowly. We did not know when the next ones would arrive. Several days of going without eating while watching others still holding on to their food had convinced them to plan better.

The boys talked often about the foolishness of them following their relatives to battle and ending up in Andersonville Prison. What had been such a keen idea had now turned into a nightmare. The two of them joked about asking to be freed, since they were not real soldiers. But they knew they would just be laughed at.

Aaron figured it was probably more dangerous to be at Andersonville Prison than to be in battle. He thought a higher percentage of men were dying here. It was strange to think that with rebels shooting at us in battle we actually would have a better chance to make it through. Although there was no way we could test his theory, it made sense to me.

I told him how the prison reminded me of my wagon trips through the fields where the battle took place at Antietam Creek. The sounds were similar, with the crying of those near death, of men begging to be shot, and the huge numbers of dead awaiting burial.

The same sun I had been grateful to see my whole life suddenly became evil. We had no shade. We were being baked every single day. It could easily have blinded us too. What I would have given for *One-Eyed Jack's* lean-to on some of those sunny, hot days.

As sport, some of the men took the mud from the storm and fashioned little dirt balls. The sun baked them hard as rocks.

After dark the prisoners threw dirt balls at the guards. It was great sport. Many prisoners played the game. Tom was dead on with his aim and the best dirt ball thrower in the camp.

The way we knew of any direct hit was to listen to the cries of the guards themselves. In just one night, judging from the shouts, the score was Tom twelve, the guards nothing. And the men inside Camp Sumter cheered with each hit.

Today *One-Eyed Jack* and his men went around bartering rain water from that storm a few weeks back. They had containers full of clean water they had saved up. I had to admit that they were certainly smart. Their prices were high, but there was always someone desperate for clean water in the encampment.

We watched daily as the bodies pile up at the south gate. At first it was just about a dozen a day. The number kept growing. Now more than fifty men died every single day.

Men loaded a wagon pulled by mules each night to remove the dead bodies. Each morning a fresh heap would be started. These Union soldiers were finally going to escape the torture chamber of Andersonville Prison, feet first. Some probably welcomed death, living a terrible life here.

Those dead men whose names were known, had pieces of paper attached to their bodies showing their name and unit. One Union soldier had been chosen as the scribe, taking names and units as the new prisoners entered the camp. He also noted who passed out the south gate.

Colored prisoners who were recruited to dig graves told us some of the grave markers had names on them — but many did not. To dig graves meant double rations. I appreciated that my colored brothers volunteered for grave digging duty.

Often the clanking sounds of the picks and shovels from the men at the cemetery was the one steady sound you could count on every single day.

George, one of the Fifty-Fourth Massachusetts Volunteers who was a grave digger, told me the only order in the whole prison was at the cemetery.

He said there were very straight long rows of graves dug each day, one after the other. About a hundred men were dumped into each long row. He said he hoped they had enough space to keep up with all those who were dying. George said two from our regiment, Smith and Rensellear, had recently passed into the beyond. He hated most burying men from the Fifty-Fourth Massachusetts Volunteers.

George said some of the men who dug the graves were so hardened to the task, he didn't think they would have noticed if someone they knew was placed in the next grave. For him it was different. He felt sorry for the poor men who didn't make it. "They fought valiantly in the battles, only to die from starvation, disease, and destitution. My wish," he said, "is to return to the Union army and personally kill one rebel soldier for each grave I have dug." He said as of today that count was 252.

The near-dead were sometimes silent and at other time were very noisy. Some men died so quietly it took their partners in the space some time to realize they were no longer with them. Others gave up all hope and died dramatically. Today a man walked deliberately into *the deadline*. He looked up to the sentry, and shouted, "Shoot me. I'm in *the deadline*." The guard warned him several times, and then shot him dead. The prisoner got what he wanted.

I knew Marcia and the Quinns would be worried because I had written letters home. Suddenly my letters had stopped. They probably thought I was dead. There was no way of getting a message to them letting them know I was alive but in a prison camp. Allen, the guard, told me it was too risky to try to sneak a letter out.

I prayed Marcia would feel in her bones that I was still alive. Sometimes that kind of feeling grows in you. There is no explaining it. I pledged to continue to write to her in my papers even in the stockade, hoping someday she could read the letters and find out that I was missing her.

Even if the prisoner count was going down at the rate of fifty dead each day, the trains were still bringing more men into the camp. Though they were not arriving every day, they came just often enough to expand the count by several hundred per train.

One day, I spotted a little bird sitting in a small opening in the tall fence. I watched it flit in and out of the hole. The creature was yellow and black. It sang a cheerful song. I do not think anyone else in the camp was aware of its presence. To me it was a sign from God telling me that I should remain cheerful with a song in my heart. Better days were coming.

Chapter 13
A Friendship Develops

Aaron became my trusted new friend. I was very thankful for his reaching out to help us find a place on that terrible first day in the prison. Besides Mr. and Mrs. Quinn, I had never had a white friend before. I guess my mother's lesson was right — about not judging people by their color. She said it was what was in a person's heart that counted most.

For a white man, Aaron was extremely open to having colored men as his friends. Like Mr. and Mrs. Quinn, Aaron was totally color blind. He only saw me as a man, not as a colored man. I appreciated his acceptance of me as a man more than he could ever realize.

Aaron talked about his growing up. He wanted to know about my life too. Our lives could not have been any more different. Here was a free white man talking to a former slave.

Aaron told us, "My mother, father and younger brothers all live on a farm in Bowling Green, Ohio. After I get out of here, I want to return to school to study to become a doctor. I can't stand seeing so many men die here of unsanitary conditions and without medicine or doctors. I want to do my part to see that things are better than this back home."

Aaron said he was able to tune out the sounds and smells of the stockade. He said he could place himself back home in Ohio, at his hunting cabin, fishing in the creek and at other familiar places in his mind where he was safe.

I was able to do that too. What helped me stay focused and alive was my ability to dream. I was able to take myself away from this awful hole and see myself at home with my friends and family. I could think of fine dinners at the hotel, listening to my mother read to me, driving Colonel

Washington's wagon, talking to Mr. Quinn, working in my shop, or Marcia's loving touch.

I think my determination to be free from slavery was helping me survive this unholy place.

Shackles do not suit me. They never have. But I felt shackled here in prison. And I do not like it. I promised myself I would be free again. I was not going to go out the south gate.

I tried to teach Bill and Tom to take themselves somewhere else in their thoughts. But it did not work for them. Many evenings the lads had horrible nightmares and could not go back to sleep. The prison life was much more troubling to them than it was to me.

Aaron, who had questioned my writing when I first arrived at the prison, had asked me recently for paper and a pencil so he could take notes on what he was seeing and thinking. He thought his notes would be important during his medical studies after the war was over.

What he had seen here led him to believe the filth of the prison was somehow related to the disease and death. He thought clean water, proper sanitation, clean clothes and clean bandages would make a difference. He said that would cut down on the illness and death.

After many days of watching, he said if the men who were coughing could be separated, they wouldn't infect those around them. He thought the same was true of those who had open sores. If they were close together, they would infect the others too. He said he thought the filthy clothes and gross bandages actually kept the wounds from healing.

Aaron also believed the mosquitoes helped carry the disease from one soldier to another. Those dang skeeters pestered us every night. They were huge and noisy. We swatted at them frantically in the dark as they swarmed around us. They sounded like they were as big as bumble bees. We laughed and said that six dead mosquitoes could feed a prisoner for a day. And we wondered how many of those huge skeeters it would take to carry one of us over the wall to freedom.

Even though Aaron seemed to have a good idea how to improve the health of the prisoners, no one in any official capacity would do anything about it. Day after day more men were taken out to the hospital, never to return. Others didn't even make it to the hospital. They were carried out cold and stiff to be piled near the south gate.

I knew Aaron was going to make a great doctor. I promised him I would give him Doctor Delany's address so they could write after we got out of this ungodly place.

Aaron wanted to know all about my injured leg. Bill and Tom listened in because they too had been curious about that. But Aaron was more interested in the physical part, not how it happened. Because of his interest in being a doctor and helping others, he asked if my leg still hurt. And then he asked if he could examine the wound.

Since it did not hurt anymore, I let him. He poked and prodded, saying it was probably now just like dead meat, with the nerves dead inside.

Aaron wanted to know how long it took to heal. He wondered out loud if it healed differently because it was a burn than if it had been a bullet wound or cut.

My bad leg was not doing well on the damp ground. It took me several minutes each morning just to stand up and stretch because it tightened up in the night from inactivity. I walked everyday just to keep from stiffening up.

We had to take turns so someone was always guarding our spot and our possessions. I knew Aaron would watch out for Bill, Tom and me as if we were his brothers. No harm would come to any of us or our simple treasures on Aaron's watch. I knew Aaron was a trusted ally of our army of four. And when we walked out of the north gate, we would all walk out together.

Today I looked for two of the remaining four men of the Fifty-Fourth Massachusetts Volunteers we had visited earlier. Charles August was in better shape than James Gooding. Gooding was very ill. August was afraid Gooding was not going to make it much longer.

Time passed as slowly at the prison as the dripping of one grain of sand at a time through an hour glass. When the sun was beating down, we looked forward to the darkness. But the sounds of the night were so awful, we couldn't wait for the sun to come up to save us.

Chapter 14
A Holy Man Walks Among Us

The most popular man in the prison was the priest, Father Peter Whalen. He didn't seem to care what your religion was or even if you had one. He was willing to stop and talk, lead men in prayer, or just offer an encouraging word or two.

The Bible he carried was tattered and worn. His robe was dirty and ragged. But he was blessed. If the devil himself had been a prisoner here, Father Whalen, I am certain, would have stopped to say hello.

The priest lived outside the stockade but came here early in the morning and stayed until late at night. There was no quitting in that man. Father Whalen wasn't concerned about the time. No one was going anywhere. If he didn't talk to you today, he could always come back tomorrow.

Father Whalen was welcomed most by those who were sick and dying. He made a special effort to talk to those on their last days on earth. His touch, I am told, was comforting. Men were said to have confessed enough sins that Father Whalen could get them quick and direct entrance into Heaven.

The priest was asked to pray for clean water, more rations, more medicine, success of the Union Army, President Lincoln, and a break in the brutal heat.

For every soul he was asked to save in the Union prisoner camp, he was asked to damn the souls of the guards and Jefferson Davis.

Catholics loved him. Protestants loved him. The Jewish loved him. Those who had no religion were willing to try some, in this desperate place. About the only ones who didn't love Father Whalen were the prison gangs and the guards. The gangs mocked him, calling him *The Pope*, and made fun of his prayers. The guards watched him close, in case he was smuggling items into the prison.

Men asked Father Whalen to pray for them, to pray for their families back home, and to pray that the dead would be taken quickly into God's arms and through the pearly gates to Heaven.

Chapter 15
Rebelling Against the Gangs

I lost count of what day it was. It wasn't that I couldn't count, but I didn't always have paper or pencils to keep track. Whatever day it was, today was the day the men in the prison rebelled against the gangs. That made it a very good day.

Representatives from the prisoners met with Commandant Henry Wirz to complain about the gangs inside the prison. Wirz agreed to make arrests within the prison, with the understanding that the prisoners had to hold trials and abide by the findings of the court.

He brought several dozen armed guards into the prison. Slowly the committee walked around and pointed out all the gang members. Several hundred men were taken to the jail outside the wall in small groups to await an upcoming trial.

When *Mosby* was taken out, the prisoners cheered loudly, yelling at him now that he was of no danger to them any longer. *One-Eyed Jack* and his thugs were part of those who were arrested.

Trials were held. New prisoners served as jurors because they had not yet built up any prejudice toward anyone in the gangs. They would be fair.

Commandant Wirz announced that he and his men were not involved except as observers. It kind of reminded me of the story mother told me about Pontius Pilate as he washed his hands during the trial of Jesus.

The trials lasted almost a week. Six men were found guilty of battery, theft and murder. They were sentenced to be hanged. The six were Charles Curtiss, Fifth Rhode Island Artillery; Pat Delaney, Eighty-Third Pennsylvania; W. R. Rickson, U.S. Navy; Andrew Munn, U.S. Navy; John Sarsfield, One Hundred Forty-Fourth New York; and William Collins (also known as *Mosby*), Eighty-Eighth Pennsylvania. By hanging them, we hoped the gangs inside the stockade would be finally put out of business.

Many other gang members, including *One-Eyed Jack*, were found guilty of lesser crimes. They were sentenced to various punishments.

The guards brought lumber into the prison. The colored prisoners helped erect a gallows. When the scaffold was ready, Commandant Wirz rode into the camp on horseback, leading the condemned men through the gate.

Father Whalen met with each of the men. He asked each of the six to repent. When he had finished, Father asked all the other prisoners to forgive them their sins and to allow the convicted men to be spared. Instead, thousands of prisoners shouted, "Hang them. Hang them all."

The gang members were made ready for their hangings. They climbed up on the scaffold and were placed right over the trap doors. Ropes were pulled down around their necks. Meal bags were placed over their heads. The encampment was as silent as I had ever heard it.

The signal was given to cut the ropes. The six men fell through the holes in the floor all at the same time. The prisoners in the enclosure cheered loudly. One rope broke, and the man climbed out from under the scaffold, obviously very much alive. The other five jerked to violent deaths.

The one spared was Charles Curtiss. He begged for mercy saying it was a sign from God that he didn't die. He pleaded that God must have wanted him spared. But it was not to be. A new rope was quickly strung over the arm of the platform. He was made ready for his execution. The trap door was opened. This time the rope held, with Curtiss joining the other five dangling by their necks.

I thought back to all the hangings of John Brown and his men. I had watched eleven men be hanged now in my lifetime. I hope these were my last. I looked away thinking what a horrible way for any man to die.

Minutes after the six dead gang members were dumped into a wagon and taken to the cemetery, prisoners took apart the gallows. They were looking for lumber for their *shebangs*. Within minutes the gallows had disappeared.

Hangings of the gang members
Andersonville Prison   James E. Taylor drawing
Harpers Weekly   September 16, 1865

Andersonville Prison Commandant Henry Wirz
Confederate Veteran Magazine 1864

Chapter 16
Expanding the Prison

At one point there was building going on outside the wall at the north end of the prison. Today the inner wall was knocked down. Within just a few minutes, word spread that the prison had been expanded with new open space now up for grabs.

The four of us decided to stay where we were. Others picked up everything they owned and ran to the opening in the inside fence. Whatever new ground was available looked very welcoming. It had grass and lots of wide open space. The new area appeared real different from the bare dirt we sat upon.

We watched in disbelief as men crammed into the new part of the prison. It filled as quickly as it opened up. In fact, so many men tried to move into the new part of the encampment, the spaces were soon filled to over-flowing. Men turned around and walked back, sadly returning to the old section only to find their space had already been gobbled up by others.

The inner wall was torn apart quickly by the prisoners for firewood and lumber for the *shebangs*.

The new spaces had expanded the terribly overcrowded prison, but it hardly mattered. By now we had probably tripled the population Aaron had told us was about 9,000 when we arrived. About twenty-five thousand men were here now.

Anderson, Georgia
July 1864

Dear Marcia

The Union gangs I told you about that had been terrorizing the other prisoners have been rounded up and arrested. Over two hundred of them went to trial. Many were found guilty. Six were hanged inside the prison earlier this month. Others will be imprisoned or tortured.

It has been hard for me to understand why Union soldiers would rob other Union soldiers here at the prison. I am hoping the attacks will stop now.

The rains have stopped, and the sun bakes us. We have no shelter. We sit on the open ground, as the sun beats down on us all the long day. My skin is burned. My lips are so dry I fear they will crack open.

As more and more prisoners are brought here, we have less to eat. Aaron thinks the prison, originally built to hold 8,000, probably has over 25,000 Union prisoners now.

My only relief is in taking trips back in my memory, to our little house, to suppers at the Willow Grove Hotel, to our wedding, and to Beall Air. Those thoughts give me a break from the horrors of my life in this prison.

I hold on to good thoughts of you, my dear Marcia and the teachings of my mother. I repeat over and over again that phrase my mother taught me from the Bible, "Be not afraid."

Men die as much from their loss of hope as from disease. They just don't want to live like this. They just plain give up. Do not worry, Marcia, my wife. Catesby will never give up.

Father Whalen, a priest who reminds me of Father Brian, walks among us every single day to encourage us and bring us prayer and God's word. He has inspired us.

I live for you, Marcia. I live to return as your husband. Every breath I take is with that in mind. I fear that you will not even recognize me when I return as I am now weak and frail.

As bad as this rebel prison is, it is no worse than the bonds of slavery or the injury that Mr. Newberry inflicted upon me. I have beaten them. I will come out of this too.

Keep believing as I do, dear Marcia, that I will return, as promised.

Your loving husband,
Catesby

Chapter 17
Attempts to Escape

It was our duty as captured Union soldiers to at least try to escape. And many men worked hard to find ways to get out of this prison.

Aaron said men dug tunnels to get past the walls, and sometimes succeeded. Many had escaped through tunneling. Some of them were chased down by bloodhounds and brought back into the stockade. The price of being caught is the stocks or the thumb hanging device. Men were tied by their thumbs and hung on a rack. They often did not survive the torture.

For each escape being planned, there were prisoners willing to tell the guards of the escape plans for extra rations. No one inside or outside could be trusted. We feared that prison officials sent in Confederate guards disguised as new prisoners to spy on us.

Some prisoners blackened their skin from the fires and marched out with the colored troops who dug the graves, hoping to escape that way.

Several prisoners were allowed to gather kindling in the woods outside the fence for fires and to help men build shelters. Sometimes those workers tried to run away when they became familiar with the guards outside. If captured, they were tortured.

Two men played dead. Their bodies were dumped on the pile near the south gate. They were the only ones who left through the south gate and were still alive.

For us four, we were not at the point to risking an attempt. We were plotting, for sure. I would not give up or give in. We are going to make it.

Others were as depressed and downtrodden as I was determined. Many gave up. They were hungry and sick and unable to find shelter or comfort.

Among those who died this week was Corporal Gooding. Now three of the four men of the Fifty-Fourth Massachusetts Volunteers who we had talked to have died.

Quite a few soldiers here were barely alive. They were living breath to breath. Sometimes men welcomed death as a friend. Sad faces could be seen everywhere.

Many of the former proud Union army now belonged to a group of starving, demoralized, hopeless men who stared into space. They had lost all hope. Some had lost their minds. A few were too frail to even raise their hands or raise their voices.

Scurvy, diarrhea, and gangrene affected almost all the prisoners. There was still very little clean water.

To some their only escape was through that dreaded south gate. Some looked forward to that day, and wished it would hurry along.

I became friends with Allen, the young rebel guard. He bartered with me, and brought in my paper and pencils when I needed them. He was from the Twenty-Sixth Alabama, a unit known as being intelligent and kindhearted. The other guard unit, the Fifty-Fifth Georgia, was hated because of their ignorance and brutality.

I asked Allen about the medicine, rations and clean water. He told me the officers, including Commandant Wirz, were all writing letters daily to Richmond asking for more of everything. He said Commandant Wirz pleaded with delegates sent to visit the prison to report back to Richmond that he desperately needed supplies for the prisoners. Allen thought things were going so badly for the Confederacy, rebel officials were guarding what they had. He didn't think officials in Richmond cared what was happening here.

He admitted the guards got the same rations that we got. They didn't get rations every day either. Allen said they hadn't gotten paid in several months. He watched helplessly and could do nothing to make our lives better, except to be my friend.

Allen was a good man who would do something to help if he could. I think his hands were tied. He helped me as much as he was able to. I could not blame him. It was not his fault. In fact, I admired him because he was at risk just getting the paper and pencils for me.

I believe he would have looked the other way if we had tried to escape.

Chapter 18
Smallpox Vaccine Arrives

When Allen delivered my paper and pencils today, he enclosed an unsigned note. It told us that smallpox vaccine was being sent to the prison. And while we thought this a grand scheme to protect us from the dreaded disease, he begged us not to take part in the vaccinations. He said the vaccine was contaminated. It was not safe to be given to the people of the South or to Confederate soldiers. It would be given to Union prisoners so it would not be wasted.

Not long after that, the guards announced smallpox inoculations would be given. We followed Allen's advice and refused to take it. The word soon was passed around the prison that the vaccine was unsafe. After a few days of trying to inoculate the prisoners, the guards gave up. Most of the prisoners refused to take it.

We were thankful to Allen for alerting us to the problem and perhaps saving our lives.

Tonight I wrote again to Marcia.

Anderson, Georgia
August 1864

My beloved wife Marcia

Each day I watch more and more men carried to the south gate. Today we counted over one hundred dead.

My friend Aaron, who is going to be a doctor when the war is over, suggests we stay as far away as possible from unclean water and sickly men. He thinks disease is spread by the unclean conditions and the darn skeeters. We stay as clean as possible and away from the sick. So far, it has worked for us.

I have made friends with a guard, Allen, who provides me with paper and pencils. This week he warned us that the smallpox vaccine they brought into the prison was unsafe. He urged us not to take it. We were thankful for that information and refused to take the vaccine.

I read in the old newspapers brought in by the suttlers of more Union victories. We hope the Union troops that are in nearby Atlanta will attempt to free us.

Men continue to try to escape by digging tunnels under the wall. We think that is too risky. If we would get caught by the rebel bloodhounds, we would be tortured and probably die. I am not willing to die here, even in an escape attempt. Our army of four voted that we would wait for a better way to find our freedom.

Marcia, please continue to believe, as I do, that Catesby will return home. Do not be afraid. I promise that I will return. Catesby always keeps his promise.

Until that time, I remain,

Your loving husband,
Catesby

Chapter 19
Two Miracles!

It rained ten days straight in August. Part of the one wall collapsed from the wet ground. Colored soldiers were called in to rebuild it while armed rebels guarded the opening.

A miracle happened at the end of the storms. Lightening hit near the north gate. Out of the ground spurted a new spring. It was a God send, bringing us plenty of clean, fresh water. The spring was quickly named *Providence Spring*. Men lined up with every container they had and waited for days to get some of that fresh, clean, cold water. Our only fear was that the spring would not last. So far, it has provided a steady stream of fresh water.

In early September, a startling announcement was made at roll call that the Union men at Andersonville Prison were going to be moved to another prison starting tomorrow. It was our second miracle.

Allen had alerted me several days before that he had heard rumors this was going to happen. My friend didn't have any of the details. He wished me well. Allen said he would not have treated a dog this poorly. I thanked him. I assured him we did not blame him.

There was now an excitement in the air we had not felt before. Certainly, wherever we were being sent, it had to be better than this.

Commandant Wirz posted the order of movement of about five hundred men each day. The handbill listed the dates each roll call group would be leaving. Our unit of ninety would move out with other groups on Tuesday, September 11. We had just another four days of this hell-hole to survive.

I wrote to pass my excitement on to Marcia, hoping this would be my last letter from here.

Anderson, Georgia
September 1864

My darling wife Marcia

We have just received news that they will be transferring our group from this sewer of a place to another prison in just four days. We do not know where we will be going. Wherever we are sent, we are expecting it to be better than this hole.

We are happy with the news, but we are not real sure of what is going to happen. The four of us continue to look for ways to escape. But we are not willing to risk our lives.

I have survived Andersonville Prison as I was determined to do. I will be marching out the north gate, as I promised I would. I will bow my head tonight and pray for those thousands who did not survive.

Maybe when we get closer to a Union victory in the war, the Union prisoners will be freed and allowed to return home. I will bless that day when it comes.

I dream of the day I will limp back in the door to our little house, call your name and say "Honey, I am home." That day will make up for all the awful days we have been apart.

I look at your pretty face in the photograph each day. Please hang on tight to the thought and belief that I will return.

Your loving husband,
Catesby

We prayed together thanking God for allowing us to leave Camp Sumter alive.

Aaron, Bill, Tom and I made a plan. We decided, no matter what, we would continue to stick together with our army of four. We also agreed we would be open to any chance of escape. But we wouldn't do anything stupid.

We were not about to get shot by some trigger-happy rebel guard when we were on our way out. If any situation came up along the way, Aaron and I would make the decision. The two lads would follow us.

The mood of the prison had changed. Men on the list to march out first walked through the camp. Everyone wished them well.

In the morning, we watch those first five hundred leave by the north gate. They stood taller and prouder than anyone else I had seen at Andersonville Prison.

We had been told only the able would be transferred. But Union men carried their ill and injured friends with them. The rebel guards did not try to stop them. We could see the men heading back toward the train that had brought us here.

When the first men left, there seemed to be no more room in the prison than before. It hardly made any difference at all. However, at least a couple of the prisoners were enjoying a few extra inches of space they hadn't had the night before.

Now men at the end of the list, having to wait a couple of months to leave, were trying to bargain to get their dates moved up. If they had cash or additional items of barter, anything was possible. Some begged, fearing they would not be alive in two more months. And as always, everything was for sale here in the prison, including swapping roll call numbers.

We watched on Sunday and Monday morning as two more groups of five hundred marched out through the north gate. We knew that we only had to endure one more night in the prison.

We walked around and said good bye to the men who remained. There was back slapping, handshakes and hugs, some from men I didn't even know. All were thankful that we had survived Andersonville Prison. And that at least we were going somewhere else.

I enjoyed the last night, wanting to remember the sounds and smells. I never shut my eyes even once. I prayed and prayed, hoping upon hope this move would be a good one. I hoped they were taking us to some rebel camp where we would be treated better than here at Andersonville Prison. Any other prison must be better than this one.

I prayed in thanksgiving for surviving and for being able to walk out of the north gate. And I hoped that Marcia still believed I was alive.

Chapter 20
Marching Out the North Gate

Tuesday, September 11, 1864

We were greeted by an amazing red sunrise at the beginning of our final day at the Andersonville Prison. We said goodbye to our friends. We went to say goodbye to Charles August of the Fifty-Fourth Massachusetts Volunteers but he had died last night. Now all four of our friends had been lost.

I met with Major Bogle and presented him with the lists of information I had gathered on the U.S. Colored Troops. He thanked me for my good work and wished us well. I had updated the records and copied them for him.

This is the complete list of the colored troops at Andersonville Prison.

> Major Archibald Bogle, Thirty-Fifth U.S. Colored Troops; E. Horst, Thirty-Fifth U.S. Colored Troops; William Moss, Thirty-Fifth U.S. Colored Troops; Warren Norfelt, Thirty-Fifth U.S. Colored Troops; D.H. Hill, Sixteenth U.S. Colored Troops; William Hopkins, Seventeenth U.S. Colored Troops; Mark Babcock, Thirty-First U.S. Colored Troops; and John Mackey, Forty-Fifth U.S. Colored Troops.
>
> Members of the Eighth U.S. Colored Troops at Andersonville include Charles Annon, Paul Blackman, George Brown, George Burton, Richard Chancellor, William Edwards, John Fisher, Joseph Ford, Lt. Colonel George French, Henry Gardner, Irving Hall, Henry Henson, Jacob Hollingsworth, William Jennings, William

Lewis, Harrison Lockwood, Daniel Phillips, George Potter, William Scott, Clement Shilton, James Smith, Stephen Thomas, John Thompson, James Walker, George Washington, Samuel Waters, Alexander Whittaker, Abraham Woodruff, and Molton Young.

Members of the Fifty-Fourth Massachusetts Volunteers present and accounted for at the prison were: James Allen, Solomon Anderson, Charles August, David Bailey, Joseph Baynard, Lemuel Blake, Jesse Brown, Morris Butler, James Caldwell, Jason Champlin, George Counsel, John Dickinson, Jefferson Ellis, Ralph Gardner, James Gooding, George Grant, Alfred Green, William Grover, Charles Hardy, William Harrison, Isaac Hawkins, Hill Harris, Cornelius Henson, William Hill, Nathaniel Hurley, Walter Jefferies, Edward Johnson, M. Johnston, Henry Kirk, John Leatherman, William Mitchell, George Morris, William Morris, George Moshroe, Joseph Proctor, George Prosser, A. Ratsall, Charles Rensellear, William Rigby, Robert Riley, Enos Smith, William Smith, Charles Stanton, Daniel States, George Thomas, William Vanalstyne, Frederick Wallace, Alfred Whiting, Charles Williams, James Williams, Samuel Wilson, Stewart Woods, and Henry Worthington.

The list, including our two white officers, totaled ninety soldiers.

I also prepared a second list for Major Bogle of those men we had already lost up to this point.

The list of the U.S. Colored Troops who died at Andersonville Prison as of September 11, 1864 is as follows:

Irving Hall	April 24, 1864
Clement Shilton	May 20, 1864

George Burton	May 21, 1864
Charles Rensellear	June 8, 1864
Henry Gardner	June 10, 1864
William Smith	June 22, 1864
Mark Babcock	July 1, 1864
Alexander Whittaker	July 2, 1864
George French	July 4, 1864
William Scott	July 4, 1864
James Gooding	July 19, 1864
William Hopkins	July 24, 1864
D. H. Hill	July 31, 1864
Jacob Hollingsworth	August 22, 1864
Daniel Phillips	August 24, 1964
William Edwards	August 24, 1864
Stephen Thomas	September 9, 1864
Charles August	September 10, 1864
William Vanalstyne	September 10, 1864

We grabbed our gear and prepared to march out. Those north gates today seemed like the gates to Paradise.

This time when roll was called, the north gate was opened. Our group of five hundred men marched slowly toward the waiting train. We marched two by two through long lines of armed rebel guards. We followed the same path we had marched down five long months ago.

I looked back over my shoulder one more time, realizing this was the last time I would ever see the prison at Anderson, Georgia.

I saw Allen standing guard. He flipped me a quick little salute so none of the other guards could see it. I did not miss it. I returned the salute quickly and then looked away.

I know he was happy that we were moving out, but sad to see a friend leave. My feelings were the same.

The train was waiting up ahead. We were crammed back into the box cars that had brought us here to Anderson Station. The car still smelled of urine, but this time I welcomed it. It was not as bad as the smells of the prison.

When we were all stuffed inside, the guards slammed the doors shut. Soon the train began to clank along the rails. We had not been told where we were going or how long it would take to get there. Most of the men dropped down and tried to sleep.

The men had much more space here than in the prison, even crammed tightly in the box car. And we knew, with each passing minute, we were getting farther and farther away from that awful prison.

Aaron offered to stand watch. I let him. I rested and fell asleep. I don't know how long I slept.

I was awakened suddenly by a horrible noise. Within seconds, before I knew what was happening, the box car started tumbling. It rolled over and over. Men banged against me. They screamed out as we crashed into the walls of the train in the dark. I had no time to try to figure out what was happening. I was being thrown around like a rag doll. I hit my head and my arms several times as I bounced around.

The noise was deafening. I tried to grab hold of something. It was difficult because I was blinded by the darkness. I got hit and clawed, kicked and bitten. I thrashed around, not knowing up from down or left from right.

I rolled around covering my head with my duffel, trying to keep from further injury. My head ached. The pain in my arm numbed my left hand. My shoulder was banged up too.

I could not imagine what was happening. Was I just having a bad dream?

The box car finally stopped. It lay on its side, with the sliding door at the top facing the sky. Part of the door had broken off. Sunlight lit the dark car.

Between the light and the dark it was hard to see. I searched for Aaron, Bill and Tom.

Screams came from men lying all around me as others scrambled to pick themselves up and find a way out. Some didn't move at all. They may have been knocked out or dead.

Other men on top of the train car were trying to slide the door open from the outside. Within a few minutes, they slid the door back all the way, allowing more light inside. They shouted for us to reach up so they could pull us out. Men climbed up on each other to reach for help. Some were lifted out through the opening.

I found Bill. He seemed to be dazed but not injured badly. I helped lift him up so that someone could pull him out. I told him to stay close and wait for us. I searched but I couldn't find Aaron or Tom.

A man reached up to be helped out, holding a long object, for others to grab. It was my crutch he was using.

In the rubble, men lay battered and torn, piled on top of each other. I called softly to Aaron and Tom, stepping carefully over others. Men screamed for help as some could not get up on their own. I helped a dozen or so by pulling them up so they could reach for the men outside and get out. With more men leaving the train car, it was easier to get around. Others lay quiet, either too hurt to move or perhaps even killed by the accident. I prayed Aaron and Tom were still alive.

A ladder was lowered into the box car and men from the top made their way down to help more men out. I finally found Tom's crumpled body lying in the corner. All I knew was that I had to get him outside. I pulled him up onto my shoulder and held him until someone from above reached down and took him out. I didn't know if he was even alive, as he was not moving. I searched for Aaron.

When I found Aaron, he was lying very quiet, not moving at all. I snatched him up and threw him over my shoulder. I called for help. The men pulled us both out of the boxcar.

I asked one of the men who helped us out to fetch me my crutch, as it wasn't needed any longer to pull men up and out.

Men on top helped us climb down to the ground. I looked around. I saw a wrecked train lying in the ditch. The train cars lay here and there, broken and twisted. Many cars had jumped the tracks.

Prisoners worked quickly to help those from the damaged cars. Suddenly it looked like the Union army was back in business, working together against a common enemy. It was something I had not seen in the prison.

I laid Aaron on the ground and looked around. Bill was nearby with Tom sitting beside him. Tom was awake now, but with a large bump on his head. His arm was hurt, but he seemed to be getting along all right.

Aaron moaned loudly and woke up. We sat and waited until Aaron and Tom recovered. I asked how hurt they were. They were both badly bruised. They said they were not too hurt to leave the area with us.

We had survived the train wreck, though some had not. We had no idea where we were. Aaron and I decided within minutes that we had to flee as quickly as we could, before the Confederates sounded the alarm. The prison had been in Georgia. We could not be sure we were still in Georgia. All we knew is we needed to go north.

Chapter 21
Our Army of Four Escapes

Men formed into small groups and started scattering in all directions. Our army of four moved out and let the others go on their own.

With one white man and three coloreds, we were likely to be noticed. That didn't stop us.

We agreed to the story that Aaron was a plantation owner and we had been his slaves. That seemed to be believable. Of course, with my hobbling along, the idea of walking all the way to Pennsylvania was frightening. It would take forever. Aaron thought we should steal a wagon and a horse to make travel easier.

I had another idea. I suggested that we should work and earn money to buy a wagon and a horse. We finally agreed that was a better solution. Shortly after that, we met a lady with a farm wagon that was broken down along the road.

We offered to help get her wagon fixed if she would give us a ride. We introduced ourselves using our real names, with Aaron telling her the slave owner story. She said her name was Toni Camp. She lived in Griffin, Georgia which she said was north, near Atlanta. That was the direction we needed to go.

Bill, Tom and I got to work fixing her wagon while Aaron talked to the lady. The work on her wagon was not major. We had it ready to go within a short time. Mrs. Camp was thankful that we fixed it for her.

She gave us a ride to her house, which was quite broken down. She said there was no one to do any work because all the men in town had joined the army. She was a widow. Her husband had died in the war. We asked to stay to help her fix up the place for as long as needed to earn enough money to buy a wagon and a horse. She agreed to sell us a horse and wagon for ten days of work. She provided meals and let us sleep in the barn as part of the deal.

I finally got to write a letter to Marcia that Mrs. Camp said she would mail for me.

Griffin, Georgia
September 12, 1864

Marcia dearest

I am coming home. I have been held in a prison in Georgia. I will tell you later about my awful five months there. I was not able to write because of that. But I have escaped. I know you have been worried that I have not written.

The four of us who are now together must be careful not to be recaptured and sent back to prison. We are at risk each day. We will work here in Georgia long enough to earn money to buy a horse and wagon so I don't have to limp all the way back to Pennsylvania.

We will move slowly north so we don't cause any alarm. Aaron tells people he is a slave owner and we are his slaves. So far that story has held up.

Be strong, my dear. Each step I take now is one step closer to holding you in a lifelong embrace. This time I will not let go until all the breath has gone out of my lungs. I told you before I would come home. I will keep that promise. I will write again as I get closer to Cashtown.

Your loving husband,
Catesby

By the end of the first week, we decided to be honest with Mrs. Camp. We told her we had been Union prisoners held in Andersonville Prison who escaped when the prison train had wrecked.

She said she was tired of the war and all the hate. She had no bad feelings toward the North. In fact, she had friends who lived near Washington City. The war had cut her off from them. Mrs. Camp regarded slavery as evil, sinful and degrading. This southern lady wanted to know what happened to "all men are created equal?" I told her I had that same question.

I liked Mrs. Camp. She spoke with an interesting accent she brought here from her home in New Zealand. She hated war. "Let's just all go on home and start over," she suggested. "Maybe the second time around we can get it right." I thought that was a grand idea.

By the time we had worked hard for ten straight days, we had Mrs. Camp's place looking much better. She was pleased with our work. Mrs. Camp gave us some extra money in addition to the wagon and horse. She provided us with civilian clothes to replace our tattered Union uniforms. I shaved and bathed for the first time in almost a year.

We parted as friends, trading addresses, and promised to stay in touch.

Chapter 22
The Slow Journey Home

October 5, 1864

We traveled roads northward in the general direction of Virginia.

The war had not been kind to the area we passed through at all. Many buildings had been torched. Others looked abandoned. Where crops would have normally stood, the fields were barren. Where animals would normally be seen grazing in the fields, some lay dead and rotting in the grass.

Broken wagons lay wasted along the roads. Canteens, caps, rifles, swords, bedrolls and even shoes lay abandoned in the ditches. We rooted through the clothing and took anything that fit.

Bridges had been destroyed, so it was difficult to cross the streams.

When our wagon went by, youngans ran out to the road to see if we were anyone they knew. And then they ran off disappointed that we were not.

We pushed hard, taking turns driving the wagon and sleeping, and not stopping except to buy food along the way and to rest the old horse. Every few days we hired out to a nearby farm to earn a meal or two or to get some additional money for our long trip.

Near Roanoke, Virginia, a farmer named Kevin Martin offered us food and a room for three nights, in return for helping him repair his barn. He gave us another horse to spell the one Mrs. Camp had given us. Mr. Martin said he too was tired of the war.

I paused again to write and send a letter to my wife.

Roanoke, Virginia
October 5, 1864

Dear Marcia

We have arrived in Virginia at Roanoke and are working for money to purchase food for our trip home.

Our story of Aaron traveling with his slaves continues to protect us from danger so far. Everyone we have met is ready for the war to be over and for the killing to stop.

Aaron, Bill and Tom will leave me shortly to continue to their homes in Illinois and Ohio. They plan to ride the Baltimore and Ohio Railroad westward from Martinsburg, Virginia to start them on their way home. I will have the horses and wagon to use to travel the rest of the way.

I will make it home as fast as I can. I promise.

Word is the war will not last much longer. The rebel troops are out-numbered. They have little food to feed their army. General Sherman's forces have destroyed a wide path to Atlanta and beyond.

My journey seems terribly long and hard. My spirits are good as I am getting closer to you. Our time apart will be short. I should be home around the first week of November.

Be strong, Marcia. I will be there soon.

Your loving husband,
Catesby

October 30, 1864

We finally pushed into the North again crossing from Winchester to Martinsburg, West Virginia, a new state formed by President Lincoln during the war. I was surprised to hear that West Virginia is a northern state putting Shepherdstown, Charlestown and Harpers Ferry now in the North.

A man at the Baltimore & Ohio Railroad depot in Martinsburg said people here were mostly for the South.

They were not happy they were now living in the North. They didn't favor President Lincoln.

I guess the line in Shepherdstown at the Potomac River dividing the North and the South has now moved somewhere else.

Aaron, Tom and Bill prepared to take the train from Martinsburg to Wheeling, and then further west on various railroads before getting to their homes.

There wasn't a dry eye as they boarded the train. They assured me I had saved their lives and helped them resolve to live through their time at Andersonville Prison. I told them we were an army of four. We all helped each other. It was sad to see them go. We all wrote out our addresses so we could stay in touch.

I wrote what I hoped was my last letter before arriving home in Cashtown.

Martinsburg, West Virginia
October 30, 1864

My dear Marcia

I am even closer now to being home. I was surprised at arriving in Martinsburg that this part of western Virginia including Charlestown, Harpers Ferry and Shepherdstown, are now in the new state of West Virginia formed by President Lincoln. This area is now part of the North.

Aaron, Bill and Tom have boarded the Baltimore & Ohio Railroad train to travel to their homes. It was difficult to say goodbye to the three man I have spent every minute with for the last six months. Now I am ready to travel on my own over roads I am familiar with on my way to Cashtown.

I think I will be home in just a few days, perhaps even before this letter reaches you. I will not stop at Beall Air as there is no one left there I want to see. I think my mother will understand.

I am most anxious to be with my wonderful wife again. I am weary, sore, tired, and weak. You may not recognize me when I arrive.

But inside I am strong. I am also very thankful to have made it this far. I have survived, like I knew I would. I will be the happiest man on the earth when I see you once again.

Soon, my love, I will be holding you in my tired, worn and scarred arms.

Your loving husband,
Catesby

I passed Beall Air. I had no reason to stop anymore. I kept going toward the bridge at Harpers Ferry. I was not surprised that Harpers Ferry was in shambles, as I had read about the Confederates destroying the arsenal buildings. But I was surprised that the building where we had been held prisoner by John Brown was still standing. I passed across the river at Harpers Ferry and then on to Frederick, Maryland. I will go north to Gettysburg, and then west to Cashtown.

Chapter 23
Home at Last

November 1, 1864

As I approached home, I wondered to myself how life would be now. Will being at Andersonville Prison harden me to my regular life? Will I have to try to return to my regiment, the Fifty-Fourth Massachusetts Volunteers? Will my wife recognize me with all the weight I have lost? Will she be happy that I am home? Will I be able to pick up where I left off?

I pulled the wagon into the lane after midnight, slowly passing the Willow Grove Hotel. I moved toward the barn.

There before me was a sight I was not sure I would ever be seeing again -- my house and my blacksmith shop. Not one light appeared in any of my windows.

I slowly got off the wagon, completing my long, hard journey. I was finally home at long last. I unhitched the weary but reliable old horses and put them in the stall. I got a bucket and gave them enough water and feed to hold them until morning. I was thankful that with God's help, the old horses had delivered me home.

The wagon could wait until morning. I limped slowly toward the house, tears of joy running down my face. I walked up the step and onto the porch as a light suddenly appeared in the window. The door opened before I could reach out for the latch.

A beautiful young lady held a shotgun pointed directly at me. "That better be you, Catesby, or I'm going to shoot."

"Yes, my darling, Marcia. It is Catesby. Honey, I am home." I collapsed into her arms. I cried and cried. I clung to her. I didn't want to ever let go.

She surrounded me with her arms. If I had died right that moment, I would have died the happiest man ever. But I was given a second chance and survived.

"Marcia, I was so afraid you would give up on me because I could not write to you. I have been in prison. They did not allow us to send letters."

"Catesby, I felt all along that you were alive. I thought it odd you did not write but I never believed you had been killed. I would have known inside the minute your heart stopped beating. You were alive in me, Catesby, every single minute that you were gone. Let me look at you. You look frightful. I am guessing that prison life did not agree with this free man. But when you rest up, I still want to have that dance you promised me."

I laughed, knowing this lady did believe in me so much that she refused to think I would die or not return.

I stumbled into bed and slept.

November 2, 1864

When I awoke, Marcia wanted to hear everything. It was easier to let her read my papers, letters and journal first. She was real quiet, except when she stopped to cry. The more she read, the more she cried. I waited as it took her hours and hours to read them.

While she read, I just watched her, trying to believe I was really home. She hadn't changed. She was as pretty as ever. Just being beside her was a wonderful gift I was enjoying.

"Oh, Catesby. How awful that must have been. And all those poor soldiers who left by the south gate."

I agreed. But I also knew that the ones who had died were now free from the awful hell-hole of Andersonville Prison too.

Marcia looked at me, wanting to be assured I was finally home.

"Catesby. I want you to tell me everything that happened," she insisted. And then she added very gently, "but not until you are ready to."

I appreciated that.

I visited the Quinns today. They greeted me like a long lost son. We talked and talked. They too were thankful I had survived, as many people they knew had received letters from the fields that their sons, brothers, fathers and husbands died in the war.

Mr. Quinn said he heard rumors that President Lincoln would probably not be re-elected. Even so, Mr. Quinn was certain President Lincoln was the best man to patch up the country when the war was over. General McClellan was running against President Lincoln. Mr. Quinn said in the last thirty years no president had won a second term.

The Quinns presented me with a welcome home gift, a journal with lots of empty pages. I was thankful and anxious to start writing on the pages.

Neither Marcia nor anyone else could ever understand what I had gone through at Andersonville Prison. I spared them the details. They knew it was painful for me to talk about. What they didn't know was that it was so awful I would not even have wished that place on Mr. Newberry.

November 4, 1864

I wanted to get back to my job at the blacksmith shop, starting slowly with short days until I got stronger. Brian had done a good job while I was gone. But he was glad to see me. He thought he still had a lot to learn.

Brian had dozens of questions waiting when I was ready to start again. He still wanted to be a real blacksmith. He needed his teacher to help him do that.

Mr. Quinn said Brian was doing well, but would never be "the best blacksmith in the Commonwealth of Pennsylvania," a title he had given me.

I wrote to Dr. Delany to ask him if I needed to try to find the Fifty-Fourth Massachusetts Volunteers and re-enlist. I thanked him for his support with my enlistment. I told him of my imprisonment at Anderson, Georgia. I gave him the address of my friend, Aaron Putnam. I asked him to give Aaron some advice since he was studying to be a doctor.

Chapter 24
President Lincoln is Re-elected

November 9, 1864

Mr. Quinn and I were excited about today's announcement. President Lincoln had been re-elected. Now he had another chance to end the war and start bringing this divided nation back together. Mr. Quinn was re-elected too.

Mrs. Quinn said that evening at supper she would have liked to have voted for her husband and President Lincoln in this election. She asked "When do you think women will be able to vote?" Mr. Quinn looked at her, but did not reply.

I joined her by saying, "I would have gladly voted for you and for President Lincoln, if I had the right to vote. When do you think colored men will be allowed to vote?"

Again, Mr. Quinn was silent. Mrs. Quinn winked at me and joked, "So, Mr. Re-elected Representative. You seem to be speechless for the first time in your life."

And he was speechless and red faced.

December 4, 1864

I got a package and a letter from Dr. Delany today. He told me my enlistment was over. He said I should stay at home with my wonderful wife. I was relieved. He thanked me for serving, saying he was quite proud of me and my contribution to the Union army. He was sorry for the time I spent as a prisoner of war. And that he would be happy to contact my friend Aaron and encourage him. He wished us well. In the package was a new Union uniform.

Marcia and I became good friends again. As expected, it took some time for us. I found I was more in love with her than before. Marcia told me over and over how important my few letters had been for her to keep the faith. She said Mr.

and Mrs. Quinn had provided her love and support while I was gone.

Maria listened to my stories as if I were the most important reporter on the war in the world. She wanted me to tell most of the terrible trip on the ship to Florida, the Fifty-Fourth Massachusetts Volunteers, and my days on the blacksmith wagon prior to our capture. She had left the Andersonville Prison part to be forgotten. I wish it were that easy.

I thought it might take me years and years of Marcia's love and tenderness to push the awful nightmares of the prison out of my head. Even when I started to feel better and got stronger, the memories haunted me whenever I closed my eyes.

At home I enjoyed the food and clean water very slowly and in a way no one could have understood who hadn't been in the prison camp. I was thankful for the roof over my head, and for a real bed. Just to have room to stretch out seemed a gift to me.

I didn't realize how much my looks had changed while I was gone. Marcia, Brian and the Quinns had said nothing about it. But when I went into town or when someone came into the shop, they would greet me by saying, "Catesby. Is that you?"

I continued to be blessed and thanked God every day. I was home, alive and had survived the awful war.

December 5, 1864

Mr. Quinn and I spent hours discussing the war and my travels. He was an important politician. He wanted first-hand information to help him make better decisions. I became an important aide to him.

Everyone wanted to know my thoughts about the war. I only had one. It was way past time for the fighting to stop.

There wasn't anything I could do about it except talk to anyone who asked me.

Very few men alive lived through Harpers Ferry in 1859, Antietam Creek in 1862, Gettysburg in 1863, Olustee and Andersonville Prison in 1864.

I knew about as much about the bloody war as anyone. Whatever caused the war originally had long been forgotten. No soldier I talked to had any idea. I wondered if the blue and gray generals knew.

I continued to read all I could in the newspapers about the battles. More and more soldiers were dying. And the newspaper reporters weren't writing at all about the thousands who were dying in the prisons.

I wondered often where the Union prisoners that transferred from Anderson, Georgia had been taken. We had escaped because of the train wreck. I think the others will just have to wait until the end of the war to make it back home.

I thought about President Lincoln and his colored troops. I hoped they were making him proud.

December 12, 1864

Mr. Quinn and I talked today about the war again. His interest was greater than it had been at the time of my enlistment. He wanted to know what the real war was like. He called me his "inside source" because I had been there.

He said "Tell me what it was like, Catesby. Tell me what you saw and what you were thinking about." And so I did.

There was nothing I told him that was pretty or sugar-coated. Like the people who had watched the battle at Bull Run said, this war definitely was not a picnic in the park.

December 20, 1864

Marcia and I talked about starting a family, knowing it might be best to wait until the war was over. As much as I agreed we should wait, I had the desire to become a father.

Marcia said I would get the honor of naming our children, as I had been cheated out of having a full name

265

when I was born. I thought that was a grand idea. I was thankful she was giving that important duty to me.

What I hadn't told her was I already knew what my children's names would be. I would name them after Aaron Putnam, my friend at Andersonville Prison, my mother, Colonel Lewis Washington and the Quinns. Those were all the important people in my life besides Marcia.

My son will be named Aaron Washington Quinn Catesby. If we have a daughter, we will call her Willa Washington Quinn Catesby. Even though I only had one name, they would each have four.

Bonnie, Marcia's sister, began to visit us regularly. I think she was starting to like me a little, though she will never admit it. She had helped Marcia while I was gone.

December 25, 1864

When Christmas came around, I made everyone gifts from the shop. For Brian I built a sign, like Billy had made for me. It said, "Brian -- Blacksmith." He loved it.

I forged a fancy bell for the tavern door for Mr. Quinn and a metal trellis for Mrs. Quinn's garden.

For Marcia, I made a large kettle for the fireplace.

Marcia presented me with a fine box for my journal. I was amazed because it was identical to the one she had hidden for me at Beall Air. Mr. and Mrs. Quinn gave me a framed certificate from the Massachusetts's legislature, thanking me for my serving in the Fifty-Fourth Massachusetts Volunteers. I will cherish that. They gave Marcia a beautiful broach.

I gave Bonnie a doll I purchased in Gettysburg. I made a set of chess pieces for the Quinn children to go with the checker board I had given them before.

December 27, 1864

For the holidays, Mr. and Mrs. Quinn took Marcia and me to a dance in York. Since we both enjoyed our first dance so much, we kidded each other about going to another dance. We were thrilled to accept their offer.

I have to admit, it was more fun than our first dance. Perhaps that was because I wasn't so nervous being with Marcia this time. I still was with the prettiest lady at the dance. And Mrs. Quinn dragged me onto the dance floor again, as she promised she would.

Catesby had the dancing part figured out a little better this time around too. I wasn't embarrassed that my injured leg wasn't up to what you might call traditional dancing. I leaned on my crutch and just kind of wiggled back and forth to the music. My way of dancing, at least for Marcia and Mrs. Quinn, was plenty good enough.

We laughed and talked. We ate and drank and danced some more. A good time was had by all four of us.

And after the dance Marcia and I returned to our home. There was no surprise goodbye kiss, like after the first dance. That's not to say there was no kissing, if you know what I mean.

January 2, 1865

My exhaustion from prison took my strength away and slowed me down some. Fortunately Brian was carrying more and more of the load.

Mr. Quinn suggested I give Brian a raise, and I did. Brian was very thankful. He asked when I thought he might be able to be a real blacksmith. I told him honestly that I didn't think he would have to wait much longer. He was doing really well here.

I noticed when I returned home that Brian's hands were becoming hardened and his arms were burned. As Billy said, he was earning the badge of being a blacksmith.

There was nothing Brian wouldn't do for me, Marcia or Mr. and Mrs. Quinn. The Quinn children loved him too. I have seen him many times giving rides on his shoulders to Kelli and Bonnie. Brian became another of my growing list of white friends. He reminded me a lot of my prison friend, Aaron. Both were honest and loyal. Both were blind to my color.

I was excited to have received a letter from Aaron saying that he was attending medical school at Ohio University in Athens. He said Dr. Delany had sent him a letter of encouragement.

Marcia asked me about the journal I had left behind at Beall Air. She had not gotten to read it. I tried to tell her the parts that I remembered. She knew how valuable my journals were to me. She cherished the letters I had sent her and saved them too. She knew to save them if anything ever happened to me.

January 7, 1865

I thought of Colonel Washington, Sam, Mason and Billy on occasion. I wondered what Colonel Washington was doing in France. Had Sam and Mason become free blacks? Where in New York had Billy set up his blacksmith shop? I wanted to search for them but I had no idea where to look.

I thought of Robert, Thom, and Mrs. Newberry too. And believe it or not, I even wondered about old Mr. Newberry. I no longer wanted to cause Mr. Newberry's slow and painful injury or death. I had forgiven his horrible actions somewhere along the way. Mother would have been proud of that. I think the system of slavery was more at fault for making owners of slaves behave like that.

I was hopeful slavery would end as soon as the war was over. I was sure President Lincoln would insist on that. And then we could have that "all men are created equal" kind of country he had hoped for.

No matter what day it was, there was a good chance I would start thinking about my mother too. I wish I could bring her back for just one day so that Mr. and Mrs. Quinn and Marcia could meet her and she could meet them. I know she has been watching over me in Heaven — probably bargaining for God to save me from that awful prison and from the train wreck. I know she was proud of me too. And I thought of General Robert E. Lee. I wondered how he was doing in this horrible war.

Chapter 25

Mrs. Ritner Visits Cashtown

February 2, 1865

Mrs. Ritner was a surprise guest at the hotel tonight. Mr. Quinn sent word over to my shop that she was here. Marcia and I joined her for supper. I hugged her because I was so happy to see her. I introduced her to Marcia.

Mr. Quinn bragged to her about my work as a real blacksmith. Mrs. Ritner was pleased everything was working out so well.

Her work with the Underground Railroad was continuing. She said there was still a need to help coloreds escape their bondage. She said after the war was over everyone needed to help the freed slaves go to school. Mr. Quinn said he would talk to me about that.

I told her how thankful I was that she had put me with such a fine family. I said someday I wanted to pay her back.

"That is not necessary, Catesby," she said. "The way you pay those kinds of debts is to reach out and help the next person who needs you. That's what the Bible verse means that says, 'Whatever you shall do for the least of my brothers, this you do unto me.'"

I nodded. I understood. My mother had read that verse to me many times. Now it made more sense. I was ready to help others.

February 13, 1865

Mr. Quinn took me to Harrisburg today to tour his office and the capitol. I was very impressed. Harrisburg is a very large town.

Mr. Quinn said he would soon be looking for an assistant because Mrs. Fedeli was leaving to go to another business. Mr. Quinn thought Mrs. Fedeli would be difficult to replace because she was such a hard worker and a trusted employee. A legislator always had a small staff, he said, so he needed to surround himself with good people.

He and Mrs. Quinn entertained often. They attended important social functions throughout his district. Often Marcia and I stayed and played with their children until they returned home. The Quinn children treated Marcia as a big sister. She was better at guarding them than I had been guarding the prisoners at Harpers Ferry.

February 23, 1865

Marcia wanted me to tell others about what had happened to me during the war. "Many of the people with information from the war will never return home to tell about it. You were an eyewitness. Perhaps you should write a book, Catesby," she suggested.

I laughed, not imagining that a free colored man could write a book interesting enough for anyone to read. And then I thought back to what Dr. Delany had said. "There is nothing you cannot do, Catesby. Nothing at all. You just have to believe in yourself."

And I said with a wink, "Maybe that's why my mother started me writing in my journal."

Marcia was right. Most witnesses took their stories of the war to their graves. I had been spared, for some reason. Was it like Marcia said -- so I could tell my story?

I wondered after Andersonville Prison if I would return hardened from my time there, different from the Catesby I had been, and unable to pick up where I left off.

Now I knew. I was still Catesby. But I was different too. Marcia said I was sadder than when I left. Mr. Quinn said I seemed a lot older than I was when I left. Mrs. Quinn thought I was a bit more serious. Brian said I got distracted easier from the tasks I was working on.

How could anyone who had driven the battle grounds at Antietam Creek, watched the passage of the wagon train of

Confederate wounded at Millerstown and Cashtown, felt the affects of the battle of Olustee and then had been held at Andersonville Prison, not be haunted by the evil ghosts of the war?

Of course, my nightmares of seeing the war had not gone away. In fact, they were there every time I closed my eyes. I could see the bodies and arms and legs piled high at Antietam Creek. I could see the dead soldiers waiting to be taken out the south gate.

I could hear the wailing of the rebel men on the wagons moving south after Gettysburg. I would smell the filth of the stockade. I could see John Brown and the other men with bags covering their faces, hanging by their necks. I wondered if they would haunt me forever.

The sights, sounds and smells were almost as real in my nightmares as they had been the first time around. I wanted to tell Marcia that I would soon be over all that. I feared that would have been a lie.

Anyone with a heart that is still beating after the war will continue to admire those who had died, regardless if they were wearing blue or gray.

I think even the rebel guards from Andersonville Prison will have haunted dreams of that awful place.

March 7, 1865

I read today that President Lincoln was sworn in to start his second term. In his speech, the newspaper reported, he said we need to not show any malice toward anyone in the South and have charity for everyone. I thought all of the people I had talked to were ready to do that.

March 8, 1865

Mr. Quinn read in the newspaper today that Doctor Delany, the man who enlisted me in the colored troops, had been named the first colored staff officer in the United States Army. I was so proud. Major Martin R. Delany. The newspaper reported that President Lincoln said Major

Delany was "a remarkable and intelligent colored man." I agreed with that.

March 10, 1865

Mr. Quinn's hotel was a place I could sit at night just to listen to the tall tales of the war. It was like a parade of liars, one trying to top the next. The more the men drank, the more amazing their stories became. I knew most had never even been close to a battle. They made out that the soldiers from the North were braver than those from the South. I knew that wasn't true. There were very brave men on both sides.

Their descriptions were empty, and more like newspaper accounts, which was probably their source of information. It reminded me of listening to similar stories in New York as I waited to board the ship to go Florida to join the Fifty-Fourth Massachusetts Volunteers.

If I hadn't witnessed the war myself, I might have believed them. If they hadn't been talking so poorly about so many brave men who were now lying in their graves, their stories would have been funny. Instead, their tales were very sad.

I wanted to stand up and scream, "You do not know. You were not there. You cannot understand. Stay silent in respect for those who gave their lives to protect your freedoms." But I bit my tongue and listened as they talked on. What I thought was better left unsaid for now.

April 11, 1865

There were fireworks all day today and into the night. It was quite a celebration. We had received word that the war had ended. Mr. Quinn said the Confederate Army and General Robert E. Lee had surrendered to General Grant on April 9 at a place in Virginia called Appomattox Courthouse.

I had never heard of Appomattox Courthouse before, but was thankful for the end to that long and dreadful war. I bowed my head and thanked God it was finished. I was sure President Lincoln was happy to finally put that behind him. I know from the newspaper accounts how much the war had troubled our president.

I didn't realize the war had dragged on four whole years. And to think, many had predicted it would be a short war. Four years seemed mighty long to me for a war to go on.

Mr. Quinn said the North needed to make an effort to mend the break in the Union. He said President Lincoln was calling all the northern states to help with reconstruction and for all the southern states that left the Union to return.

Chapter 26
Invitation to Visit Washington City

April 12, 1865

Mr. Quinn invited Marcia and me to go to Washington City with him and Mrs. Quinn. He was to meet with President Lincoln on Friday afternoon. Mr. Quinn, as the representative from Pennsylvania on a national committee, was to help discuss reconstruction plans to bring the nation back together. That same evening Mr. and Mrs. Quinn were going to take us to the theater.

As we prepared for the trip, a messenger came from Cashtown with a telegram addressed to both Mr. Quinn and myself. I was shocked but pleased in reading it. It was from Major Martin Delany. It read as follows:

Wilberforce, Ohio
April 12, 1865

Mr. Quinn and Catesby

President Lincoln has asked me to appoint a committee to travel to Anderson, Georgia as his representatives to help close the prison there. I would like you both to travel by train to Georgia with the other committee members on April 15 from Washington City, if possible, to help with that task. I want Catesby there because he will be the only one of the committee who has been there and understands what happened at the prison.

There will be others on the committee, but I would like Representative Quinn to be the chairman with Catesby as his assistant.

Please let me know by return telegram if you are willing to take this assignment.

Very truly yours,
Major Martin R. Delany

Mr. Quinn and I discussed the matter with Marcia and Mrs. Quinn. We decided it was an excellent idea and another way to help President Lincoln.

We sent a telegram back to Major Delany that we were pleased to be asked. We would be delighted to serve.

Mr. Quinn said we could ride the train to Washington City with Mrs. Quinn and Marcia. And then he and I would travel on to Georgia from Washington City with our wives returning to Pennsylvania together.

April 13, 1865

This morning, Brian took us to the train depot. We rode the train to Baltimore and on to Washington City with the Quinns. Talk about an adventure. We certainly enjoyed the trip. Marcia had not been out of the area so she was looking all around and watching the scenery pass us by. She would point at a deer on one side of the railroad tracks and then quickly try to get my attention to see something else on the other side of the tracks. I have to say riding on the train seat instead of in a dark, smelly box car was very pleasant for me.

We stayed in the famous Willard Hotel in Washington City, rooming right next door to the Quinns in a real hotel room. I had told everyone I had brought Colonel Washington to the Willard Hotel when he testified before the Senate Committee five years ago. But that time I had to sleep at the livery with his horse.

The Willard was the fanciest hotel in Washington City. The furniture was almost too pretty to sit on. Marcia walked around touching and smelling everything like it wasn't real. I wondered if this is how my mother felt taking care of the

Beall Air mansion for Colonel Washington. The hotel was by far the fanciest place Marcia and I had ever visited.

April 14, 1865

Mr. Quinn surprised us at breakfast this morning by saying that we too were invited to the White House to meet President Lincoln at a reception. I could not have been more excited. A chance to meet President Lincoln was a long-time dream. I had gotten close before, but not this close.

I had brought my new Union uniform from the Fifty-Fourth Massachusetts Volunteers to wear to the theater, to show that I was part of the president's Union army. Marcia and Mrs. Quinn both said I looked very handsome in it.

We rode by buggy to the White House. I was as nervous as I had been on my wedding day.

We were shown into the White House where the President and Mrs. Lincoln lived. We were taken into a large room filled with many people. There was a band playing spirited songs and a long line of people making their way up to talk to the president. As I looked around I noticed Marcia and I were the only coloreds not working as servants in the room.

Mr. Quinn led us to the end of the line. He introduced us to the official White House greeter, telling him we were first-time visitors here. The greeter told us, "You will be shaking hands all along this line with people you don't know. Just shake all their hands, smile and be polite."

As we approached the president, I heard Mr. Quinn say, "This is Catesby, and Mrs. Catesby, Mr. President." With that Mr. Lincoln held out his hand to greet Marcia. He took her hand and lifted it up to kiss. And then he reached out to me and shook my hand.

"Major Martin Delany wrote me about you and your enlistment to thank me for freeing the slaves, Mr. Catesby. I appreciate your contribution to the Union Army. Mr. Quinn tells me you unfortunately spent time as a prisoner in Andersonville Prison. I am sorry you had to endure that. I am pleased that you and Mr. Quinn have agreed to go to the prison to help us close it down. Thank you."

I was quite surprised the president had heard of me from my friend Dr. Delany. Of all the four million colored slaves, he had heard of me, Catesby, a Union blacksmith. It didn't seem possible.

Marcia squeezed my hand as I responded. "Thank you, Mr. President, for all you have done for my people. You will never know how much it means to us to finally be free. I know that what you said was true, that all men are created equal. It is a pleasure to be able to serve in your army."

Later Marcia looked me in the eye and asked, "Catesby. You always spoke so highly of President Lincoln. Did you know he also knew about you?"

"No, my dear. I had no idea."

"That lady over there is the President's wife," Mr. Quinn said, pointing to a short, plump lady standing with some men by the fireplace. And then Mrs. Quinn teased me saying, "Catesby. I didn't know you were so famous."

Mr. Quinn said it was time to leave. We rode a buggy to the Ford's Theater. It was close by. We were there in just a few minutes.

The play we were to see was called "Our American Cousin" starring the famous actress Laura Keene. Never having been to the theater, neither Marcia nor I had any idea what was going to happen. For me, meeting the president was the highlight of the day and perhaps my life.

The theater was crowded with persons dressed in very fancy clothes. Many Union soldiers were there and nodded at me. I was happy I had been able to wear my new uniform.

It was exciting to see the scenery and to try to figure out what was happening in the show. I know it was causing people to laugh a lot.

At one point along the way, all the people on the stage stopped and the play was held up so President Lincoln and his wife could be seated in the box above the stage over to our right. I got a good look at the president. He bowed to the audience. The audience stood and clapped wildly. The orchestra played a lively tune Mr. Quinn said was especially for the president called "Hail to the Chief."

The box where the president sat was draped with red, white and blue decorations and had a large painting of George Washington on the front.

I had seen his portrait at Colonel Washington's mansion house. Mrs. Quinn whispered and told us that the president was sitting in the official presidential box.

Marcia and I enjoyed the play. People talked during the breaks about how happy they all were that the awful war was now over.

After the second break, the play had barely gotten started up when I heard a loud noise. And then a man leaped from the presidential box down onto the stage. He yelled something and then ran off. The actors and actresses stopped the play, and watched. We were all quite surprised by the event.

The theater became very noisy. People were running around saying President Lincoln had been shot. I looked up to where the president had been sitting, but people had my view blocked. I couldn't see anything.

"My God," I thought. "Who would want to shoot the president? The war is over. He said we should reach out and help patch up the Union. It made no sense to think he had been shot."

Mr. Quinn told us to wait as he had business to attend to. He would be back shortly.

Within minutes, police were in every aisle, with drawn guns. Mrs. Quinn told us to duck down under our seats, so we would not be shot.

When Mr. Quinn returned he informed us that the president was critically injured. He had arranged for a detachment of five soldiers led by Colonel Obadiah Downing of the New York Cavalry to carry the president across the street where he would be treated by a doctor.

Mr. Quinn told us the president had been shot in the head at close range, had lost massive amounts of blood, and would most likely not survive.

I told Mr. Quinn I was quite sure I had seen the man who had jumped on stage before. I remembered Colonel Washington point him out to me at the hanging of John Brown. Colonel Washington said his name was J. B. Wilkes.

We returned to the Willard Hotel, all exhausted and worried about President Lincoln. I didn't sleep at all. In the morning we would be leaving to go to Andersonville Prison.

Ford's Theater – Assassination of Lincoln
Drawing from Harpers Weekly   April 29, 1865

Chapter 27
Returning to Andersonville Prison

On our way to Anderson, Georgia
April 16, 1865

Dearest Marcia

Mr. Quinn and I are expected to be in Anderson, Georgia by tomorrow afternoon. Mr. Quinn was given a package full of information for the committee when we arrived at the train depot. He has been going over the materials with me. We have had several meetings with the committee already here on the train.

Everyone is quite troubled by the death of our president. We are also determined to continue to serve him on this important committee.

It is amazing to me that you and I met President Lincoln just a short time before he died.

I am told to expect between 500 and 1000 Union soldiers at Andersonville Prison. That is certainly a far cry from the more than 30,000 soldiers who had been there in August before they sent men to other prisons.

Our committee's plan is to move those remaining Union prisoners by train to Vicksburg on the Mississippi River. There we will meet other prisoners from many other stockades in the South. All the men will be carried to Cairo, Illinois on board several large ships. There the committee will provide help for the men to return to their homes.

I am wondering if I will recognize anyone who is still there. I hope my friend Allen, the rebel guard, is still at the prison so we can talk. I wonder if Major Bogle or any of the U.S. Colored Troops will still be there.

I have really mixed thoughts about returning to the prison. It is a place that brings horrible nightmares to me. I remember thinking when I left it would be my last time there. Now I am returning because I know I will be helping Major Delany and President Lincoln. ˋ

Mr. Quinn said Major Delany was right in sending me, since I know Andersonville Prison better than any man on the committee.

This morning Mr. Quinn told me one of his best kept secrets. Remember the slave catcher I told you about who had come looking for me after I got to Cashtown? The man sent by Mr. Newberry didn't leave because I had papers from Mrs. Ritner or because Mr. Quinn had important connections as he had told me. The man left because Mr. Quinn paid him $2000. Mr. Quinn legally owns me.

All this time I have been owned by Mr. Quinn. He chose for me to be free instead. He said my freedom was his gift to me. He suggested when we return home I should remind him to give me that contract so that we can keep it to show to our children.

I was happy that he told me but I cried too. It was an amazing thing this white man, my friend, Mr. Quinn, had done for me. Every day since I have come to Cashtown, Mr. Quinn has helped me like he would have helped his own son.

When I get home we need to pay him back the $2000. I know he won't want it, but it is due to him. Even if it takes me years, I am determined to pay him back. Each month we must set aside a portion of our money to that end. I will repay him every penny of that $2000 if it is the last thing I do.

I miss being with you already, Marcia, but now that the war is over, you do not need to worry about me. I will not be in any danger of being shot or captured.

Your loving husband,
Catesby

P.S. I must have left my journal in your bag as I don't seem to have it with me. Please keep my letters so that I can add them to the journal when I get back home.

Anderson, Georgia
April 17, 1865

My dearest Marcia

We arrived today at Anderson, Georgia. I am happy to be here. I know this time I do not have to stay.

From the time we left the Anderson Station depot walking to the prison through the north gate, it was like I was getting a second chance. I wish Allen could see me finishing a job he would have liked to have done himself, closing this evil place once and for all. But he is not here.

Major Bogle has been released along with all of the U.S. Colored Troops who survived Andersonville Prison. I'm told of the 90 colored troops I had recorded, sixty survived. That is a remarkable number. I am proud so many of my brothers made it out too.

Members of the following units are still here at Andersonville Prison:

> Twelfth Ohio Volunteer Infantry, Seventy-Second Ohio Volunteer Infantry, Fifty-First Ohio, Thirty-Fifth Indiana, Ninety-Fifth Ohio Volunteer Infantry, Ninety-Third Indiana, Fifth Michigan, One Hundredth Ohio Volunteer Infantry, Forty-Fifth Ohio Volunteers, Seventeenth Michigan, One Hundred Fourth Ohio, Twenty-Ninth Indiana, Eighty-Ninth Ohio Volunteer Infantry, Sixth West Virginia Cavalry, First West Virginia Infantry, Fifth West Virginia Infantry, Ninth West Virginia Infantry and a few others.

There are no guards on the platforms. The gates are wide open. There is plenty of space for the few remaining prisoners who are still here. The spirits of the prisoners are high. They cheered our arrival.

Most of the six hundred Union prisoners left are in such poor condition that they cannot leave under their own power. The committee is arranging for wagons to carry them to the train.

I did recognize several men who are still here. They were quite surprised to see me. They told me that with five hundred men a day being transferred out, those left tried to hang on.

Many of these men were very disappointed when their date of transfer arrived, because they were too weak or too sick to leave. These men had waited from last September until now. Many others died waiting.

Father Whalen is still here, which doesn't surprise me any. He will be happy to get home, but only when his work is done. I thanked him on behalf of all the prisoners. I told him he was truly a blessing during the awful days the prison operated.

He walked with me to the cemetery I had heard so much about but had never seen. I prayed silently over the rows and rows and rows of graves, each one representing a brave Union soldier who will never be going home. Some graves were marked with names. Many had no names.

Father Whalen was sorry for the awful conditions of the prison. He said he had spoken to every official Richmond had sent here to check on the conditions, but no one had done anything to help improve the situation.

I told him Allen, the guard, said that Commandant Wirz and other officials had tried to get more rations and medical help but no one in Richmond listened to their ideas.

I accepted his apology on behalf of all who had survived. I reminded him that he had done a lot of good to help us overcome the evil. He had given us hope and faith.

Father Whalen said Union troops in the area around the first of January chased off the last of the rebel guards. The prisoners have had plenty of food, medical help and fresh water since then.

It is amazing to feel the hope every single soldier has to be finally going home. Our being here is a miracle to them.

Mr. Quinn has been a grand leader, giving instructions to the committee to help remove the remaining prisoners. He asked me if I wanted to burn the prison on my way out. I am considering that idea.

The committee walked with me all through the enclosure. Mr. Quinn allowed me to tell them what it was like to be imprisoned here. I was honored to have been given that chance. The committee asked many questions, but none I could not answer.

Telling them my story at the stockade was easier than telling it to you back home. I wish, Marcia, you could have walked with us and listened in today.

Mr. Quinn stood proudly and listened to me talk. Tonight he thanked me for being his assistant on this important mission.

The committee will stay here a few more days. And then we will board trains to move west to the ships waiting along the Mississippi River.

Our task here is almost over. I will be returning to Cashtown soon. Thank you for agreeing with Mr. Quinn and Major Delany to send me on this trip.

I look forward to seeing you.

Your loving husband,
Catesby

Cemetery at Anderson, Georgia

Anderson, Georgia
April 21, 1865

My darling Marcia

Father Whalen led us praying the Lord's Prayer as a group today. And then Mr. Quinn and the committee loaded the prisoners onto wagons. The last of the Union men have left the awful stockade at Anderson, Georgia.

I stood alone in the enclosure for several minutes before leaving thinking of how different it felt, how much space I had all to myself, and how God hadn't presented me with something that I could not handle. I thought of President Lincoln and how proud he would be of Mr. Quinn and this committee.

I was the last person out. I got to close this chapter of the war. I left by the dreaded south gate, staring that awful "call to death" in the face as a last defiant symbol of the prison. Never again will anyone have to struggle to survive this stockade. And then I hobbled out to catch up with the last wagon going to Anderson Station.

I did not burn the stockade, though I had seriously considered it.

The committee placed all the men onto the train. I was the last one to board. I looked back at the stockade and gave it a little salute, happy as Mrs. Ritner had said, to offer help to those still in need here.

This train ride was quite different from the railroad box cars I had been jammed into coming to and leaving Andersonville Prison. Each committee member and each prisoner had a seat to sit on during the entire train trip. Many soldiers were too weak to sit, so they laid across the seats.

Soldiers thanked Mr. Quinn and me for helping them return to home. They were the same thoughts I had when I was finally able to leave the prison. All were thankful they had survived. They were finally going home to their families and loved ones.

They talked of wives and children they had not seen in several years. One man had a new son at home he had never seen. Another said he was married the day before his unit marched to war. He had not seen his new wife since October 1862.

I wondered if their families would recognize the men who are riding on this train. Most probably did not look anything like the men who left to go to war. The war and prison life had changed them.

Many cried like babies, knowing they were free from that awful prison. They just wanted to get all this behind them and start over.

These Union soldiers finally had reached the point for the first time since the war started that they no longer feared death, injury or capture from their enemies.

Within several days we will reach the docks at Vicksburg, Mississippi. Mr. Quinn will work with the other officials to fill the waiting ships to take these honorable Union war veterans home.

The committee members continue to question me about the prison. There is some interest in trying to bring charges against the prison officials due to the violations of the code of conduct in dealing with prisoners of war. Those charges may be filed against Commandant Wirz and several others from Andersonville Prison. From what Allen had told me, I thought Commandant Wirz was trying to help us.

It has been an honor to serve on the committee at the request of Major Delany. Some members said they found my information valuable to their understanding of what happened at the stockade.

Marcia, my spirits are raised by the desire of these soldiers to help restore the Union. They have no hate toward the rebel soldiers or the people of the South.

I will write more when we arrive at the ships. I look forward to being with you.

Your loving husband,
Catesby

Vicksburg, Mississippi
April 23, 1865

Marcia Dearest

We have arrived at Vicksburg. Several steamships have already left, loaded with Union soldiers who are going home. This last ship is waiting for us.

There are about 2,000 Union soldiers ready to board the *Sultana*. Men from other prisons including those from Cabaha Prison in Selma, Alabama will join us on the ship.

Many of these Union men are so frail, only the thought of going home has given them the energy to continue on. It is like everything they have gone through has been worth the sacrifice to get them to this day so they can finally rejoin their families. Soon they will be home.

There is no fear in these men. They only want to go home and be left alone with their loved ones. They want to catch up on the days they missed, get their strength back, and try to forget this dreadful war.

You may remember me telling you of my trip aboard the steamship *Maple Leaf* when I vowed never to leave dry land again to board a ship. Men here say the Mississippi River will be a much smoother trip than my voyage on the ocean.

As a member of the committee, it is our duty to board last. I will make sure every one of these men has boarded this ship. With all that they have gone through, I promised Mr. Quinn I would not lose any man at this late date. I will take roll as they board.

I am told we will be loading tomorrow evening, with the ship leaving port by 9 o'clock. Our men will be the last soldiers to enter the ship.

These men have not been home since the war started. This is one of their last steps in going home. They will finally be free. Just like Catesby.

As weak and ill as these men are, their spirits are high. If they were able, they would be singing and dancing. They had feared they would never make it home. Now they know they will be home within a couple of weeks. I remember how I felt when I finally returned home. I am happy that they will be experiencing that joy soon.

We are scheduled to arrive in Cairo, Illinois on April 29. From there we will organize the men's transportation to their homes. Our committee will be the last to leave. I think that Mr. Quinn and I will be home around the tenth of May.

Mr. Quinn has told me several times that I have been a valuable assistant to him. When we return, he said he would like to hire me as his assistant in his office in Harrisburg.

If that happened, I would turn control of the blacksmith shop over to Brian. What do you think about that? Mr. Quinn said he would pay me a good wage. I could still make a percentage of the money Brian brings in from the blacksmith shop.

I am excited about the possibilities but would like to discuss the matter with you first.

I am very proud to have served Major Delany and President Lincoln on this committee. It has made up for all those months in Andersonville Prison where I questioned just how much I was helping the Union cause. Bringing six hundred Union soldiers home also helps me to pay my debt to Mrs. Ritner for helping me.

My next chance to write will be on board ship, but I will not be able to mail it until we reach Cairo. I miss you and will see you very soon.

Your loving husband,
Catesby

The *Sultana* Steamship photo   April 26, 1865

Chapter 28
The *Sultana*

April 27, 1865
Daily Argus Newspaper

Memphis, Tennessee...An explosion was reported on the Mississippi River seven miles north of here around 2 a.m. today aboard the *Sultana*, a 1700 ton steamship carrying Union soldiers home from the war. The ship's boilers burst causing a fire that sank the ship. Officials at the scene fear as many as 1500 of the 2500 passengers have been lost.

Information on the disaster, believed to be the worst in American shipping history, is sketchy. Officials at the scene report the ship was designed to carry less than four hundred passengers. The steamship carried only one life boat and 76 life preservers.

Soldiers were trapped by the explosion, burned by debris from the ship and boiling water from the ship's four boilers, or drowned in the icy flood waters before help could reach them. Many of the dead were burned beyond recognition, hindering efforts by the medical units to identify them. The ship's records were destroyed in the ensuring fire, thereby making it virtually impossible for officials to know all the names of those who had boarded the ship.

The ship's passengers included those who survived imprisonment at Anderson, Georgia (Andersonville Prison) and Selma, Alabama (Cahaba Prison) and twenty members of a committee sent by President Lincoln to close Andersonville Prison. Among those not accounted for and feared dead are Pennsylvania State Representative Harold Quinn, the committee chairman, and his assistant, Mr. Catesby, both of Cashtown, Pennsylvania.

The *Sultana* was traveling from Vicksburg, Mississippi to Cairo, Illinois. The ship left Vicksburg on Monday night, April 24.

Rescue operations are continuing. All Memphis area hospitals including Gayoso, Adams, Overton, and Washington Hospital are treating victims of the disaster. The Ladies Sanitary Commission and the Sisters of Charity are also on the scene.

A statement issued by President Johnson in Washington City, reads as follows: "I think it is a cruel irony so many men who endured confinement as prisoners of war have died on their way home. I have sent a special relief force to the scene to help those local organizations who are working to identify the dead and care for the survivors. I praise the work of Pennsylvania legislator Harold Quinn and his committee. And I asked the nation to pray for all those who were lost and injured in this tragic accident."

Officials of the Merchants' and People's Steamboat Line, owners of the *Sultana*, were not available for comment.

A board of inquiry has been appointed to investigate the disaster. Major General Cadwallader C. Washburn will lead that commission.

Union soldiers from other prisons had been carried earlier by other ships and are expected to arrive at their destinations soon.

Addendum

This is a historical novel. Catesby, Jim, Sam and Mason lived at Beall Air and were slaves of Colonel Lewis Washington. Mr. John Allstadt, his son, and his slaves Henri, Phil, Ben, Levi, Jerry, George, and Bill lived nearby. They were all captured and held hostage by John Brown and his men at Harpers Ferry in October, 1859.

The events depicted including the raid at Harpers Ferry, the trial and execution of John Brown, the performance by J. B. Wilkes at the reading room, the slave auctions in Sharpsburg, the photographer wagons at Antietam Creek, the meeting of President Lincoln and General McClellan at the Grove farm, the Underground Railroad activities of Mrs. Ritner, the passage of the Confederate wagon trains through Millerstown (today called Fairfield) and Cashtown, the Gettysburg Address, the assassination of Abraham Lincoln at Ford's Theater, the prison at Anderson, Georgia and the explosion of the *Sultana* are actual historical events.

Many of the characters of this book including Catesby, Abraham Lincoln, John Wilkes Booth (aka J. B. Wilkes), John Brown, Robert E. Lee, Clara Barton, Alexander Gardner, Dr. Martin R. Delany, Commander Henry Wirz, Mrs. Ritner, Father Peter Whalen, Colonel Obadiah Downing, John Earnest, Mr. Mickley, Mrs. Ella Washington, and Colonel Lewis Washington are all real characters.

The list of U.S. Colored Troops held at Andersonville Prison and who died there are from the actual prison records. The six men who died by hanging at Andersonville Prison are also from prison records.

Doug Perks and Jim Glymph are also real people who can be found most any day at the Jefferson County Museum in Charles Town, West Virginia.

Many of the other characters of this novel are a figment of my imagination.

This is my third novel. My other two "The Perfect Steel Trap Harpers Ferry 1859" and "The Virginian Who Might Have Saved Lincoln" were both published by Infinity Publishing. "The Virginian Who Might Have Save Lincoln" is also now available on audio books, published by Spoken Books Publishing, a division of Infinity Publishing.

My fourth historical novel is in the works. "A House Divided Against Itself", the story of two brothers who fought against each other at the Battle of Second Winchester, will be out sometime in 2009.

For more information about me and my books, please visit my website at www.boboconnorbooks.com.

I appreciate any feedback from those who read my books.

Acknowledgments

This book could not have completed without the help, continued encouragement and support of the following: James Taylor, Doug Perks, Jean Libby, Jim Teague, Judy Reed, Jack Snyder and the staff of the Old Charles Town Library. You all, in your own way, are very helpful to me on a regular basis. Thanks.

I appreciate very much the generosity of Mort Künstler, renowned Civil War artist, for allowing me to purchase the rights of his painting for the cover of this book.

Special thanks goes to Tom White at the George Tyler Moore Civil War Center in Shepherdstown, WV for helping me with important research on the U. S. Colored Troops at Andersonville Prison.

I also appreciate very much the expertise Eric Johnson, blacksmith, contributed to this story.

To Charles Crawford, I offer my gratitude again for his expert scans.

Thanks to my editor, Melanie Rigney, for her constructive suggestions to help improve this manuscript and for taking me on as a project. Mel, may God Bless you real good!!

Kudos to my expert webmaster, Jackie E. Sanders, for maintaining my website at www.boboconnorbooks.com. Jackie, you are indeed a wiz!!

I am always grateful for the support, encouragement and love given to me on a daily basis by all my friends and family, including but not limited to Kelli, Craig, Rachel and Doug, my six grand children (Lexi, Lacey, Owen, Lainey, Kyle, and Claire), my mother, my sister and my brothers and their families.

And as always, a special commendation goes to Rebecca Boreczky, my mentor and teacher, for getting me started in publishing. Thanks for encouraging and nudging me to publish.

Bob O'Connor

2007 Photo by Denise Barnes Walker

My first published article was written when I was in eighth grade for the Illinois Historical Society magazine. At age 62, I now have had over two thousand articles published and three books.

But I haven't quit my day jobs – at the Jefferson County Convention and Visitors Bureau in Harpers Ferry, WV and at the City of Charles Town.

My six grand children, Lexi, Lacey, Owen, Lainey, Kyle, and Claire, my two children, my daughter-in-law and son-in-law live nearby.

My mother, Willa, who is very instrumental in who I am today, lives in Dixon, Illinois, where I grew up.